The First Seal

Book 1 of
The
Apocalypse Prophecies

Sean Deville

First paperback edition 2020

Paperback published by Amazon.

Visit the author's website at **www.seandeville.com**

Readers advisory

This novel is based on the biblical book of Revelation.

It is an apocalyptic work of horror fiction. As such, it seeks to attain a realistic account of the times we are in. This means it contains graphic descriptions of violence as well as what some may consider to be profane language.

There will be death, there will be slaughter… there will be blood and gore.

Whilst the work contains religious themes, it does not proclaim to be an accurate representation of the various religious texts.

It's make believe, for something that I hope never occurs.

Revelation 6:1-2

And I saw when the Lamb opened one of the seals, and I heard, as it were the noise of thunder, one of the four beasts saying, Come and see.

And I saw, and behold a white horse: and he that sat on him had a bow; and a crown was given unto him: and he went forth conquering, and to conquer.

List of Characters

Civilians
Damien/Legion
Ari Stone
Giles Horn
Detective Inspector Hargreaves
Emily Ralph
Vicky Ralph
Lucy Richards
Veronica Richards

Demons
Baal
Kane

Inquisitors
Lilith
Lucien
Father
Librarian
Cardinal Esposito

TOP SECRET

THIS IS A COVER SHEET

FOR CLASSIFIED INFORMATION

ALL INDIVIDUALS HANDLING THIS INFORMATION ARE REQUIRED TO PROTECT IT FROM UNAUTHORIZED DISCLOSURE IN THE INTEREST OF NATIONAL SECURITY OF THE UNITED STATES.

HANDLING, STORAGE, REPRODUCTION AND DISPOSITION OF THE ATTACHED DOCUMENT WILL BE IN ACCORDANCE WITH APPLICABLE EXECUTIVE ORDER(S), STATUTE(S) AND AGENCY IMPLEMENTING REGULATIONS.

UNLAWFUL VIEWING, REPRODUCTION OR TRANSPORT IS A FEDERAL OFFENCE UNDER 18 U.S. Code § 798 AND CARRIES A MINIMUM TERM OF LIFE IMPRISONMENT.

(This cover sheet is unclassified)

703-101
NSN 75690-01-21207964

The Defense Intelligence Agency

NSN 75690-01-21207964

A confidential report on the Middle East

To: General Peter Robinson, Head of the Joint Chiefs of Staff

From: General Steven Sandhurst, DIA Director

As I am sure you are aware, the present situation in the Middle East is grave. Not since the Yom Kippur War have we seen such a potential threat to the Jewish state of Israel.

There are more pressing issues, though. Whilst we strongly suspect that Iran was responsible for the complete recent destruction of the Saudi Arabian oil infrastructure, their use of third-party mercenaries has put plausible deniability between them and the financial devastation that is now threatening to bring down the house of Saud. The present unrest in the Saudi capital and other cities threatens our ally in the region. If Saudi Arabia falls, the balance of power will tip rapidly in favour of Iran.

The United States cannot allow this to happen.

Our analyses show that, without direct U.S. military intervention, Saudi Arabia, Kuwait and Qatar will all fall to internal uprisings brought on by the destabilising influence of Iran. It is our opinion that merely relying on sanctions on Iran is no longer enough, and along with the NSA, we have received compelling chatter that Israel itself is at risk of insurrection. Whilst Israel can defend itself more than adequately against any combined conventional military assault from its neighbours, it is highly vulnerable to a concerted and coordinated internal attack on its infrastructure.

We strongly believe that, should Israel be hit by a devastating terrorist attack, it may well resort to the use of nuclear weapons in response. There is no doubt that this will bring both Russia and China into the equation, which would risk a global thermonuclear exchange.

I would urge the Joint Chiefs of Staff to once again try to persuade the Commander-in-Chief to authorise our military to intervene more strongly in the Middle East. This is not a time for isolationism and we feel that it is now imperative that we act swiftly to deplete the military capability of Iran. The head needs to be cut off the snake, and it is now time for us to strike decisively against the Iranian threat. If we don't act now, we risk losing influence in the entire region, which would have a devastating effect on world energy supplies and the world's financial markets.

Although they are loath to admit it, Israel needs our help, and I would advise that the DOD considers deploying further assets to the area.

Regards

Steven Sandhurst, DIA Director

1.

Boston, USA

He never thought the apocalypse would look so beautiful.

Although daylight, the sky was black with the soot from a thousand ravenous fires. Professor Ari Stone stood close to the cliff edge, looking down at the shattered city below him. If the Metropolis had once been recognisable, the conflagration and the devastation hid its identity now, leaving nothing but anguish and ruin. He knew what this was; had read and written about it for nearly thirty years. And yet he was surprised that what he had considered glorified fiction had come to pass.

"*Do you see*?" a powerful voice said from out of the ether. He didn't know the source of the voice, but was sure it was not in his imagination. "*Do you see the truth that was prophesied?*"

"Yes," was all Stone could manage, although his voice sounded alien. The air stung his eyes and the smell of the people burning infested his nasal passages, clogging them, corroding and irritating the delicate flesh.

"*When will you believe*?" the voice demanded.

"This isn't real," Stone insisted. "This is just a dream."

The voice mocked him in reply. "*You think you know what is real? If that's the case, then you really haven't been paying attention.*"

Stone felt himself turn, the motion not of his own creation, the body filled with aches that were not familiar to him. Before him lay a mighty golden throne, with a man seated high up. The face of the man was vague, constantly changing, never revealing his true identity. To the right of the man floated a set of iron scales, upon which rested a glowing, if tattered, scroll. Despite the way it hovered, one side of the scales sank beneath its presence. On the throne, the man sighed, shaking his mighty head in resignation. He spoke, but Stone was unable to hear what was being said.

"*Then I saw the lamb, looking as if it had been slain, standing before the centre of the throne. He went and took the scroll from the right hand of him who sat on the throne,*" the ethereal voice proclaimed. Stone knew the words, had read and written them enough times.

It was then that Stone realised he was holding the scroll, the paper of which disintegrated at his touch, only to reform its solidity. It felt unusually heavy, as if wrapped around lead. He tried to throw it down to the earth, but it seemed joined to him, tingling against the hot skin of his palm. Seven wax seals held the scroll closed, each one marked by symbols that were incomprehensible to his human eyes. Stone had no control here. He felt more like a passenger in somebody else's body.

"*Poor, pathetic little lamb. You have yet to realise the devastation that will soon befall your kind. The scroll will open,*" the voice said. "*The seals will break, and you will be there to bear witness to the final wrath against the arrogance of your species. You will deny your part in it, but you will be instrumental in dooming an entire planet.*"

"I refuse," Stone insisted, only to be met by horrific laughter. "I refuse to bear witness. Choose somebody else."

"*The fool thinks he has a choice. You have already been chosen by a power you could never understand. You cannot defy what is written.*"

From the sky, the sound of great trumpets blared, almost deafening in their intensity, and pain tore through his mind. Stone didn't need to put his hand to his ears to know they were bleeding, but he did anyway, a feeble attempt to try to block out the noise. Beneath his feet, the ground shook, the cliff edge breaking away, crumbling as the reverberations destroyed the cohesion of the land. At the sound of the trumpets, the man on the throne vanished into dust. The throne shattered into millions of shards that cascaded to the floor all around Stone's feet.

"Why are you doing this?" Stone pleaded. This wasn't supposed to happen.

"*Because your kind have all fallen from his grace…and because I can.*" Was this what the voice was, some spiteful child playing with his toys? "*You have been given # every opportunity, and despite that, you tumble towards your own annihilation. You were given free will and yet you abused the gifts that you were blessed with.*" The dust around Stone's feet began to swirl in miniature tornadoes. "*Better for me to relieve you of the burden of your suffering. Now is as good a time as any, even though I know it dooms us all.*"

"No. You don't get to have that right."

The ground at his feet began to churn, the earth erupting outwards as decayed hands thrust themselves upward, clawing into the air. Some of them grabbed Stone, pulling on his feet and calves as whatever was down there tried to pull itself free. It was too late for Stone to run, the hands extending into arms as a multitude of corpses made themselves known.

"*I have every right. And I will cause them to eat the flesh of their sons and the flesh of their daughters,*" the voice continued. Before he was dragged fully down to the ground, Stone was there to witness the sky opening up and the great fire descending. It was as if the clouds themselves had caught fire.

"No," Stone begged. "You don't have to do this. We can change. Just give us a chance."

"*Oh, but I do have to do this*," replied the voice. "*And you will be there to witness it all. Humans will never change. You will pay your penance and I will have my fun.*"

Decaying flesh grabbed his arms, nails breaking the skin as they easily shredded the feeble fabric he wore. The scroll was ripped from his grasp and flung into the air, where it burst into flames. The fire did not consume it, though. If anything, the parchment seemed to feed on the fire rather than the other way around.

"*I will laugh as the first seal breaks. I do this for I am vengeance. I am spite. I am everything you little crawling monkeys crave to be,*" the voice cried out. As he was pulled beneath the surface, Stone gagged on the dry dirt that waterfalled into his mouth, stifling the final scream that so desperately wanted to be heard. "*I don't think I have ever witnessed anything that has disappointed me so. You are barely worthy of my torment, but what choice do I have? We all have our part to play.*"

That was how the nightmare always struck him. At first it had been a rare event, but over the past few months it had become more frequent, hitting two or three times a week. Stone's doctor had told him it was due to overwork and the morbid subject that he spent his time on. That made sense, he supposed. He had been pushing things of late, travelling to promote his latest book, and forcing the ideas out onto paper faster than perhaps he should have. There was a desperation in his actions, too few people willing to read his latest work. His appeal was fading, the younger generations having no interest in what he wrote.

Then there was the medication that had been prescribed, and the stuff he had acquired by more illicit means. Amitriptyline for the depression that constantly threatened to consume him. Adderall to help him write, to help get the carnival that played in his head onto the computer screen.

Sitting up in bed, he wiped the sweat from his forehead, the world still blurry around him. No doubt the prolonged travel was contributing to this, putting strains on a body that was well past its best years. But the speaking tour usually made him almost as much money as his books, and he couldn't reject how much he enjoyed educating the minds that came to hear him speak.

He could deny it all he wanted, but recognition, and the pay cheque that came with it, was a powerful motivator for why he carried on writing about these morbid subjects.

Tonight was the last of this leg of his U.S. tour. It was a full house, all tickets bought and accounted for. This was a smaller, more intimate venue than the others he had graced with his presence, but that was fine. Talking to huge crowds never felt right to him, despite their profitability. The hundred present tonight should open up some healthy discussion. As conceited as it might be, Stone thought of himself more as a purveyor of ideas rather than a writer. Often, he could better express concepts in words than he ever could on paper, because the written word couldn't respond to direct challenge.

So long as he was paid for it.

Hey, a guy had to eat.

Stone knew his subject matter, which was definitely fortunate considering the fevered responses his writings sometimes promoted. Controversy sold books, at least according to his agent. And what could be more controversial than dissecting the strongly held religious beliefs of billions of people?

Stone was about to discover that life had other ideas planned for him. Nothing would spare him what was coming.

2.

London, UK

Blood and pain.

That was all Lilith ever seemed to dream about these days. These weren't nightmares; instead, they were often accurate memories of the retribution she had wrought on those who threatened the stability she guarded. Those lives were forfeit by the very nature of their corruption, and she was happy to bring God's vengeance crashing down on those who threatened the safety of the world.

She brought that vengeance now, and she was enjoying every second of it.

Two sets of footsteps echoed down the stone canal path, hers and the man she was chasing. He was young, fit, and athletic, but he had no hope against her training and stamina. Despite the black aura that surrounded him, visible only to some like Lilith, the pursued man knew he was no match for the chasing assassin. That was why he ran, fear driving him into a primal need to survive.

The general public might not know of the religious warriors lurking amongst them, but a select few of those who followed the path of the Little Whore did. Lilith was feared by them as much as she was despised.

The canal was too wide to jump, and swimming would not be a means to escape her vengeance, so all this man could do was run along the litter-strewn path and hope for some sort of salvation. Already he was tiring. Lilith could hear that his breathing was ragged, the injured and bleeding arm clutched against his chest, shock undoubtedly looming over him like a shroud. No matter how hard he pushed himself, Lilith was clearly gaining. This vile specimen of God's universe had minutes at most. Better that he cherish them whilst he still could, because Lilith was going to savour every second of what was to come.

Killing one of the possessed was both a necessity and a mercy. It was also a damned fine way to spend an afternoon.

Three minutes ago, things had been different. The man and his two accomplices had chosen this spot because it was apparently deserted, the ideal place to dispose of the abducted that hopefully lay alive, bound in the back of their car. The abandoned brick structure next to where they had parked was a suitable venue for the end they wanted to bring to their prisoner. These three, these demons, had not expected Lilith to be waiting for them and had been woefully inept at defending themselves against her devastating attack.

Lilith had taken the three as they exited their vehicle, surprise and speed an effective weapon. She could have offed them from a distance using her sniper rifle skills, but she preferred the old-fashioned ways. Before they knew what had hit them, Lilith's first throwing knife had taken the largest of them in the neck, severing arteries, veins and muscle. A killing blow worthy of her years of training. It didn't matter how strong you were when blood was pumping from such a grievous wound.

The second knife had landed before the woman it struck had been able to pull the gun out of its holster. The satanic-infused woman had briefly stood there, shock etched on her face, the blade embedded in her left eye, the precision of the throw incomprehensible to the now running man. He too had tried to pull forth a weapon, but the final knife thrown had sliced through his wrist, making the hand useless, the gun dropped to the dirt. Flight had been the only option left to him. He wasn't powerful enough to stand toe-to-toe with Lilith, and he knew it.

Lilith wouldn't have it any other way. It was good to feel the air coursing into her lungs. She was the alpha predator here, and what use was the hunt without the excitement of a chase?

Now Lilith watched as the demon she pursued stumbled, his body hurtling to the ground with a pained cry. In seconds she was upon him, a knee firm in his back. Her enemy tried to writhe free, but she gripped an ear to keep him under control, the pressure she exerted below what was required to rip the organ from his head. There were so many ways she could hurt this creature that she was almost delirious with the opportunities presented to her.

It was such a shame the unwilling host body would have to die, too.

"You were warned to stay away," Lilith stated. Despite her exertion, her breathing was controlled. "And yet your kind persist. If you had remained hidden in the shadows, I might have been willing to ignore you." That was a lie, of course. Once Lilith got the scent of them, she never relented.

"Bitch," the demon managed, although it was a pitiful insult.

"You could have lived for at least a few more days, maybe weeks. If only you had behaved. Imagine the human delights you could have tasted." That was why they came, to defile the perceived purity of this world. They didn't realise that humanity was doing a pretty good job of that without them.

"My master will see you burn," the demon roared. He tried to throw her off, but Lilith was strong, much stronger than she looked. Her hand was like a vice and the other suddenly held yet another knife against the base of the possessed man's neck. That stilled the demon. He had heard the rumours of the inquisitors, and knowledge of what was coming was no salvation. His fate had been sealed the moment Lilith had stepped from her concealment.

No, that wasn't correct. His fate had been sealed the moment he had chosen to rise from the safety of the fiery pit. The forces of chaos feared Lilith. Some chose to fight when she appeared to them, others, like the desperate entity beneath her, chose to flee. It all ended the same way for them.

"Perhaps he will," Lilith admitted. "And when you see him, you can give him my regards. But first, I will have your name." She slid the knife across the skin, opening up a wound as a taste of what was to follow.

"I'll tell you nothing," the demon insisted. The demon's defiance was useless, for they always revealed themselves.

"Oh, come now. Must we play this game?" Such stubbornness. Did she really have to go through this again? "You know what I will do."

"Go fuck yourself," the demon roared, wriggling beneath her. The knife moved effortlessly, slipping under the right armpit, thrusting deep and rendering the arm useless.

"I'm in no rush. You know what I am. You know what I am capable of."

"I will not tell you my name, whore."

Lilith sighed. "O holy hosts above, I call upon thee as a servant of Jesus Christ, to sanctify my actions this day in preparation for the fulfilment of the will of God."

"What are you doing?" the demon implored. It sounded panicked now, trapped in a situation it could never have envisaged.

"I'm giving your host the last rites. What might these words do to you, I wonder? You will return to Hell, whatever I do, but I suspect being blessed might taint you." There was no knowing for sure, but the demons always seemed to fear the words.

"No, you cannot."

"I call upon the great Archangel Raphael, master of air…"

"Wait, please."

"Please? Did you just beg?" Lilith twisted in her position and brought the knife deep into the possessed man's right buttock. "Did you listen when the one you you abused begged you to stop?" She withdrew the knife, twisting it as she did so.

"Berith, my name is Berith."

"You have my thanks, and I release you." They always gave their name. Good, the ritual would have taken longer than she risked spending here.

Before he could object further, Lilith pushed the knife forwards, its pointed edge easily slipping through the flesh, breaking between the vertebrae, severing the cervical spine. From experience, Lilith knew such an injury would bring death, but it would be slow and drawn out. That would give her time to savour her one true indulgence.

With exaggerated effort, she turned the man over, saw the desperation in his searching, dying eyes. The muscles of his face still worked, but the rest of his body would be limp, the connection to the brain severed. The spine had been cut low enough to paralyse, but high enough to keep the heart pumping and the lungs breathing. Lilith preferred this way of killing, to bathe in their terror, the black shroud pulsing as the demon's hold over the captive began to weaken.

She used the knives whenever she could. Whilst a bullet was efficient, it rarely left her prey in this vulnerable state. The knife was pure, the weapon she was first taught to use at a young age. Even among her own kind, there were few who were her equal.

The demon tried to speak, but she pressed a gloved finger against his lips.

"Hush now. There is nothing for you to say." She waited, knowing that the change would come. This body was infected, the disease hot within it. But without the host, the infection could not survive and so it would flee back to the hot place where it would once again begin its tormented eternity.

At least that was what she had always been told by those who trained her. She hoped the bastard thing would suffer back down in the heat.

There. The black cloud that briefly swept across the whites of his eyes was further proof that this fiend had indeed been touched by the dark ones. Then the horror and the pain melted away, to be replaced by a look of peace and gratitude as the darkness around the felled man dissipated, the possession ending. The infection had been forced out, sent back to its realm of agony.

All Lilith saw in the face now was thanks. Being possessed by demonic forces was something the most evil of men should never be condemned to, even if they went into it willingly.

"Thank you," the man said, tears in his eyes, his breath laboured and heavy. "Thank you for sparing me." There was no way for her to know what this victim had been forced to watch as the demon rode in his body.

Another soul saved.

"Go with whatever god you cherish," Lilith said, slipping a hand over the man's mouth, fingers holding his nostrils closed, the knife still clenched and ready. It took less than a minute for unconsciousness to take him, and she held him there whilst he died. Not once did he try to struggle. Nothing she could do was equal to the torment of having that corruption churning away inside.

There were ways to free a body of its evil captor so that the person lived. But they were time-consuming and haphazard, and often left the remaining host broken and useless. With seven billion souls at stake, one had to take the quickest path. Lilith was a surgeon, cutting the infection from the world. Let the exorcists from the other religious orders pray their way to salvation. If you considered the survival rate of exorcists, you could perhaps see why Lilith's methods were much more effective. Exorcists were trained in words, not in violence, and violence was the only effective tool against the servants of Satan.

She could remember the name of every demon she had sent back. It was a long list.

Lilith searched the corpse then, knowing what she would find. Inside his wallet, she discovered the brutal proof of his identity, reinforcing the concern that had been growing over the past few weeks. The identification stated he was an agent of the British intelligence service MI5, so likely the others she had killed might be, too.

Demons were getting bolder and stronger. It was unlikely that the agent of MI5 had willingly allowed himself to be possessed. The organisation had long ago been purged of those who followed the teaching of Satan. It wasn't just demons that the inquisitors dealt with. They were known to hunt down those who spent their days worshipping the true lords of the Sheol.

This should not be happening. More proof that the seals holding closed the Gates of Hell were weakening. More proof that she was right about what was happening to the world. Lilith had seen that her superiors would not listen to her unless she could gather hard evidence. She suspected that they wouldn't listen even then.

To possess a member of MI5 was a worrying development. That suggested a coordinated purpose rather than just random selection by the agents of chaos. She would report this to her Order and hope that her words were believed. She wasn't optimistic. As organised and as ruthless as her Order was, it was mired in its own dogma. Demons, she had always been told, were never organised, working for their own interests rather than for some higher purpose. They were hedonistic, drunk on the emotions they could drag from the humans they terrorised. Throughout her training, she had been told that demons were loners, predatory wolves stalking the land of the living to obtain their *fix*.

Usually that was the case, but the day they learnt to organise would be a terrifying day for humanity.

Lilith was certain that day had already arrived, but those who were deemed her betters didn't agree. They would either listen or they would dismiss her concerns as they had so many times before. No matter what, she would continue her battle against the darkness because, even with its growing futility, there was nothing else for her to do.

Standing, she left the wallet open on top of the corpse, her gloved hands not leaving any residue of her presence. When it was eventually found, the MI5 identification would no doubt create an uproar in the secretive government agency. The knowledge she had acquired during her youth told her that there should have been no other cases of infection in that organisation. And yet, here was clear evidence. The auras of all three had exuded the proof she needed that the impossible was happening. Demons were working together.

Unfortunately, the proof of her eyes would unlikely persuade the leaders of her sacred Order.

Lilith gazed down at the corpse, wanting to understand the full picture of the dangers she likely faced. She could see the edges of it, an image of evil that shrouded the world she protected, but the bulk of it was unknown to her. If this was all planned, and if the demons she had dispatched over the last few months were indeed working on some coordinated agenda, she was determined to get to the bottom of it.

But first, there was one more thing to do.

Retracing her steps, she made her way back to the car, the two bodies still lying where she had left them. A quick search showed that only one of the three beasts she had slain was a member of that most elite of security organisations, although one of the other two had been a Detective Constable in the Metropolitan Police Service. This was more troubling, proof that the foul demons were seeking positions of authority. To what end, Lilith could only speculate. Curiosity drove her to search the woman's corpse further, using the knife to slice clothes from the body. Across the cadaver's back, a thick red rash spread over the skin. The more powerful the demon, the more chance there was for the human body to reject its presence.

Whatever these demonic bastards were up to, it was not for the betterment of human kind.

With the vehicle unlocked, the car boot yielded easily, revealing the terrified male teenager who cowered bound within. How many people like this had been tortured and mutilated to feed the desires of those who dwelled within the pit? Hell was supposed to keep them in check, these vile foes of Christ. That was why the legends said it had been created. And yet, so many of those supposedly trapped in their dark prison seemed able to find a way out into the light.

"You don't have to worry anymore," Lilith said. The lie came so easily to her, for she felt this soon to be man had suffered enough. She would have rescued him, but he was already too damaged, the fingers on both hands removed by tortures already inflicted. The demons had done other, unspeakable things, leaving a broken boy with bloody pits where his eyes had once been. Such a shame. He could have realised so much potential.

If the information Lilith had received was to be believed, the teenager was special in a way that neither he nor his parents could ever appreciate. He was a rarity—someone whose genetic code was locked tight against the forces of possession. Even if he wanted to give himself willingly, no king or prince of Hell could occupy this form. His abduction, cruel treatment, and eventual despatch served a dual purpose. Firstly, it gave those from the depraved place a relief for the craving they sought. And secondly, it removed the danger this youngster represented to those who occupied the nine circles.

Just as Lilith could sense those with the demonic cancer within them, so these sons and daughters of Satan could sniff out those resistant to their possession. And if Lilith had got to the victim in time, maybe he could have followed her path.

Her Order mostly recruited from those who were immune to the temptations brought forth by the scourges of Satan. Some of those were born specifically from carefully selected and ruthlessly protected bloodlines. Others, like Lilith, were collected from the carnage that demons often left in their wake. Lilith didn't have to examine what further horrors had been perpetrated on this victim's flesh. She could see much of it on the teenager's exposed skin. Lilith also had the memory of what had been done to her before she herself had been rescued nearly twenty years ago. That memory was a suitable motivation for the battle she waged.

Without the fingers and eyes, whoever this teenager had been was of no use to her Order. And whilst she could have let him live, what kind of life awaited him? He was traumatised beyond measure, having endured what nobody should ever suffer. Better to end it now and send this teenager to the beloved and gentle waiting arms of Christ.

Those were her standing orders. Besides, the demons would just keep coming for him. He was marked now.

Bending down, she removed the duct tape from his mouth, the cries of anguish finally freed. So young to experience such pain, and likely his mind was already on the brink of shattering. He was too lost within himself to try to repel her seemingly caring embrace, and she placed her hands gently on either side of the teenager's head. For a second, the teenager seemed to calm, his essence meeting hers. In that brief moment, they made a connection that Lilith had no choice but to betray. A quick twist, and the neck snapped easily.

The only life she would leave the eventual authorities was whatever non-sentient creatures skulked in the surrounding dirt, or the skies above.

***

To look at her, few would realise that Lilith had been responsible for the death of over a hundred people, but those who knew of her kind were never fooled. Of the naïve public, some would call her killer, a vicious force that cut a swathe of carnage across a whole country. Other more logical minds would call her guardian, the last remnant of a defensive line that had kept evil at bay for more than a thousand years. Most people wouldn't call her anything, because the battle for the soul of humanity was hidden below the placid surface of pumpkin spiced lattes and dopamine-inducing social media.

The war for the fate of mankind was never televised or reported. It had always been hidden by a cloak of secrecy. That allowed Lilith to hunt those who chose to hide in the darkness.

By the modern laws of man, Lilith was guilty of numerous violent atrocities, but she had no need to fear the police or the country's security services. Lilith was a ghost, moving from city to city, bringing the fight to those who had earned the feel of her blade against their throat. That was her favourite method, to use the laser-sharpened steel to separate the flesh, opening up blood vessels and letting the life flow from them freely. To look in the eyes of her victims as they bled out before her was an addiction to which she willingly succumbed.

She was sure the almighty would allow her this one small pleasure. The demon who had tried to run away from her needn't have bothered. There had been no chance of him getting away.

There were other ways she killed, all as ruthless and as efficient. No life was safe when it reeked of the corruption of the ones who ruled the world below. It didn't matter who they were. Man, woman or child, she would end whomsoever her Order demanded. And recently they had been demanding a lot. Perhaps the rumours were true, the whispers she snatched from those who lived these secret lives. Despite the denials from her superiors, it was said that the seals holding closed the gates of Hell were weakening.

That would be a problem.

That would mean the end of all things.

That was why she was here, on the outskirts of London. More deaths to add to her body count. More blood to stain the fetid earth. More dark souls to send back to their rotting makers.

Just because the demons were spawned from Hell, that didn't give them any special powers. When you possessed a human's body, you took on all its traits and weaknesses. Only the strongest of those from the dark place arrived with anything close to supernatural powers. That was why her religious Order had been so effective against them over the centuries. With rare exceptions, her enemies were no greater threat than the average man or woman.

It was difficult for those trapped below to escape into the light of the free world. That didn't stop thousands of them trying, though.

As it was, there were enough of Lilith's kind at present to hold back the trickle that made it through. But they wouldn't stand a chance if the gates were flung wide. If those seals ever broke, it wouldn't matter how many vermin she dispatched. As skilled as she was, Lilith and those who fought with her could never win against such numbers.

She belonged, body and soul, to the Order of Tyron, a secret and most likely forgotten remnant for most in the Catholic Church. Only a rare few knew of its existence. Any books depicting or recounting the Order's deeds were locked away deep in the Vatican vaults, lest the world learn of the true power the Catholic Church could still wield. The Order of Tyron was the shield of man, one of the last defences against the growing forces of darkness that pressed against the sanity of the world. Depleted, over-stretched and hideously outnumbered, those who served the Order did what was asked of them because there was no other way.

It was the only life Lilith knew. Her kind was kept hidden, for the world would reject the truth she represented. Her given name was Lilith Wrath, born of pain and trained in blood. No civilised society would accept the tortures she had been forced to endure to earn her place in the inquisitor ranks.

A memory flashed briefly into her thoughts. She had once been like the boy, abducted, broken, and abused. Only back then, the man who saved her had not been forced to end her miserable suffering, but to prolong it a thousand-fold.

Her title was inquisitor. She was a hammer of God, sent to smash those who would defile the Lord's holy name. And she would not stop until the war was won, or until she was dead and buried in the cold, unforgiving earth.

Only a fool would ever claim the war could be decisively won, but she fought it anyway.

3.

Saudi Arabia

After a whole day, parts of Saudi Arabia were still on fire. Not since Saddam Hussein had set his oil fields ablaze had so much devastation been wreaked upon the oil production capability of the Middle East. The world's stock markets had reacted accordingly, plunging as fears of a prolonged oil shortage began to emerge.

A lot of people had just lost a lot of money, with pension funds across the globe reeling from the impact.

Saudi Arabian oil facilities had been attacked before, and the lessons from those attacks had clearly not been learnt. The air defence systems, comprising Patriot missile batteries as well as Crotale short-range missile systems and M1097 Avenger systems for point defence, had proven inadequate to stop the previous attack on the Abqaiq and Khurais oil facilities. Those defences, although recently bolstered, were once again useless against the more sustained attack that was yesterday thrown against them.

In reality, there really was no effective way to defend against such an attack, and everybody knew it.

This time, the assaults were far more widespread, comprising hundreds of drones and cruise missiles which overwhelmed every major oil facility in the Kingdom of Saudi Arabia. The first target hit was the newly completed Jazan refinery, quickly followed by the Luberef facility. Within minutes, before the alarm could be raised across the country, the Riyadh refinery was also ablaze. The first storage tank to be hit at Riyadh caused an explosive cascade that spread to fifteen other storage tanks as well as to the refining structures themselves. The result was utter devastation.

Across the region, pipelines were also shattered. The plan was simple—the eradication of Saudi Arabia's ability to extract, transport and refine the crude oil products it was so dependent upon. This was an economic death blow, the first stage in a war the Iranians had now decided they were willing to wage.

Before those watching could catch their breaths, the Abqaiq plant, Ras Tanura and Jubail refineries were also burning furiously. Deep in the deserts, several pumping stations were hit for good measure, their remoteness no defence against the coordinated and well-planned act of war. Although the Houthi movement in Yemen once again claimed responsibility, nobody was in any doubt that it was Iran who masterminded the attack.

In parts of the country, it began to rain oil. And that wasn't the end of it.

Shipping was also attacked. In the Strait of Hormuz, with a displacement of over six hundred thousand tonnes and carrying four million barrels of freshly loaded oil, the oil tanker *Herald of Faith* was sinking and abandoned after being hit by three perfectly aimed torpedoes. The torpedoes were fired by an Iranian-owned but Russian-built, kilo-class submarine that was steaming back to a safe port to escape the vengeance of any allied naval ships that might be in the vicinity. Although there were numerous western ships patrolling the waters of the Persian Gulf in the hope of protecting the vital energy corridor, they were not in the right place to stop the attack.

That burning and sinking super tanker couldn't be blamed on the Houthi rebels.

The Strait of Hormuz hosted the transport of nearly a quarter of all the world's oil, and it was effectively a no-go area. There was more trauma to come. When you had your enemy on the ropes, the classic tactic was to keep on hitting them. This time, unfortunately, as so often happened, the enemy hit back.

The leaders of Iran were soon to learn they had made a monumental strategic blunder.

***

Ashkan Khazenifar knew little about the attacks, but had dreamt about the great fire now raging in the Hijaz, the western part of Saudi Arabia. The prophetic symbol this represented was hard to overlook, though he did his best to ignore the implications.

The Last Hour would not come until fire emits from the earth of Hijaz, which would illuminate the necks of the camels of the Busra.

His part in the great plan seemed small, but he knew he would not fail, for his faith was unquestionable. The hot sun beat down on him, but he did not complain, for he had lived his whole life in such temperatures. Now he was about to end that life in a heat that would rage a thousand-fold. As a loyal member of the Iranian Sepâh, his only real regret was that he was destined to martyr himself on the day of his youngest son's birthday. There was so much he still wanted to do with his life, but when honour and duty called, what could a man faithful to Allah do but heed that call?

Ashkan knew his family would be well cared for, so long as he was successful in his mission. In the nights that led up to this fateful day, he often found himself wondering what his two sons might make of his sacrifice. Would they understand? Would they honour him as the martyr he hoped to be, or would they curse him for abandoning them to the evils of such a world? Ashkan hoped they would one day understand.

He hadn't been in the country long, having crept across the highly porous Iraq/Saudi border three days before. There was a time when such a journey would have been impossible, with Iraq a mortal enemy of his beautiful country. But Iraq, riddled with Shia militia, was all but an ally of Iran now. Iraq, once a constant thorn in the Iranians' side, had become a useful buffer against the land armies of the Kingdom of Saudi Arabia. That buffer would be needed, because to all intents and purposes, Iran had declared war on a nation that possessed considerable military power. The Saudis would hit back.

Not only was that a risk, but they were also backed by the Great Satan himself, the cursed United States of America. Iran had plans for them as well.

Ashkan stepped into the street, the slim bomb vest that had been constructed for him easily hidden under his robe. It was made from thin blocks of Semtex coated in steel ball bearings, designed for maximum human casualty. It would also send Ashkan straight to the afterlife. The outfit was stifling, but he easily went unnoticed amongst the people who were likely reeling from the assault their country was already under. The oil was only part of it. With much of the oil infrastructure closed down, the financial toll on the Kingdom would be catastrophic. No doubt they would have to go cap in hand to the hated Americans who would already be pouring extra troops into the region.

Let them come, thought Ashkan. They will all fall before Allah's might.

It was money that was always going to be Saudi Arabia's Achilles heel. Unemployment was high, with people kept pliant by the promise of bread and circuses funded by the billions brought in by the country's great oil wealth. Those who objected were brought into line by the brutality of the Mutawa, the Saudi religious police. That control would fail if the majority of the people went hungry.

It was so easy for regimes to fall. Ashkan suspected that was what the Iranian hierarchy was hoping for.

The Saudi kingdom still had its wealth but presently couldn't extract it from the ground. That was why Ashkan was here, to further hit the Saudis where it would hurt them the most. He wasn't alone either. He couldn't see any of his brothers, but he knew they were near, and they would not fail, either. They would come after his explosion. Dressed as fire fighters, they would bring the carnage further into the heart of the structure.

His job was to destroy the security at the main doors and to provide the pretence for this additional incursion. With the lobby of the immense sky scraper filled with the dead and the dying, who would argue when first responders arrived? Whilst Ashkan would martyr himself through suicide, his brothers would come with guns to kill as many as they could find.

Attacking the Tadawul Stock Exchange only made sense during the day, when it was full and busy in its trading. The huge building towered above him and he knew he had mere moments left before those he loved would give him the title Shahid. He was suddenly sure his sons would honour his name. How could they not? This was the will of Allah.

It was mere minutes from here to where he had stayed the night before and the desire to back away grew unnervingly strong. He knew he would not succumb to that weakness. He was human; he was frail and fallible, and his mind could rebel all it wanted. As long as his feet carried him forward and his thumb pressed down on the trigger taped to the palm of his hand, he would not fail his country or his God.

Hiding any concerns that lurked in his heart, Ashkan climbed the steps that led up to the impressive structure.

There was no way for him to know that the war he was helping spark was being orchestrated by minds that desired to see humanity fall. If only he had been in possession of Lilith's powers. If only Ashkan had been able to see the black shroud surrounding the man who had sent him on this mission, perhaps then he might have been able to understand the way the minds of men were being manipulated.

If only he could have seen the part he was playing that would hurtle the planet to the end of all time.

4.

London, UK

"Armed police, get your hands up. Get your fucking hands up now." Damien had not been surprised that he would eventually be found. He just hadn't expected it to be this night. It was a shame, really, because he hadn't finished displaying the two bodies he had recently killed. His breath lingered around him as he sighed, his bare flesh hardly feeling the cold. Damien raised his hands, a sly smile falling across his lips.

Let the fun commence.

"On your knees, get on your knees." Damien thought about it for a second, and eagerly complied. A bullet was not something he wanted to encounter right now. He had to survive this because his task in this world was incomplete. There was so much of this life he wished to experience. He had for so long lurked in the shadows, hiding away from the world as he and his hidden accomplice picked off these victims. It would be interesting to feel what fame and notoriety were like.

"Get your face on the floor, get your face on the damned floor."

"On your belly, on your belly," another voice ordered.

With the ground biting into his legs, he arched his head around to see how many of them were here. My, they certainly *had* pulled out all the stops for him. Damien felt almost honoured.

"Do not look at us, do not move," men screamed, half a dozen surrounding him now that he had failed to comply fast enough, weapons pointed threateningly at his face. He spotted the hesitation. Perhaps Damien's height and heavily muscular frame were daunting for them. If not for their guns, he would have tried to fight them off. Instead, he let the arms grab him roughly as they tackled his body fully to the ground. His face was planted in the dirt and debris that had accumulated over the years since the abandoned factory had closed.

Something sharp dug into his abdomen, but he ignored it along with the knee pressing in his back. His arms were manipulated behind him, which was of more pressing concern. He put enough tension in those arms to make the person on top of him work for it.

He had no idea how they had tracked him here. They would no doubt tell him in their own good time, gloating over their own brilliance. The weak liked to do that. They liked to prove their supremacy if given the chance.

"Easy, guys," Damien said.

"Shut it," came the response.

"You got him?" one of the officers asked.

"Yeah, I got him. He's not going anywhere. Are you killer?" Those words were followed by an unnecessary tug on his right arm as the cuffs descended on his wrists. There was chaos all around him as further officers attempted to make safe the area. Oh, what delights they were about to find. This room had once been a staff canteen, able to seat well over fifty people. It was presently barren of furniture, with the police free to roam its full expanse.

The real treat was to be found in the adjoining office.

"You could at least let me get dressed," Damien said in mock protest.

"I said, shut your damned mouth," came the response, a gloved hand pressing down hard on the back of his head. Damien felt his cheek thrust across the ground, likely grazed. He blinked as debris got in his eye and made it water. That annoyed him. He didn't mind the dirt, but Damien didn't want anybody to think he would weep for what he was about to be accused of.

"Sarge, you have to…*Jesus*!" somebody said from the adjoining room. Then came the sound of vomiting, somebody obviously traumatised by what Damien had prepared. If only they could understand. If only they had let him finish. It would have been better if he and the one he carried had been able to complete the masterpiece he had only recently begun to create.

Despite the persistent memories it would carve in his captors' minds, Damien knew each and every one of these officers would willingly gaze in awe upon his art. They would deny it, of course, calling him a host of vile names, but inside their hearts, they would weep with the beauty only he could create.

"What's your first name?" the officer riding him asked. Damien spat dirt out of his mouth in response. "I said, what's your first name?"

"I am the I am," Damien said. It was so clichéd, but it seemed like the right thing to say. At least they didn't need to search him, what with him being naked save for the blood that completely coated his body.

Damien's latest victims had died two hours ago. The police would soon realise how close they had come to saving two lives. He hoped such knowledge would haunt them, for they were interfering with his precious and vital work. Those lives weren't even valuable, both a threat to the world and the people in it. Damien would explain that to them, but he knew they wouldn't listen.

He wouldn't hold that against them. There was no way their feeble minds could comprehend the magnitude of the task he had been set. But then, Damien would show them the true monster that lived within him. Then they really would have something to talk about.

If he was honest, Damien expected rougher treatment. Perhaps a boot in the ribs, or even a kick to the head. The fact that those arresting him seemed restrained, despite the evidence of his brutality on display, meant they were likely wearing body cameras. That was a shame. There was a certain invigoration about the body blows he was expecting, but alas, they never came. Instead, Damien was dragged to his feet, and a blanket thrown over his shoulders. He didn't mind being naked, but apparently the police did. Maybe he made them feel inadequate. Even with the cuffs, two men kept hold of him with his body restricted between them. Without their guns, he could have easily killed every last one of them. Never mind.

He loved how intimate it all was. Damien reckoned he could get used to such treatment. Not his other half though. That part of Damien wanted only to kill.

The officer with the sergeant's stripes got right in his face, his foul breath washing over Damien. The sergeant was calmer than the others, a level head to settle the vigilante justice that could so easily be unleashed here. Cameras could be turned away, a resisting body flung down a flight of steps. Damien was big, but bones could be broken and fingers dislocated.

"Tell us your name, lad. Let's not have any more nonsense."

"You can call me Damien." There was little point lying, although he declined to give them his other names. Damien wasn't the name he was born with, but it suited him. It seemed apt, considering.

"Well, my friend, let's get the official stuff out of the way, shall we? I'm arresting you on suspicion of multiple murders. You don't have to say anything, but it may harm your defence if you don't mention something that you later rely on in court. Anything you do say may be given as evidence." A spit hood was suddenly pulled over Damien's head. He could still see through it, but the world was now a haze.

"You honestly think I would spit at you?" Surely such activity was reserved for drug addicts and animals.

"I don't know what you are capable of," came the sergeant's response. "But we wouldn't want to give these fine lads an excuse to use any unnecessary force, now would we?"

"That's a shame. I was kind of looking forward to that."

"Save it," the sergeant said. "Nobody is impressed by your bullshit."

The sergeant watched as his prisoner was dragged away before venturing into the adjoining room, where three of his officers stood ashen-faced. He didn't want to enter that room. He wanted nothing more to do with this maniac. None of this had been expected, as the officers first on the scene held back and called in backup. The anonymous tip-off had proven itself, and inside the factory they had found the man half the Metropolitan Police had been hunting for the last fifteen months.

Forty-seven murders, many of them still unknown to the police. All were male and included both adults and children. There hadn't been a sexual aspect to the killings. Things had been much worse than that. The killings had been so random that nobody had been able to establish a consistent pattern. Damien would likely be able to tell them the pattern, but the sergeant didn't put much stock in the murderer giving them the truth.

In the room of death, two bodies hung by their feet from the beams above. The bodies were cold, pale, the blood drained out of them into a bath that had been placed beneath. No doubt that depraved bastard had enjoyed the bath. Maybe he even found the blood invigorating. But where were the victim's clothes? Unlike the room in which the arrest had been made, the floor here was clean, swept of all but the faintest traces of dirt. A thick, clear plastic sheet had been spread out so that the killer could begin his collection. The sergeant suspected Damien had been interrupted before he was finished, as not all the organs had been removed from the bodies.

The sergeant stood there, mesmerised, surprised by how little the scene affected him. The impact would come. It always did. Later, though, when he was alone. At least they finally had him, and the streets of London could once again lay claim to safety.

Now they just had to get the bastard talking.

***

Lilith regretted the death of the teenager. It had been unfortunate, but necessary. His life would have been one of useless pain and torment, made worse by the yet undiscovered corpses that had once been his parents. The demons would have killed them, slowly, in front of their victim to freshen him up for the fun that was to follow. It had been better to spare the teenager any more of this world. He was an innocent and the Lord on high would tend to his wounded soul.

There was also the risk that the poor soul would be kidnapped again by the persistent demonic forces. The demons she had dispatched would not find it easy to return for quite some time, but there were others that would love to taste the young man's fear. Their numbers were too numerous to count, and Lilith could only protect so many.

That had always been the way of her Order.

When she was well away from what was now a crime scene, Lilith informed the authorities of her actions. The text she sent was via an anonymous burner phone purchased nearly twelve months earlier. The message went to the number 61016, the number for British Transport Police, and relayed the GPS coordinates of the bodies she had left at her unsuccessful rescue attempt. No doubt the police were already on the scene, tearing their hair out, trying to understand what had occurred. Whilst MI5 would undoubtedly try to usurp the investigation, the presence of the dead police officer would hamper their attempt to play power games.

The two agencies would have to work together under the mutual umbrella of their humiliation.

Both organisations would want to keep this as quiet as possible due to the embarrassment it would cause. The DNA of the three dead adults would be all over the teenager, along with fingerprints. The truth that they had kidnapped and tortured the youngster would be there for all to see.

Lilith had returned to the safe house she used whenever she was forced to come to this dismal city. She owned no property herself, but had access to countless addresses scattered across the UK. Inquisitors were rarely in one place for long, their mission seeing them follow a trail of abductions and murders that demons invariably left in their wake. Most of the time she acted on the intelligence provided by her Order. But sometimes, as with today, she was able to hunt out the infestation using her own training.

Being able to see the darkness around the possessed helped in that regard. It was a skill only some inquisitors could claim. Whenever she discovered a demon, and when time permitted, she would put that individual under surveillance. Sometimes she would kill them outright. Opportunity occasionally allowed that. With regret, she now saw that she should have taken that action when she first saw the corruption around the man who she discovered worked for MI5.

Her possessions were not hers. They were merely on loan from her beloved Order. One day, the weapons she carried into battle would either be abandoned at the scene of her death, or returned to be used by her replacement. When she was dead, she would have no need for such trinkets. Lilith would be a curiosity for the law enforcement organisation that found her cooling corpse and she would end up cremated without anyone present to mourn her passing.

Lilith had to admit that the day's events troubled her. Not the killing of an innocent; that act barely registered on her conscience. No, her unease rested on the identities of the others she had killed today. In her mind, the forces massed against her kind were becoming organised, working together to further some scheme that was a mystery to all. She knew she could not solve this conundrum on her own, but she also knew that the hierarchy of her Order appeared slow to adapt, painfully set in their ways.

Demons acted in a set, defined pattern. That was how it had always been, so why would things change now?

The house she borrowed was the typical terraced affair found across much of London. It looked normal from the outside, but its structure had been hardened against attack. The windows were bullet and blast-proof, with the external walls strengthened by a second steel-reinforced layer that had been added years ago. The front and back doors, so innocent in appearance, were designed to withstand everything except the most persistent of attacks. Although the front door gave the appearance of being opened by a key, that was purely for show. The inquisitive often ignored that which gave off the appearance of being average. Instead, the door was opened via a hidden retinal scan reader that was programmed with the biometrics of all the inquisitors who were likely to use the property. Lilith was aware of two other similar properties in London she could use if this one became compromised.

She knew that one of them presently housed another inquisitor, although she hadn't seen him of late. His name was Lucien, and he had graduated the same year as Lilith.

Inside this house, her haven included more of the same deception and subterfuge. Hidden panels, hidden rooms, all containing the tools she needed to fight her never-ending war. She never saw the people tasked to service these residences, but knew that whenever she arrived at a property, it would contain everything she needed to sustain her. Most importantly of all, the basement allowed for a secret escape—a hidden grate that provided access to a series of disused tunnels below. Ancient cities like London were often interlaced with such subterranean mysteries. The ones beneath this building had been installed in 1875 to run gas pipes through.

The residence would also have all the weapons she needed for ridding the world of demonic hordes. Hers might have been an ancient Order, but they embraced all that modern technology could give them. They were part of the Catholic Church, and therefore not short of funds.

The idea was that inquisitors would never need to interact with the world at large except in the pursuit of their mission. Lilith, however, as with many of her fellow inquisitors, rejected this approach, choosing instead to venture out into the world and see first-hand the corruption that dwelled there. Such actions were frowned upon, but not forbidden because it was understood that a knowledge of society and the people she helped defend were, for some, important in maintaining the cover that the Order of Tyron required.

The number of people outside the Order who knew of its existence could be counted on the fingers with which God had blessed Lilith.

She sat cross-legged and naked on the padded rug in a living room that held no other furniture, waiting for her satellite phone to inevitably ring. The call would be encrypted over the Vatican's own secretive satellite network. People forgot that the Vatican City was a nation unto itself, with a reported wealth of nearly fifteen billion dollars. Of course, it was worth much more than that, easily able to establish a covert international communications network impervious to the ever-listening ears of the world's security services.

The phone resting on the rug in front of her rang as expected. Lilith picked it up.

"I'm listening," she said.

"Report," the voice on the other end demanded. This man she had never met, and hopefully never would. He was Lilith's handler, the person to whom she directly reported. His name was Bishop Rizzo, but Lilith knew him mainly by the generic codename John. Even that she would never use over the phone, and the Sicilian accent that punctuated his words confirmed the falsehood behind the fake name. Lilith knew other things about him, too. From his voice alone, she could tell he was a man of weak stature. This was not an individual trained in battle.

"It was as I feared. Three were working together."

"That is unusual. Are you sure you are not mistaken about this?"

"Who are you talking to?" Lilith had no time for such foolish notions.

"Right. Did you rescue the boy?"

"He is with Christ." She could almost sense the anger bristling at the other end of the phone. Anger not with her, but with the opportunity lost.

"Were you too late?" This implied that the teenager was dead by the time Lilith had arrived at the attempted rescue. Not too foolish a question given the often-volatile nature of the demonic mind, and she accepted that John had to ask. He, like Lilith, had people to whom he had to answer.

"No, the boy had been rendered useless. The vermin had cut off all his fingers and thumbs. Blinded him, as well as doing other things."

"Again?" It was not the first time Lilith had encountered this type of defilement. She also suspected she wasn't the only inquisitor to have reported such occurrences. The demons were learning; adapting.

"They know how to act against us. We can expect to see this more often." Whilst many of the Inquisition were born into the role, those like Lilith were conscripted from the children rescued by other inquisitors. As haphazard a technique as this seemed, the resultant inquisitors were often of the highest calibre, for they had first-hand experience of the dangers the world faced.

First, they had to survive the training.

"But that suggests a coordinated approach. Demons work alone." John seemed to believe the words he spoke. Lilith no longer did. "Demons always work alone."

"Clearly not anymore. My recent experience says otherwise. Has my last report been relayed to the Cardinal?" Lilith was referring to the man who headed the Order. In the entirety of its existence, the Order of Tyron had never been commanded by anyone from the inquisitor battalions. That honour always went to the select few who worked their way up through the Vatican ranks, chosen sometimes through merit, but at other times through politics. All, however, had to go through a trial to prove they were immune to the corrupting influence of the demon spawn, as did any at the highest ranks in the Vatican.

In times of old, that was an arduous and unpleasant process. Now it was done with a simple blood test to prove the candidate was genetically incompatible with the demon hordes. It would not do for the head of the Order to fall to possession. The Catholic Church had suffered enough of that over the last few decades, causing the church to be riddled with scandals not of its own making. And still those in control could not imagine the demons working to some ordered plan.

Sometimes Lilith wondered if those in charge were bloody idiots. The other possibility that occasionally occurred to her would be a disaster for the world, so as usual, she pushed it to the back of her mind.

"Yes. Though I have not been told what was made of your report."

"Have other Inquisitors reported similar findings?"

The voice at the other end paused before responding. "There have been rumblings," came the eventual reply. *Rumblings*? So, her fellow Inquisitors were finding exactly as she was. "You should not concern yourself with such matters."

"How can I not, with what I am seeing?"

"You presume too much," John insisted. "You are here to follow orders, nothing more."

"Have you ever battled with the dark ones?" Her words carried no malice, but it was sometimes important to remind the bureaucrats who the soldiers were in this fight.

"You know I haven't. I am not worthy of that honour."

"Then do not tell me what I do or do not presume. I request a conclave be organised." She knew such a request would be denied, but she asked anyway. At least it would be on record. Every word she said across this secure phone network was recorded and logged.

“Don’t be ridiculous. There hasn’t been a conclave of active inquisitors in over two hundred years. The risk is too great.” Indeed. Having the Orders warriors under one roof was risky, even with the precautions they would take.

“That may be, but I request it anyway.”

“Very well,” John replied wearily. “But don’t hold your breath.” With that, the conversation was ended, the line going dead. The temptation to hurl the phone across the room so that it might smash against the stone fireplace was strong. Instead, she switched it off and placed it with exaggerated caution on the ground before her.

To feel temptation was acceptable. Acting on those temptations was where the problems always started.

5.

Inquisitor training camp, 20 years earlier

They stood naked in the rain, the gathered children all of similar age. Where they all came from, Lilith didn't know and didn't care. Her own anguish was the only thing consuming her. For nearly a year, she had not felt the wind against her skin. This was the first time she had been outside the oppressive confines of the concrete catacombs that had been her home since her salvation. For twelve whole months Lilith hadn't seen the sun. Now, the surrounding night was a cloak of blackness only punctured by spotlights that swept the perimeter wire of the camp. That wire, so tall to her young frame, was there to both protect and contain.

This camp was her new home, hidden away from the world. At least the air smelt fresh, although it was tainted by the subtle scent of smoke. She tried not to breathe too deeply. There was only one thing ever burnt here.

"You twenty have been deemed worthy of continued training," the man standing before them said. To Lilith, he was a giant, huge in stature and width. One of his arms hung oddly at his side, as if damaged, possibly the result of some grievous injury long ago received.

Lilith feared him, as well as the stick he carried. She knew what damage such an implement could inflict, the souls of her feet scarred from previous punishments. Some of those beatings had been warranted, others random lessons given to teach the harshness of life. At first, on her rescue, she thought she would be spared any more pain. She had been wrong.

There was something else to fear. The burning brazier behind Father glowed red hot, the coals in there stoked and ready despite the falling rain.

"You will call me Father, for I am here to guide you," the man continued. His piercing gaze searched the twenty helpless recruits for signs of defiance. As the months progressed, he would also search them for weakness. The frail ones, those who had not passed the first of the tests, had already been disposed of. These twenty would become ten, and then five, only a quarter of his present class likely to survive. Through over two decades of overseeing the training, Father claimed he knew who was going to make it from day one. Some had been born to this place, others brought here after surviving their ordeal at the hands of the defiled.

They would become inquisitors, or they would be broken. Many would die, while some would earn enough respect to take up lower positions in the Order. But only the best would go on to bear the name inquisitor. Every year, a class of up to forty new recruits would replace those who graduated. Not much of an army to defend the world, but it was all their Order's resources would allow.

"Your life here will be unrelenting, gruelling, and filled with agony. Many of you will say this isn't fair, but such complaints are pointless. You must learn that all life is suffering. To deny that is to deny the very will of God." Father struck the air with his cane, the space seeming to separate as it interrupted the downpour. To Lilith's left, a girl whimpered, the weakness in her flesh made audible. Lilith made no such noise, for she was determined not to fail. Having been kidnapped by those with the stench of sulphur, an unyielding vengeance burned within her young and once tender heart.

She was prepared to make this sacrifice so that she could one day wreak her vengeance on those that had defiled her.

"The people of the world do not deserve our protection because they have become corrupt, decadent and weak. But protect them we will, for that is our purpose. That is why we are here, to keep the order and protect those fallen from God's grace." From the sides, cloaked figures appeared, three on each flank, to stop the errant from making a break for it. Nuns, consumed by their devotion, unrelenting in their brutality. Effectively, these six figures had been Lilith's and the other children's parents for the last year, and this would be the last time she would ever see them. Every one of these nuns had stood where Lilith now stood. Rejected trainee inquisitors, devoting their life to nurturing the future generation in penance for their failures as children.

Having been a late arrival to the ranks assembled, the nuns had been particularly vicious with Lilith. Not out of malice or sadism, but out of a devotion that demanded only those worthy be considered for inquisitor ranks. Lilith had borne their blows and their cruel words silently and with an acceptance that surprised the harshest of them.

In her year of confinement, not a single tear had escaped her eyes. Out of earshot, the nuns would often comment that they had never seen a child as strong as the one called Lilith.

"Who will step forth and take the protective mark?" Father asked. His words sounded gentle, in complete contrast to what was being asked. Despite her own doubts, Lilith felt her feet move, a step taken, an indication of her true devotion. Father smiled. "See?" he said, beckoning Lilith to come closer. "This is how it begins. There can be no hesitation, no doubt. Whatever happens in your life is because God wills it." Lilith came close to her new teacher, pride threatening to blossom within her heart. She crushed it, for pride had no place here. That was an emotion for those who lived out in the world. The weak and the selfish. Those on whom the Beast preyed.

Lilith felt a hand descend on her shoulder. It was harsh, calloused, squeezing harder than was necessary. She made no complaint.

"What is your name, child?"

"Lilith."

"Ah yes, after Adam's first wife. Sent out from paradise because she would not submit. Do you know why you were given this name, child?"

"Because inquisitors do not bow down to anyone except God." The pride came again, so seductive, so addictive. It would soon be driven from her for good, and she craved that moment. Should a seven-year-old be able to think such thoughts? Well, think them she did.

"That is correct. Lilith, do you claim your chance of a place amongst us?" Father kept his grip on her as he guided the tiny child over to the brazier. She could see the iron rod sticking out with the promise it held.

"Yes. For God, not for man." It was easy to remember the words. They had been repeated countless times, ever since she first learnt her new place in the world.

"For God, not for man," the rest of the children said in unison.

One of the nuns detached herself, the eldest of them, the one chosen for the task. Now properly positioned, Lilith could feel the heat from the brazier. As the elder nun approached, her wrinkled face was lit up by the glow, and for the briefest of moments, Lilith thought she saw delight there. It must have been a trick of the shadows, though, for there could be no such thought in any of the nun's minds. Their actions might have seemed cruel, even heartless to the uninitiated, but that was far from the case. The children needed to be prepared, made ready for this day and the ones that followed. Only the strongest could survive.

On her third month in the place of the concrete rooms, Lilith had noticed that one of her group had gone missing, never to be seen again. Nothing was said of the disappearance except that, whilst the meek might inherit the earth, only the strong could protect it.

Lilith watched the nun as she picked the hot iron from the simmering coals. She knew she should feel afraid, but she felt nothing, her whole body overtaken by a numbness that was strangely empowering. She did not flinch as the branding iron was brought towards her. Lilith's eyes never wavered from its glowing tip.

"Do you give yourself to God until your dying breath?" Father asked.

"Yes," Lilith said, her voice audible over the falling rain. The iron sizzled as the water fell upon it, just as it sizzled when it was pressed against the flesh of her yet unformed breast. The pain was all-consuming, but still nothing to what had already been done to her. Not a sound made its way past her clenched teeth.

"Let this be an example to you all," Father roared. "See how she accepts the mark. As you are branded so you shall be reborn. Who is next to bear this holy seal?" One by one, the children stepped forward, only two crying out at the injustice being inflicted upon their body.

Even at that tender age, Lilith held no pity for those who let pain overcome them. Only the sturdiest could hope to bear the final brand that would be delivered at the end of the training. Those who lacked the strength in this moment were unlikely to survive and it was better their struggles were ended quickly. Father was not one to tolerate or forgive any kind of weakness.

Inquisitors were flesh made steel. Their training started at such a young age to eradicate the frailties that made humans such enticing morsels for the dwellers of the netherworlds. It was perhaps ironic that inquisitors, once trained, were more merciless and ruthless than anything that came out of the Pit.

6.

Slough, UK. Present Day

"But mum, I don't feel well." At only eight years old, Emily Ralph was a little young to act so deceptively, but she really didn't want to go to school today. Of late, school felt wrong, not the safe place it was supposed to be. Seated at the kitchen dining table, the face she made could have won her acclaim on Broadway. Unfortunately for Emily, her mother wasn't easily fooled.

"Oh really? And what's up with you today? Bubonic plague? An attack of the screaming abdabs?" Emily's mum, Vicky, had the power that many mothers seemed to miraculously possess, the power to know when their offspring were trying to pull a fast one. She also had years of training as a psychologist to back up that intuition.

"My belly hurts," Emily protested. It didn't really, but she reckoned she was a good enough actor to fake it. A cool hand descended upon her temple. Oh, no. Emily had forgotten about the dark detective arts her mother possessed. Emily put an extra grimace on her face for good measure.

"Well, you aren't hot and you seemed well enough to wolf down your breakfast this morning."

"It just came on." Foiled by her own greed.

"Oh, it has, has it?" Vicky seemed to tower over her daughter, the piercing stare one of the many weapons at her disposal. In the background, Vicky barely seemed to register the announcement on the radio news about the attacks on the Saudi Arabian oil infrastructure. As with most people, the events that shaped the globe often occurred unnoticed by them.

"Well…" The hesitation and the guilt were setting in.

"What have I always told you, pudding?"

“Not to lie.” The jig was up. The cat was out of the bag. Emily didn’t quite know why a cat would be in a bag, but it was running around freely now.

“And what are you doing now?” The words were calm, Vicky’s face unflustered.

“Perhaps not telling the whole truth.” Her mother sat down next to her. The father wasn’t on the scene anymore, not since the cancer had taken him two years ago. Whilst the life insurance helped, the loss of her father’s income meant Vicky was struggling to keep the family’s head above the financial waters, despite her own career. It wasn’t easy to raise a kid alone and succeed in her chosen pathway in life, not in this economy.

“So, what’s going on with you? Why don’t you want to go to school?” Emily wasn’t aware that people felt there was a surprising strength to her. It wasn’t easy to lose one of your parents at such a young age, and yet Emily had seemed to weather it. If not for the child’s fortitude, Vicky sometimes wondered if she herself would have been able to drag herself out of the pit into which life had thrown her.

The pain often showed in Vicky’s eyes. She was obviously tormented by the memory of her partner’s last days; the agony he had endured. Emily could easily recall how her dying father had looked at the end, the forced smile trying to hide the truth of his condition. She wondered if her mother would ever be able to love another man again. She wasn’t yet wise to that part of being human, but Emily had a suspicion that love had a habit of making an appearance when you were least ready for it. That was what one of her favourite films had told her, anyway. Her father had been a rock that had been shattered by disease. Even towards his end, his prime concern had been his family.

Emily knew she was her mother's reason to keep on going, and normally she tried not to provide anything in the way of trouble.

"It's my teacher." There, she had said it. Now would come the dreaded inquisition, the disbelief that adults often retreated into whenever children threatened the stability they thought they had created around their lives.

"What, Mrs Rawlinson? What's wrong with your teacher?"

"There's something…" Emily hesitated. "There's something weird about her." Oh boy, was there!

"But you always liked her." Emily knew her mum had met the teacher several times, and always commented that she was likeable.

"She's just odd now." Emily didn't have the vocabulary to really express her reservations about the woman who, until recently, had been a fabulous teacher. There was something definitely amiss with the woman, as though there was a sickness feeding off her. Not a physical malady; her teacher still seemed healthy and vibrant. This was something that Emily suspected only she could detect. Nobody else had mentioned it, or shown any sign of seeing what had been so visible to Emily for nearly a week. This was why Emily had been hesitant to mention it.

The only word Emily had in her limited vocabulary to describe Mrs Rawlinson now was *evil.*

If she concentrated hard enough, Emily was sure she could sometimes see a darkness surrounding the once amiable fifty-year-old. Sometimes that darkness would spread, touching the children around her as Mrs Rawlinson moved around the classroom. How was she supposed to explain that to her mother?

Oh yeah, you know, my teacher kind of looks wicked. And then there were the eyes, the black shapes that Emily swore she had seen floating across them on occasion.

"Does she ever shout at you?" Emily wasn't the kind to cause a problem in class. She was one of the good kids, well liked and of a friendly disposition, and that meant she found it easy to make friends. Adults often proclaimed that Emily was a delight, and Vicky clearly didn't feel there was much to argue about in that regard. As children went, the child was considered an angel by many.

Well, most of the time. Children grew up, although Emily had yet to hit the puberty rapids. No doubt her mum was not looking forward to the time when hormones started to crash through her loveable child.

"No, nothing like that. Do I really have to go to school?"

"I think so, honey," Vicky said, although a tinge of regret crept into her voice. Emily would have liked to spend a random day with her mum. Would it really hurt for both of them to have some surprise time off once in a while? No, it probably wouldn't, but that wasn't going to happen today.

"Okay," Emily said, but she didn't try to hide her reluctance. Would there be more questions about what had happened to cause this reaction?

Emily wasn't surprised when the front door suddenly opened, but she was glad for it.

"Hello," a familiar child's voice shouted. Emily brightened then, the arrival of her best friend a welcome distraction from the grilling she was receiving. Lucy Richards wandered into the kitchen as if she owned the place, her blonde hair as unruly as ever. Lucy's harassed mother, Natalie, followed in her wake, an apologetic look plastered across her face. Emily received the playful hug from her friend that she was expecting, and the two girls skipped off into the adjoining living room.

Vicky frowned, watching them leave, then turned to Natalie when she spoke. "Sorry, I keep telling her she needs to ring the doorbell." It was an apology for the way Lucy had sauntered into a house that wasn't hers.

"It's fine," Vicky said genuinely. Natalie and Vicky shared the duty of taking the two children to and from school, and today it was Natalie's turn. "Although a minute ago Emily insisted she didn't want to go to school." The words were said in a mother's huddle, voices lowered so that the two girls wouldn't overhear.

"Really?"

"She said she felt ill."

"Emily doesn't look ill."

"She isn't. Turns out she's worried about Mrs Rawlinson."

"Why would she be worried about her teacher? The woman's a blessing." The words reassured Vicky. If none of the other kids had noticed anything wrong, then maybe there wasn't anything to worry about. Especially as their daughter's teacher wasn't a man.

Vicky chastised herself for falling into that media-inspired trap. Men, in general, weren't the danger in the world. Only some of them were. You had to be able to still trust, or else you risked raising your kid in a protective bubble that would harm them later in life.

"Emily says she's odd."

"Well, Lucy hasn't said anything. Now if they were talking about the headmistress they have at that place, I could understand it." Neither mother had the financial means to send their children to private school, so they had to make do with what the state provided. So far, they had been lucky, partly because where they lived put them in the catchment area of one of Slough's better primary schools. The headmistress they were referring to, although short in stature, seemed to instil a healthy dose of fear into the children and parents alike. The woman in charge was likely the main reason the school did so well.

"Keep your ears peeled, could you, just in case?" There had been something in the way Emily had spoken those words that had spooked Vicky. *She's odd.*

"I doubt Lucy would tell me anyway," Natalie complained. "She's turning into a right little madam."

"I'm sure you were just as bad."

"I was terrible!" Natalie beamed. "I don't know how my mother survived my tantrums." The designated driver turned to face the living room. "Emily, Lucy, come on. We have to go." This dragged the two youngsters from whatever they were doing. Emily gave her mum a gentle hug as she passed and then she was off after Lucy, bag and coat collected by the door.

Vicky followed them out, her own demanding job beckoning. She knew she would give anything to protect her daughter, but it would be a lot easier if the man who had promised to cherish her was still alive.

***

"I want to be an Instagram model when I grow up," Lucy proclaimed proudly in the back of the car.

"Do you even know what an Instagram model is?" her mum asked. A glance in the rear-view mirror reassured Natalie their seatbelts were fastened.

"I'm going to grow a huge butt and flaunt it."

"Lucy!" Natalie tried to sound shocked, but there was no disguising the humour that crept in there.

"Me and Emily will both grow huge butts and be an Instagram sensation." Lucy empathised the last word, throwing her hands up in the air in celebration.

"I don't want to have a big butt. I'm going to be a vet so I can cure sick kittens," Emily said. "And when they are well, I will make kitten videos to show everyone how good I am."

"You could put them on Instagram," Lucy insisted. Emily could tell her friend was obsessed.

"Instagram's boring." Emily's statement resulted in mock horror from her friend.

"How can you say that?"

"It is. You should read more books."

Lucy rolled her eyes. "Books are for old people like mum."

"Hey, watch who you call old, you." Emily was often surprised by how little her peers read in their free time.

"I'm not going to grow up," Lucy decided. "I'm going to stay a kid, so I don't have to worry about responsibility."

"You can't not grow up," Emily advised.

"I can if I want. I will stop growing. I will use magic."

"You don't know any magic."

"I am sure I can learn." Lucy sounded adamant. "I will search the internet for spells to stop me growing old."

"But then you will have to stay in school forever." The thought of spending more time than she had to in Mrs Rawlinson's class filled Emily with dread.

"Oh, I hadn't thought of that."

"Emily," Natalie interjected, "your mum says you think your teacher is odd."

"She is," Emily insisted.

"Mrs Rawlinson smells," Lucy said, backing up her friend. Emily was grateful for that, but it was obvious Lucy didn't see the truth behind the situation.

"She does not," Natalie said disarmingly. Emily agreed with Lucy's mum. She had been around the teacher enough times to know there were no body odour issues emanating from her teacher. Smelly pits she could deal with.

"You shouldn't say things like that about people," Natalie continued. "You could hurt their feelings."

Lucy wasn't going to accept the wisdom of her own mother. "But she does. She wears too much perfume. Pooh, pooh," Lucy suddenly grabbed her nose and began to writhe around as if she couldn't breathe. Natalie caught the antics in the mirror, as well as Emily not trying to hide the deathly seriousness in her face.

"What's odd about her?" There it was, more questioning. If there was something going on, the adults never relented until they got to the bottom of it.

"It's hard to explain," Emily answered. She wished she hadn't started with her masquerade. "She just isn't the same. I don't like her anymore."

"Well, I like her," Lucy announced. "She gave me top marks for my story."

"I read that story," Natalie remembered. "It was very good."

"Was that the story about the goat?" Emily had been there when Lucy had read it out to the whole class. Most of the kids had been in stitches. Who would have thought goats could be so funny?

“Yes. When I’m on Instagram, I will have a big butt and tell stories about goats.” That got Emily laughing, which seemed to drown out the voice of concern that stayed in the child’s head.

“Maybe you should have a page about goat butts,” Natalie pointed out.

“Nobody would want to see that.” Lucy sounded amazed at the very idea. Emily knew her friend wasn’t going to waste her time on something nobody would want to see. What would be the point of that? You see, there it was again. Adults, they didn’t have a clue.

7.

London, UK

Damien wasn't naked anymore, which was a shame. His skin and hair were also clean, the arresting officers insisting he shower himself. Damien found such cleanliness disagreeable, preferring the natural smells that nature could provide. The paper shell suit he wore bulged in complaint at the mass it was trying to cover. Another disadvantage of his pending incarceration, Damien realised. He wouldn't be able to wear the clothes he preferred.

Life could be so tedious sometimes.

Whilst he had waited in the holding cell, Damien had given serious consideration to soiling himself and his environment with his own faeces. He suspected if he tried that, they might have set the hose on him, so there was little point to such belligerence. It finally occurred to him that such an act was beneath him, given his lineage.

He had a part to him that was a killer to be feared. Smearing shit all over the walls of his cell was the act of a drug-addled barbarian. Best not bother with that idea then.

At present, he sat alone in an interview room, his hands shackled in front of him. Those who had put him here thought the metal could protect them. That was a mistake. It was another declined temptation though. It would have been so easy to show them that his strength could break him free from their attempts to constrain him.

The brightness of the room bathed him. His buttocks were already irritated by the hardness of the chair he sat on. He'd always found it difficult to sit like this for prolonged periods, the normal world not really made for someone of his size. Sitting implied inaction, and Damien had too much to do to waste his time lounging around.

There were people out there he needed to kill.

Unfortunately, with his arrest, he would find himself with a lot of enforced free time. If they had only given him a few more days, there was so much more he could have achieved.

Just as his mind began to drift away to savour the memories of his previous slaughter, the door to the room opened and two men walked in.

"Good afternoon, Damien," one of the men said, both sitting down. The fact that they were still calling him Damien showed they had yet to track down his true identity. They would struggle with that. His details wouldn't be on any criminal database, and he lived off the grid, floating through the cracks, flourishing in the black economy. He was also an immigrant to this country, having snuck in years before.

It was only recently that Damien had realised why he had been drawn to this sceptic isle.

"Is it afternoon already?" His question wasn't answered.

"Do you need anything? Food or refreshment?" the same man asked. Damien shook his head. He wanted to get this over with.

"Right, let's get started. I'm Detective Inspector Paul Hargreaves, and this is Detective Sergeant Black." Black glowered at Damien. Was that an attempt at intimidation? Damien would have liked Black to try that with his guts coiled around his ankles.

"You two make a nice-looking couple," Damien said, pleased with his own attempt at defiance. Neither officers rose to the bait. Instead, Hargreaves pulled out a disc and placed it into the recording device that rested on the table.

"Right Damien, you've just seen me remove the seal and place the disc in the recorder."

"If you say so."

"This interview is being video and audibly recorded, and may be tendered in evidence if your case is brought before a court. We are in an interview room in Hammersmith Police Station. I am Detective Inspector 1791, John Hargreaves. Beside me is Detective Sergeant 1342 Dereck Black. We are both attached to the Special Investigations Unit in charge of investigating the crimes for which you have been arrested. At the end of the interview, I will give you a notice explaining what will happen to the discs and how you can obtain a copy of them."

"Peachy," Damien interrupted.

"For the purposes of the recording, Damien, can I get you to introduce yourself with your full name and your date of birth?"

"Damien Morningstar. I do not know my date of birth." That was actually true. He had no notion of when he had been brought onto this fetid planet.

"Come now, let's not play games," Black admonished.

"Unfortunately, it is the truth."

"And the name you use, Damien Morningstar? Is that for real?" Hargreaves was looking at him doubtfully.

"It is the name I took for myself. It is better than what my father of record used to call me."

"And what was that?" Black asked.

"Shit."

"Pardon, could you repeat that?" Black was also taking notes.

"Shit, or Little Shit on a good day. The father who raised me called me Shit."

"Okay. For the purposes of the interview, we will refer to you as Damien. Is that okay?" Hargreaves asked.

"You can call me what you like. Except for Shit, of course. I tired of that long ago." Damien's smile wasn't as infectious as he hoped it would be. "I must say, you are both being very polite."

"I'm glad we can accommodate you," Black added. The sarcasm was not well hidden.

"Damien, you are not represented by a solicitor at this interview. Can you confirm that one has been offered, and that you declined?"

"Most certainly." A solicitor would only tell him to keep quiet. "I have so much to share."

"Thank you, Damien. Let me remind you that you have a right to free and independent legal advice, and you can speak to a solicitor in private at any…"

"That will not be necessary." Damien had no time for such legal nonsense, as he saw it.

"…at any time, day or night. If you do want legal advice, then the interview can be delayed. If you do not know a solicitor or you cannot contact your own solicitor, then you can ask to speak to the duty solicitor. I will thus ask again. Can you once again confirm that you do not wish to speak to a solicitor at this time?"

"That is correct." My, weren't they both being cautious?

"Is there any reason why you have declined a solicitor?" Black asked.

"Why delay the inevitable?" Damien wanted to sit back in his chair, but the chair prevented that. It felt too small for him. The room was also too warm, not the chill he preferred. "Plus, I've never met a solicitor that I would piss on if they were on fire."

"Do you know many solicitors?" Black asked.

"You would be surprised." He'd killed two that he knew of in his slaughtering rampage.

"Before I start to interview you, I must caution you again." *Seriously, get on with it*, Damien wanted to scream. "You do not have to say anything, but it may harm your defence if you do not mention something when questioned that you later rely on in court. Anything you do say may be given in evidence. Do you understand that?"

Boring.

"Yes," Damien answered.

"So, Damien, how many people have you killed?" Black asked.

"Now that's more like it. Why didn't you start with that?" Damien gave a thumbs up to show his approval.

"Just answer the question, please," Hargreaves said sternly.

"But where would be the fun in that? I'll tell you what, you two come up with a number and I'll tell you if you are close." Damien was determined to enjoy this.

"We aren't here to play games. This is a serious matter," Black said, leaning across the table. A gentle hand from Hargreaves restrained him. Interesting dynamic there, thought Damien.

"You might not be here to play games, but I am. All life is a game."

"Murder isn't a game," insisted Hargreaves.

"But my dear Inspector, that's the best game of all." Both men looked sickened by the smile Damien presented to them. "The hunt, the kill, and everything that follows. You two don't realise that, because you have a mistaken view of the world."

"We have you present at the scene of two obvious murders. You were naked and covered in their blood. Your fingerprints were found on the knife we suspect was used to disembowel them. I don't think your game has ended very well for you." Black seemed pleased with himself.

"I'll admit, you have caused me some inconvenience. I do wish you could have given me more time. If you let me go, I promise to return in about, ooh, a week or three. There are people out there who urgently need killing."

"Somehow, I don't think we will be able to take you up on that," Hargreaves responded. He had a cool head, this Inspector. Damien could tell. No doubt many a criminal had tried to goad him in the past, and likely all had failed.

Hargreaves had one of those manners that would suck the information out of most prisoners.

"Well, I had to try."

"Do you admit to murdering those two men?" Hargreaves was here for one thing. A confession.

"Well, you see, that's a difficult question because I did, and I didn't."

"What the hell is that supposed to mean?" It was evident to Damien that Black was too passionate about his job. The sergeant had yet to learn the subtle skill of distancing oneself from the proceeding. It would be interesting to see how both officers reacted when Damien showed them the truth.

"These hands," Damien said, holding up his fingers, "are guilty of the crimes, but this mind remains innocent. A nice little riddle for you there, gentlemen." He wiggled his sausage-like fingers in emphasis.

"For the recording, can you explain what you mean by that?"

"Oh, I can do better than that. I can show you. Would you like that? Would you like me to reveal one of the rare mysteries of the universe? People will flock to hear of the time you were there when

Damien Morningstar revealed to the world his secret. It will be a story you can tell your grandchildren."

"And what secret is that?" Hargreaves asked.

"Hold on, I'll be right back." Damien seemed to shrink into himself, his face being swallowed up by his hands. The huge body began to shiver, an uncontrolled tremor running through it. Restrained as they were, both arms went into spasm, Black pushing his chair away in an involuntary reaction.

Finally, the contractions ended and Damien lifted his head back up. His eyes were closed.

"Damien, what just happened?" Hargreaves demanded.

"Damien isn't here right now," came the response. The voice was different, lighter, not the thundering bass that had occurred throughout the interview.

"What the hell is this?" Black demanded. In answer, their captive opened his eyes. Whereas before, the irises had been a dark brown, now they were a light blue. The body had swelled further, the material over Damien's biceps ripping.

"As I said, Damien isn't here. You can call me Legion."

8.

Off the coast of the Falkland Islands

Wilson Smith had been fishing these waters for nearly ten years. As the captain of the fishing trawler, *Castero*, he was on the hunt for calamari in the waters north west of the Falkland Islands. The seas were rough and cold, but nothing he and his crew couldn't handle. They were destined for a good catch, which was good news for him and his men. Despite the violence of the water, there was nothing better than being at sea.

Unfortunately, his crew were going to be disappointed this trip.

"Skipper?" Sitting in the comfort of his cabin, Smith was interrupted by the voice over his radio. Wearily, Smith put his book down and picked up the radio handset from the table beside him.

"What's up, Gary?" Gary was his first mate. A reliable man, which was who you wanted in such treacherous waters. You needed people you could rely on because this was also dangerous work and it was not unheard of for people to die.

"Skipper, the sea…it's pink."

"Probably just an algae bloom," Smith replied. It wasn't like Gary to worry about such things.

"No, this is something more than that. You need to come up here and look for yourself." There was definite concern in Gary's voice. If Gary said something wasn't right, you could take that to the bank.

When Smith came out on deck, he was amazed by what he saw. For as far as he could see, the water was a bright, almost fluorescent pink. It was only now visible due to a bank of ocean fog finally clearing. That in itself had been a rarity for this region. There was a definite smell too, as if the air itself was rotten. Smith found himself almost gagging. So much for the bracing sea air he loved.

"The fish are all dead," Gary told him. Smith hadn't spotted it at first, but on closer inspection, he could see the shapes bobbing in the water. Most of the fish were hidden by the algae bloom that had so obviously killed them.

"We can't catch anything in this," Smith declared. This was a disaster. The fish were dead either because they had been poisoned or because all the oxygen had been sucked out of the water. Easy to catch, but no way they could be fed to any living things. Most likely, every single one of them would be toxic.

"I've heard from another trawler five miles from us. It's the same there, too." Five miles! How big was this bloom? Smith had heard of such things before, but never in waters so cold. And never so far out to sea. Normally, it was associated with the run-off from land pollution. Such an occurrence shouldn't be happening out here. They were in the middle of fricking nowhere.

"Let's see if we can find the edge of it," Smith ordered. There were things other than fish dead in the water. It looked like all manner of marine life had been slaughtered. "*Jesus*, that smell." Was it from the decaying fish, or was it a by-product of the algae?

"Any idea what could have caused it, boss?" Gary asked.

He did, but he didn't voice his concern. He wasn't one to share his Anglican religion, but the quote from the Bible he knew so well suddenly haunted him.

Hosea 4:3 ..."Therefore shall the land mourn, and every one that dwelleth therein shall languish, with the beasts of the field, and with the fowls of heaven; yea, the fishes of the sea also shall be taken away."

No, surely it couldn't be that.

The waters were also unusually calm. Normally, standing here would have seen Smith moistened by the spray as the boat cut through the waves.

Further up towards the bow, one of his deck hands screamed in pain. Out of curiosity, the deck hand had run a boat hook into the water to drag out some of the thick, carpet-like goo. He'd then made the mistake of touching it.

"What the hell happened?" Smith demanded, coming to his man's aid. In agony, the fisherman held his hand up, the flesh visibly bubbling where it had touched the algae.

That changed everything.

"I want everyone inside until we get clear of this," Smith commanded. Sod finding the edge of this, they needed to escape it before someone else got hurt.

9.

Slough, UK

Emily sat with Lucy on the edge of the playground. The break was nearly over, which meant they would need to be back in the classroom. She knew she was being silly about it, but being around Mrs Rawlinson made her nervous. If Emily was honest, the actual way her teacher acted had hardly changed. It was just the blackness that surrounded her.

It made Emily feel icky to look at.

"You're very quiet," Lucy said.

"I'm thinking."

"What are you thinking about?" Lucy prodded.

"Stuff. Important stuff."

"You read too much," Lucy advised.

"No, I don't."

"Yep. You read and read. It's not healthy."

"How can reading not be healthy?" Emily was astonished by the idea.

"It makes you ponder." Lucy was clearly very proud of that word.

"Makes me what?"

"Ponder. That's what you are doing now, pondering." Lucy sounded like she was convinced that pondering was a source of many of the world's ills.

"I am not," Emily insisted, though she wasn't quite sure what she was being accused of. From the corner of her eye, she saw two of the boys in her class walking over.

"Are you still worried about Mrs Rawlinson?"

"No," Emily lied. She didn't want to talk about that. The boys were closer.

“What are you doing alone over here?” one of the boys asked. He had ginger hair and a nervous smile.

“We are talking, Richard. You should not interrupt ladies when they are talking.” Lucy put exaggerated annoyance into her voice.

“What are you talking about?” Richard insisted. The other boy, Simon, hung back. Simon didn’t seem to want to be part of the conversation. He was new to the class, having only recently moved to the area. It was well known that Richard had taken it upon himself to befriend him and make sure nobody picked on him. Emily thought that was a really nice thing to do, because some of the kids in her class could be really nasty. Nobody bullied Richard, though. He was too big for that. If he’d had a less agreeable character, Richard would have been the ultimate bully.

“Politics,” Lucy suddenly exclaimed.

“What are politics?” Emily thought Richard’s question was quite valid. What exactly were politics?

“You wouldn’t understand.” Lucy threw her hand up and looked dismissively away. “Boys don’t understand such things, do they, Emily?”

“No. Boys only understand about farts and eating their own snot.” Emily couldn’t resist getting dragged into Lucy’s random fantasy.

“We do not.” Richard sounded mortified. “Why are you being mean?”

“Because it’s ‘be mean to boy’s day’. Everyone knows that.” Emily had no idea how Lucy came up with this stuff.

“There’s no such thing,” Simon managed.

“Yes, there is, because boys are dumb,” Emily added.

"And they lie," Lucy pointed out. "They lie all the time. I often can't believe a word they say."

"And they sleep a lot and don't do anything." Emily didn't know how she knew this piece of wisdom, but she was sure about it.

"Sleeping isn't a bad thing." Richard stood with his hands on his hips. *You're wishing you'd never come over here, aren't you*? Emily thought. *But you can't figure out how to break off from the conversation.* He was taking Simon round and making sure everyone had met him. And now he had to deal with Lucy when she was at her best.

"Yes, it is. You can't eat ice cream when you are asleep." Emily knew this would win both boys over to her cause.

"You shouldn't eat too much ice cream, though," Lucy replied. "My mum says too much ice cream will make you fat and give you a big butt."

"I thought you wanted a big butt?"

"Emily," Lucy scolded, "not a fat butt. You need to get a butt by doing squats."

"What the hell are squats?" Richard was lost in the maddening world of girls.

"Squats are an exercise to give you a big bottom."

"Why would anyone want a big bottom?" Richard couldn't think of anything worse.

"It's so Lucy can be famous on Instagram," Emily said, although she could kind of understand Richard's point of view. She could never say that out loud, though. Lucy was about to respond, but the bell went, stating their break time was over. That meant going back into the classroom, an end to their freedom.

Simon ran off, finally freed from the awkwardness the girls represented. Emily watched him go, running past two teachers that had gathered near the main entrance. Mrs Rawlinson was one of the two.

It was then that Emily noticed that Mrs Rawlinson was watching the children intently, a serious look etched on her face, eyes scanning the children that were careening towards her. For less than a second, Emily felt herself catch her teacher's gaze, and a shiver ran down her spine. Then Mrs Rawlinson's eyes fell on Simon and a sick, predatory grin formed. There really was no disguising it.

As crazy as it sounded, the blackness surrounding Mrs Rawlinson was more noticeable today. And that blackness pulsed as if it were alive, reaching out to touch Simon as he made his way past someone who should always be able to be trusted. Emily felt her breath catch in her throat. She'd never seen the darkness so strong. It almost engulfed the top half of Simon, if just for a moment.

"Emily, we'll be late," she heard Lucy say, but Emily was mesmerised. Why couldn't anyone else see how evil her teacher was?

10.

Silicon Valley, USA

For we wrestle not against flesh and blood, but against principalities, against powers, against the rulers of the darkness of this world, against spiritual wickedness in high places - Ephesians 6:12

Those were the words written in large letters on the frosted glass of the conference room where Giles Horn sat alone, waiting for his board of twelve directors to arrive. Truth be told, he hated every one of them, but they were a means to an end, an irritation he could put up with. That they didn't truly understand his vision didn't matter to him. His only concern was that they worked tirelessly to make his company one of the most successful and powerful in the world. That was why such meetings were infrequent affairs required for only the most important of matters.

The company Horn owned, as vast as it was, belonged to him and him alone.

He had no doubt that they would do exactly as he commanded, for the penalties they would pay for any defiance were extreme. Some of them were leftovers from when Horn Senior had founded this company, but that cretin had been dead in the earth over ten years now. Horn did not miss him, just as he didn't miss that soulless lush that had masqueraded as a mother.

Any claim that his biological father had over Horn's success had long since been buried. Horn was his own man, and the company he now controlled was vastly superior to the one he had inherited. It had more than quadrupled in size under his stewardship. He had even renamed it.

Abaddon International Incorporated, or AII for short. It was kind of a joke to Horn, based on a newspaper article that had done the rounds a few years back. The article's creator had taken objection to the private security contractors Horn employed, giving Horn the nickname *The Angel of Death*. Horn hadn't been offended. If anything, he found the term flattering, and had renamed his company accordingly. He'd still bought the newspaper and sacked everyone, closing the fledgling news organisation down. To top off his vindictive spree, the reporter in question had been arrested a week later. The child pornography the police found on his computer was unknown to him, but there was no way the police could believe that.

There were no more negative press pieces about Horn after that.

AII rested at the top of a pyramid structure of seven corporate behemoths, each covering a different aspect of the overall business. Industrials, technology, telecom, materials, financial services, healthcare and energy. Each of these had ten further subdivisions, owning hundreds of smaller companies overall. Some of the most popular brands in the world were owned by Abaddon, and most people didn't even know it.

A large chunk of his corporate empire had been acquired at no cost on a fateful day three years back. But that was a story for another day.

The renamed company, and his growing reputation, helped remind people who they were dealing with when they met Giles Horn. In truth, Abaddon was an empire. It was vast, probably one of the largest corporations in the world. Because Abaddon was privately owned, it was difficult to know exactly how much money it made every year, but some experts reckoned it was close to four hundred billion dollars.

Those calculations weren't even close.

There were still those who underestimated Horn, and those who chose to oppose him quickly regretted the poor choices they made. Horn was ruthless against anyone who went against him. For those who worked for him, he demanded unflinching loyalty. To question Horn without good cause risked having your life destroyed, such was his level of financial power. Threaten his business, and a whole legion of less than scrupulous minions would be turned against you. Lawyers, private detectives, as well as low-level street thugs who could effectively be used to menace and threaten even those with the strongest moral conviction.

Chief amongst those he could call upon was Lucas Kane, a man of unusual talent and unquestioning devotion.

Lucas Kane was Head of Security for AII, and if Horn willed it, Kane would make his boss's desires a reality. Kane was instrumental in ensuring everyone who worked for the company understood the importance of Horn's latest vision for the human race.

Even with his resources and his reputation, Horn still faced obstacles. Rival corporations, foolish journalists, principled politicians and those who sought to profit at his expense—all fell before him. And all the while, Horn moved ever closer to his ultimate goal.

Horn knew that none of his board of directors understood the legacy he was creating, nor the technology that he had developed to achieve it. Few people did. It required a level of genius that rarely manifested in the minds of humanity, a blessing passed on to Horn from his dear departed father, according to those who didn't know any better. In truth, the genetics of Giles Horn Senior were the only useful inheritance from the dead patriarch. Those genetics had allowed another to take control of Horn Senior at that most critical of moments… the conception of the man Horn Senior would call son.

Horn's true father was not of this world.

Horn possessed an astonishing intellect and was not afraid for the universe to know it. Such a genetic blessing came with advantages and disadvantages. His mind could conceive of things that most of the *plebs* couldn't comprehend, and could then sift through his eidetic memory to search for viable solutions. When no answers could be found, he had the ability to consume vast amounts of information in a single sitting, his focus rarely wavering from the burning question that had formed in his mind.

There was no denying he was destined for the role in which he found himself. Kane would confirm such, although the glorified bodyguard was somewhat biased in his opinions. Kane's loyalty bordered on total, unwavering subservience.

The disadvantage, if it truly was one, was Horn's inability to relate to those who were deemed lesser than him. This manifested as an almost unshakeable feeling of superiority over his fellow man, and he considered the majority of the sentient beings on the planet to be beneath him. This arrogance and lack of empathy allowed him to hold much of the human population in utter contempt, seeing them merely as cattle to utilise for his own ends. Whilst his company purported to make products that improved people's lives, all Horn cared about was his market share, the bottom line, and the accomplishment of his destiny.

Such pride sometimes made him reckless and quick to anger. Angering Giles Horn was not a path to personal or financial wellbeing. If you got on the wrong side of him, he would come after you until you were a shattered, broken ruin.

Horn's path in life had changed the day of his father's burial. That was when he was introduced to the truth of who he was, of the destiny he was put on this planet to fulfil. He was given knowledge that would break a lesser mind from three strangers with black eyes. They delivered a message that Horn had been compelled to listen to.

There might have been billions of humans on the planet, but the civilisation they had developed was a dead end, created by an overuse of exhaustible resources. The promised saviour of technology couldn't save them, and their pending demise would be long, drawn out, and thoroughly deserved. Only intervention could hope to solve the crisis in overpopulation and climate devastation. Who better than an individual of Horn's intellect and lineage to help bring about that intervention? Especially if he could make a healthy profit in the process.

More important than that was the increased power he knew it would bring, propelling him to the dizzying heights he was destined for. Horn was meant for great things, and those who survived his grand scheme would bow down before him.

At times an idea would come to him out of the ether, a devious scheme to further his agenda. Often, such a thought would become all-consuming. On the last such occasion, Horn had retreated from the world for several weeks to become a virtual recluse, refusing to communicate with anyone. Instead of complying with his scheduled engagements, he had withdrawn to an isolated home he'd had purpose-built deep in the Eldorado National Forest. When you had the level of wealth he possessed, such constructions were easy to finance.

What he had come up with in those weeks of solitude was an idea that had morphed into a technological reality. His eventual creation had been revolutionary and the answer to so much of humanity's problems, as he saw them. The only way to save mankind was to control it and guide it on the path to salvation. That would be his message, even though he knew there would be no salvation for the billions who would cry out to him. Already, his wealth was funding a massive public relations campaign to warn that humans were either going to obliterate themselves through nuclear fire or be slaughtered by a vengeful Mother Nature. Only the science offered by AII could save the world from that terrible fate. Horn cared little for the fate of individuals, nor did he care long term about his billions. For he was convinced he was the son of the one who would bring terror to the earth, Horn standing shoulder to shoulder with he who would bring forth the apocalypse. Some of humanity would be left alive to serve those who deserved nothing but the deepest reverence. Acolytes and the oppressed would be forced to worship him.

Despite his own brilliance, Horn still had the needs that came with being part of the human species.

His desires were another way he differed from Horn Senior. Lust was his primary vice, although he quickly became dulled and bored with the women who, sometimes unwillingly, shared his bed. Men were also not spared his crude, and in some areas of the planet, illegal advances. If not for Kane and his army of dedicated minions, Horn might have been one of the many faces rolled out in the "me too" scandal. But no-one was left in a position to point the accusatory finger at him once Kane had dealt with them.

Threats, intimidation, violence, bribes and murder were all used to allow Horn to continue his hedonistic and destructive ways. The perversions he desired were the pressure valve his genius needed. Without such release, that brilliant mind might have turned on itself.

It would have been better for the world if it had.

The idea he had come up with in those weeks of isolation was a work of brilliance. Horn had thought long and hard about what to call his latest technology. In the end, he called it the Redeemer, the name popping randomly into his head. It didn't look like much, a hologram-based, surgically implanted tattoo about the size of a postage stamp. That had evolved over several months into a microchip the size of a grain of rice.

The revolution was in what it did. It contained a wireless transmitter that connected the host body to a virtual cloud that he had also developed. The implant was both a receiver and transmitter, allowing the user to throw away all their credit cards, passports and identification. Whilst he knew the nations of the world would be slow to trust and rely on his technology, his billions at least gave him the chance to bring his marvel to the world.

The implant would also act as a verification mark and allow those with portable scanners to check an individual's full medical history. Added to that was the ability for real time tracking, via an extensive satellite network, everything controlled by a supercomputer buried deep in a bunker on the outskirts of Geneva.

The name Horn gave to that computer couldn't be more apt.

The Beast.

There were plans in the works to make his creation as good as mandatory for the people of the world. Despite the power he held and the people he was acquainted with, to release that now would create too much opposition. There were ways around that. The Redeemer was a small piece in the cosmic scheme he was concocting. All part of the plan to keep his true father happy.

On the conference desk in front of him, a newspaper was open to a report of his most recent corporate acquisition.

Abaddon International Incorporated buys Securescope Biotech for $3.2 billion

The international giant just bought the world's largest producer of implantable technology.

May 12, 2019 08:30 AM Eastern Daylight Time

In a move that surprised markets, Securescope Biotech, the world's largest producer of implantable security technology, announced today that it had agreed on a full takeover by the multinational giant Abaddon International Incorporated. Shares in Securescope rose 11%, and marks the continued expansion of the private company owned by the secretive billionaire, Giles Horn.

This acquisition is just another in a spate of recent purchases that has seen Abaddon International spend nearly fifteen billion dollars on acquiring firms that had been marked down as competitors to their recently announced Redeemer technology. By buying Securescope, Abaddon International has now become the world leader in implantable bio wear, both in scientific innovation and manufacturing capacity.

There are also unconfirmed reports that Abaddon International has secured a multi-billion-dollar contract to supply its Redeemer technology to the U.S. Department of Homeland Security. If this is true, then it adds more weight to the growing international desire for the Redeemer.

One step further towards his goal.

Any fledgling company that threatened his technology was bought out or destroyed. Any established rival found themselves victims of sustained and brutal industrial espionage, often masquerading as misguided terrorist attacks. And although Horn was known to let his anger get the better of him on occasion, protecting the

AII interests through violence was a tool he left to minions such as Kane.

The Redeemer encryption was based on the DNA of the person implanted, making it totally unbreakable and totally secure. At least, that was what Horn had been assured. Whilst conventional technology couldn't read it, Horn had that covered, too. He promised to change the way commerce and banking were done in the United States, and from there, the world.

The organisation he had inherited years ago now owned three of the largest banks in North America, as well as the contracts to supply airport security technology to a host of European countries. The essential companies he didn't own were controlled by powerful men who willingly bowed down to him. Despite *their* billions, these powerful businessmen gave him their utmost subservience.

Just think about it. No need for cash or wallets full of credit cards. With his technology implanted, a person's own biometrics became a secure means for engaging in any and all transactions. Once implanted, the implant merged with the body, sending out microscopic tendrils that snaked into and intertwined with the body's own peripheral nervous system, giving it another added security feature. The danger with the alternative implantable microchip technology was that criminals would resort to hacking limbs off or engaging in butchery to remove the chip. That wouldn't work with the Redeemer. Once implanted, it had a failsafe mechanism in that it wiped itself clean should it be detached from a living host.

What had initially been deemed a flaw in its design quickly became an eager conversation point. When activated, the small chip glowed briefly, giving the skin above it an irradiated orange colour.

And when the end finally come, and the Redeemer chip's real purpose was revealed, then the fun would really start.

Although they didn't know it yet, the governments of the world would delight in the benefits the Redeemer would bring them. Total surveillance of everyone implanted would be made easier by the 5G technology he was also helping to establish across the globe.

By selling this device at cost price, Horn knew he would get control of virtually all transactional banking, as well as making his own credit card company the world leader. A credit card without the inconvenience of an actual card. And as with everything Horn developed, the microchip was deemed safe, reliable and likely to become high in demand. There were side effects with the earlier variants, but nobody mentioned those in Horn's presence.

Horn had insisted on this security when he passed his blueprints and ideas over to the team of scientists who had perfected it, and had overseen many of the experiments personally. Evidence of the inevitable human casualties that came with such advancements was destroyed without a trace. He didn't care about the test subject riddled with cancer. The medical incinerators on the many acres of his corporate headquarters were ideal for eradicating such evidence.

This all took time and patience. Horn knew how to funnel money to the people who made the political decisions. Some of that had been legitimate, others less so. Whilst cash was never handed over in crude brown envelopes, the digital equivalent was part of the price of doing business as far as he was concerned. Again, it was Kane who dealt with such matters.

The present incumbent in the White House would not have won the election without the millions Horn had given him.

Distribution of the Redeemer would be the first order of business in today's meeting, and Horn expected everyone to be on board with the phased rolling release that he and his strategists had planned. Horn wouldn't tolerate any attempt to block the progress of his plan, which was why he had never taken his company public. If he had, he was well aware he would have been crowned America's richest man, so mighty was his international empire.

The second order on the agenda was the continued expansion of his company's business premises to the Middle East. Because Israel was the only stable democracy in the region, the decision had been made years ago to site the regional headquarters and prime manufacturing plant in Megiddo. Horn did a lot of business with the Israelis. He liked to imagine that his mother would have been proud of him, but if she had been still alive, she likely wouldn't have given a damn. Whilst he had never adopted his mother's Jewish faith, she herself hadn't been that faithful to its creeds, the contents of the bottles she frequently imbibed from having been her true religion.

At the age of thirty, Giles Horn ran a company valued at several hundred billion dollars. He ran it with an iron fist, keeping it private and out of the greedy hands of the stockbrokers. With the implementation of the Redeemer chip, he intended to one day make his baby the biggest company in the world. But that wasn't the important thing. The aspect of life that kept him up at night was his ultimate dream, his blueprint for the world.

The chip was only one part to finalising his mission to bring in his new world order and make his true father proud. What more could the Antichrist ask for?

***

Kane stood outside the conference room and scrutinised each of the twelve board members as they filed into the room. He towered above each and every one of them. Some looked away from his glare sheepishly, others trying to defiantly match his gaze, only to all ultimately fail. Kane was not someone who looked away first. He may have been blessed with handsome features and a muscular frame, but the truth of him was evident in his eyes. Upon meeting Kane, nobody would ever come away from the encounter thinking that he was anything but a danger to those who dared cross him. There was violence in the man, bubbling away almost visibly just beneath the surface.

If you were to learn that Kane was a killer, you wouldn't be surprised.

With everyone accounted for, Kane entered the room and closed the door behind him. This was not his time to shine, so Kane stood discreetly at the back, his hands folded in front of him. Although he didn't need a weapon to kill everyone here, the Glock 17 that rested against the small of his back was a welcome presence. He rarely went anywhere without it and had the required documentation and training to justify the gun's ownership and concealed carry. It hadn't taken Kane long to become proficient with the weapon, even though they didn't have such devices where he came from.

He also had an army of corporate lawyers behind him should local law enforcement ever take objection to his concealed carry. In all the time Kane had been associated with Abaddon, he had never had to worry about the police. The corporation had enough contacts bought and paid for, enough politicians in its back pocket and enough law enforcement officers secretly on the payroll that Kane had little to fear in that regard.

There had been a time when the person known as Kane wouldn't have considered harming another human being, never mind killing one. Those days were long past, to Horn's great delight. Kane was only useful because of his ruthlessness and his loyalty. He had skills that couldn't be found in the armies of university graduates who flocked to the company in the hope they would be given a chance to work for a multinational behemoth. Kane's skill set could only be derived from the field of battle.

Standing guard, he drowned out the useless noises the board directors made. The brave ones would raise their objections. Those who wished to curry favour with Horn kept their mouths pretty much shut. They thought that would protect them, but Kane knew that the silent ones were those that needed watching. Despite the monetary reward their positions gave them, there were always some who craved more. The lure of power was the breaker of many an oath.

The one called Kane could understand that. He'd met countless thousands like them in the eons he had spent before becoming Horn's trusted aide. They all wept their regrets when they learnt the fate due to them down in the Pit.

He didn't listen to the directors' words, but instead watched their actions intently. Words were a fiction that could be used to massage the truth behind them. The face that spoke those words held the true intentions. Horn was in no danger here, for Kane knew none of these idiots were armed. Directors had to go through a full security screening before being allowed into a room with Horn. The protection of Giles Horn was the only thing that mattered to Kane and he knew he could not fail in that mission.

For Horn to die or be harmed under his watch would be unthinkable. Although there was always another candidate for the end times waiting in the wings, none had Horn's power, wealth and influence.

Kane knew how to read the desires that lurked in the hearts of men. And women, although there were only two present. Horn was often heard saying he didn't care if some politically correct social justice warrior found that gender disparity disagreeable. Their opinions were about as consequential as the lint that one finds on occasion infesting one's navel. Horn always said he hired based on merit and not his own warped opinion of the worth of the female mind. Kane reckoned the fact there were any women in the room at all displayed how truly impressive the two female board members must have been.

The only person in the room Horn hadn't chosen was Kane. Kane had been chosen for him by powers far greater than anything Horn could muster.

What those on the board didn't properly realise was that Horn wasn't your average business owner. Kane had frequently witnessed Horn demand total obedience from those under him. Horn occasionally tolerated dissenting voices so long as the opposing view had value and brought a perspective that Horn might not have considered. With that view expressed, Horn would then insist that those around him then acquiesce to his final ultimatum. Horn always had the final say, and you could pity the poor soul who didn't realise that. Should Horn's opinion ever sour towards someone, those who lost his confidence wouldn't last long and then Kane would have his fun.

Only Kane and the three rich men with black eyes could consistently have any real chance of persuading his employer to take a different course of action.

Today, Kane was the added pressure needed to stifle any bubbling dissent because Horn's mind was evidently already set on the matter. Positioned as he was, there was no denying the nervous glances that some occasionally cast Kane's way. The security chief was an unknown variable, a randomness that those under Horn's employ rarely had to deal with. Although none of those present had ever seen Kane practise his art, the rumours were there for all to hear. None of those rumours truly reflected what Kane was willing to do for his master, however.

If they knew the true identity of the mind that presently called itself Kane, most in the room would wet themselves in terror.

Pity those that were thrown to the mercy of Kane, for he had none. As civilised and lawful a country as the USA was, there were ways to make people regret their very existence. The pain Kane could bring into someone's life was legendary, or at least it would have been if anyone had been willing to share such stories. If you had dealings with Kane and lived to tell about it, silence was usually the wisest path to follow. Still, stories got out, which Kane didn't mind. It was not a bad thing for people to be afraid of him.

It saved a lot of time.

Kane wasn't alone as an enforcer. With nearly three hundred thousand people under Horn's employ, Kane oversaw a whole security structure that protected the infrastructure, the intellectual property and the secrets that could ruin Horn. Although he wasn't able to hand pick each and every one of the five thousand operatives in the security and private contractor divisions, he had been instrumental in devising the hierarchy and the overall structure that protected this corporation. Those at the top answered to him, and he answered to Horn.

AII paid well to those who protected it, *very* well. That had not been the case when the company had been under the steerage of Horn Senior, a man who believed that people should be remunerated to the bare minimum. The younger Horn was different, believing that loyalty was fickle, but that money spoke volumes. Even so, Horn did inspire an almost cult-like devotion in many of the people who worked for him. He was charismatic, energetic, and seemed open to believing the welfare of his employers was paramount. Kane knew this to be a ploy, of course, a way to control those who would ultimately bring Horn the rewards he wanted.

Kane was loyal because he had no choice in the matter.

If you performed well for the Abaddon corporation, you and those who worked with you were richly rewarded. If you failed, the nature of that failure was addressed. Sometimes the failure was an important lesson the business could learn from, a flaw in the systems and processes. In these cases, the punishment amounted to a reprimand at most.

Should anyone actively work against the company, then the retribution was swift and without end. Kane was particularly adept at hunting out those who aimed to hurt his master's growing masterpiece.

The last person who had acted against the corporation's interest had been a man called Brian Wei. A second-generation immigrant from China, he was a computer programmer of no real particular note. Working away in the IT section of one of AII's research arms, it quickly became apparent that Mr Wei was engaged in espionage. Not for another competing company, it turned out, but for the might of the Chinese government.

Kane was forced to send a message, and a very public one. After being reported missing from work by his superior, it was two weeks before parts of Brian Wei started arriving at the Chinese Consolates-General in San Francisco. Wei was still alive when the first part of his left index finger arrived in airtight packaging. When the final package with his eyes arrived, Kane reckoned the Chinese hod got the message.

Don't fuck with Giles Horn.

Kane didn't partake in that particular barbarity personally; he had people to do that for him. Which was a shame, because it was the kind of thing that he really excelled at. That was one of the things he missed about being in the Pit. As much as the air up here smelt fresh, and the souls were ripe for the torment, Kane had to admit he would enjoy getting back into the swing of things when he eventually returned to the other place.

Like with all too many people lately, the body Kane rode in had no say in the matter. Occasionally, Kane opened the door to the mental cage in which he'd locked the body's owner. Just a fraction to give that hapless and pleading mind a taste of what was being done with his body. Such anguish. Such misery. Unlike with many of the possessed, this body was ideal for Kane. Kane could exist in it for the duration of the host's natural lifespan if required.

Sometimes the desire to hurt someone just for the sake of it would overcome Kane, and he would allow himself to carefully indulge himself. When that happened, Kane would throw the cage door wide and make the human mind *see* what it was that made Kane so special. Forced to watch such horrors would be a special kind of torture for the one trapped in the brain Kane had hijacked.

In the Pit, Kane went by another name. Plurson, Chief Torturer of Hell, and breaker of the strongest of mortal souls. Despite his proclaimed position, he was still relatively low in the hierarchy, a bureaucrat rather than a leader of Hell's denizens. He was thus not a demon of great power, but one of experience. He was a soldier and a protector to Giles Horn, sent here by Horn's other protectors decades ago.

Plurson's presence on earth had long been planned, the host body Kane picked through scrutiny rather than necessity. Thus, the host body held the requisite genetic flaws that allowed successful long-term possession. Still, if he'd had a choice, Plurson would have preferred to have been back in the comfort of the other place. Being the one who inflicted the agony came with certain advantages. As the life of a demon went, his had been relatively rich, full and free of suffering.

And now he was here, listening to monkeys talk and sporting a name that wasn't his. Even Horn knew him only as Kane.

"Right then, people, let's get this done," Horn said to finish the meeting. Kane found himself audibly sigh with relief at those words. The meeting had been tedious to Kane, but as the loyal minions filed out of the room, he saw the satisfaction on Horn's face. The meeting had gone as planned.

"Not many objections today," Kane stated. "I think they are learning."

"They know better than to disagree," Horn said. "Although I think your presence helped. One or two of them were wavering. They do seem to need a constant reminder of who is in charge."

"I am pleased I could be of service. Only a fool would go against you now." Kane was loyal to Horn, but only because he did the bidding of other's.

"But I thought you knew, Kane, the world is full of fools."

"I'm sure you will correct that." Kane had great faith in Horn's abilities. How could he not? Despite the failings of his biological parents, Horn was said to be descended from the most formidable of lineages.

“That’s why I’m here, after all.” There was mischief in Horn’s words. Kane still remembered when the billionaire had learnt the truth about who he was. Lesser men would have been broken, but not Horn. He had seemed delighted. “After all, I need to make my true father proud.”

“That’s a tall order,” Kane advised. As much as he despised the weakness of human flesh, there was something refreshing about Horn.

“He put me here to rule. And that’s what I intend to do.”

Kane never corrected Horn when he said such things. Horn thought he was the son of Satan, but for all the time Kane had spent in Hell, he had never seen or heard of a being who held such a name. There was no shaking Horn’s belief that he was the Antichrist, and as a lowly minion, who was Kane to contradict that belief.

11.

Hopi Indian reservation, Arizona

They were now in the fourth world, the previous three having been destroyed by fire and ice. The age of the lone wolf was over. So had said the Shaman when Ahote had asked for advice the other day. The answer wasn't exactly what Ahote was hoping to hear.

At a young age, Ahote had tried to get out into the wider world, but the world of the white man was harsh and unforgiving. Ahote's size and toughness were the only skills he had. His descent into alcoholism and violence had seen him punished by judges and courts who had no right to judge him. At the age of thirty-two, freshly released from the state penitentiary, Ahote did the only thing he could do. He went back home to his people so he could heal and try to get himself right with the world. He expected to find himself an outcast, but instead he was welcomed.

The young are foolish; it is only natural they should make mistakes.

Truth was, he never should have left. The lure of the mighty dollar and the riches that waited in the greater world were merely lies sent to test him. And he had failed those tests, teaching him that the white man's world was a sick and desolate place. At least, back on the reservation, he had some idea of who he was.

His addictions followed him back, though, and he became a favourite with the local tribal police. The monkey on his back refused to leave. It wasn't as if he wanted to behave this way, but, as the Shaman pointed out more than once to those who would listen, the evil spirits had infested him. That was why he went to the Shaman in the first place, the ritual a last hope to rid himself of the evil that had latched onto his soul. He had mentioned his predicament to the elders, but they had replied with riddles and prophecy.

If anything, they seemed preoccupied. There was talk of the end times, for the blue star Kachina was visible in the sky. Ahote could barely remember what he had been taught as a child, but the night sky was definitely different to what he remembered before being locked up for ten years behind concrete and wire. You don't get to see the stars when you are incarcerated in a prison cell.

It was hardly surprising to find that the ritual didn't work. Ahote remained addicted to the liquor that was slowly killing him.

Ahote's one saving grace was that he was a sleepy drunk, rather than a violent one. He got merry rather than vicious, his eyes drooping after his body had reached its limit. He tried to resist it, but his hopelessness and the pull of the brew were too much for him. Under the effects of the regular alcohol infusion, the world didn't seem such a bad place, and he stopped cursing his ill fortune to be born into what he considered a backward and abandoned time.

He became a regular at his nearest bar and had enough good sense to leave his truck at the trailer he called home. He had enough problems with the law without getting arrested for another DUI. Those at the bar tolerated him, for some were in the same predicament.

Sometimes though, if he had been allowed to consume too much, he would often forget that he had left his vehicle at home and would wander the venue's car park in a futile attempt to find a truck that wasn't there. So regular was this that some of the other locals at the bar would sometimes come out and watch him stumble about in the dark.

Sometimes it was amusing; other times pitiful.

Presently, Ahote was once again in the car park of that bar, only this time he was looking up at the blue star that shone in the sky. It was one of the brightest things up there, a beautiful blue sapphire pulsing in the dangers of deep space. And every night, it seemed that little brighter, the result of a distant supernova. To many of the elders, it was a sign that the end times were at hand, a warning that the day of purification would soon be upon them. To Ahote, it was an almost hypnotic distraction that seemed to fascinate his addled neurons.

It often drew him out of the bar, a lonely beacon to draw in those who had been abandoned by fate. With tears of unknown origin in his eyes, Ahote let the light wash into him for a few more seconds, and then he turned and trudged back to the warm safety of his favourite drinking hole. He still had money in his pocket. He might as well spend it on something worthwhile.

12.

Boston, USA

"What does the first seal in Revelation actually represent?" Stone looked out at his audience expectantly. He had no idea who would be willing to speak up, and who would sit there trying to avoid his roaming eye. Most of these young minds were unknown to him. He knew that they would be full of their own ideas, seeking the information his seminar could offer. Some of those present would no doubt be deeply committed to their faith, but he reckoned at least half the class were atheists. There would also be arrogance out there, watching him, waiting for the moment they thought was right to strike. Such an action would be a mistake on their part.

For some reason, his talk on the Book of Revelation always seemed to draw the biggest crowd.

"It's a trick question," one of the apparently smarter ones in the audience answered. Too many people thought that this age was when the Son of Perdition would walk upon the earth, more so now with recent events happening in the world. Stone relished being the one to tell them that, despite their beliefs, there was little in the original religious texts, Christian or otherwise, that adequately predicted when the end of the world would occur.

"Go on," Stone prodded.

"Well, it depends on how you view the Book of Revelation. If it's purely a historic account, then it's surely talking about the death of Christ."

"That's one interpretation, yes," Stone agreed. "There are others, of course. Alexander Keith thought that the opening of the first seal represented the rise of the Roman Emperor Nerva, who saw in the so-called Golden Age. That was the time when the Christian religion flourished across the Roman Empire." Stone took his glasses off and rubbed the bridge of his nose. "I was hoping one of you would give a juicier response than that, though." Some in the audience laughed, which was always a good sign.

Laughter was better than shouted jeers. He was ashamed to say he had been heckled out of a few places recently. Reasoned argument he could crush, but the baying, mindless mobs he had no time for.

"The Antichrist," another in the audience shouted out. You couldn't talk about revelation without mentioning the Antichrist. Besides, that was why most of them were here. Even those with no belief in God found the idea of Satan's offspring thoroughly compelling.

"There we go. We can't have a lecture about the Book of Revelation without getting into the hard-core Doomsday mythology. Yes, there are many biblical scholars and laypersons alike who believe the depiction of the first seal breaking is warning of the coming Satanic bastard."

Stone clicked forward in his PowerPoint presentation, bringing up a copy of *The Deeds of Antichrist*, a painting by Luca Signorelli.

"The confusion then comes as to who the Antichrist is," Stone continued. "If we are viewing the text as a historical account, we then have to determine what time scale it was written in. Many experts now consider the author of this section of the Bible to be John the Apostle, a man who went by many names. John of Patmos, John the Elder and even *The Beloved Disciple*. It's disputed, of course. The Bible always is. We will never know for sure when and by whom the verses were written."

"Isn't the Bible supposed to be the literal word of God?" came another question.

“By some, yes, although you would have hoped that God would have been a bit less vague in his teachings.” Another laugh; he was doing well. “Let us not forget that the Bible, as it now exists, is an amalgamation of multiple authors. It has been re-written several times, changing over the centuries. It is also a translation. Take the New Testament. Most likely, it was originally written in Greek. And not the Greek language of today, but Koine Greek that emerged around three hundred BC. To make matters worse, this itself might have been a translation from both Hebrew and Aramaic. That would then have been translated into Latin to keep such arcane knowledge away from the eyes of mere peasants.”

“So, you’re saying it isn’t the word of God?” someone near the back shouted. The audience liked that one.

“Who am I to question such an all-powerful entity?” It was obvious Stone wasn’t being self-deprecating in his words.

There were about a hundred people in the room. Normally, his lectures were deemed to be controversial by those with a fundamentalist Christian belief, so it wasn’t unknown for people to protest. Stone could understand why some would feel threatened by what he had to say. He had spent much of his career as a scholar trying to demystify the biblical texts and make them more understandable to the everyday person. That often meant the awe that could be found in the words got stripped away.

At the same time, he felt it was his duty to try to nullify the power that the Revelation of St John seemed to have in parts of the west. Despite the rapid decline in the adherence to religious dogma, there were some who had taken John the Apostle’s writings and had turned it almost into a doomsday cult.

To Professor Stone, the Book of Revelation wasn't prophecy. It was history. And poorly told history, at that. So, to counter the opposition, he turned his argument into a work of fiction, and when the first book was released, it saw him both acclaimed and reviled.

"Do you believe Revelation to be a prophetic book?" asked someone in the front row. The man sat ramrod straight, his piercing eyes never abandoning Stone. There was an intensity to the man, as if he had a bursting desire to share some curious secret. Stone had noticed him from the start, and if he was honest, the Professor found the man intimidating.

"To be candid, no," Stone replied. "We as a species have been believing in end of the world scenarios for centuries, and we seem to still be here. The Norse mythology called it Ragnarok..."

"You are mistaken," the intense man interrupted. "We are in the Great Tribulation. The first seal will break at any time." There was a murmuring in the audience. Stone could already tell that phone video cameras were being activated. Was this the confrontation that some people were looking for?

"I don't really think..." Stone attempted, only for the man to rise up from his seat. Even though the interloper didn't seem to have an ounce of muscle on him, Stone felt a twinge of alarm spark in the back of his mind. The weakest of men could have a knife concealed upon them. He might even worry about a gun, but that was unlikely in such a venue. Everyone had been screened by security before being allowed entry.

"But when you see Jerusalem surrounded by armies, then know that its desolation has come near. Then let those who are in Judea flee to the mountains, and let those who are inside the city depart, and let not those who are out in the country enter it, for these are days of vengeance, to fulfil all that is written." Despite Stone having the only microphone in the room, the power in the stranger's voice seemed to dominate the space.

"Mark 13:14," Stone said.

"Yes. Are the signs not there?"

"Who even are you?" Stone asked. He cast a glance out at the audience, rolling his eyes in mock theatrics. That brought the majority in the room back to his side.

"I am the one who has come here to ask you to repent."

"Get the fuck out," someone shouted from the back, but Stone put a hand up.

"And what have I to repent, exactly?" In response to the question from Stone, the stranger stuck a bony finger out at the professor.

"You have denied the word of God. Your books are a blasphemy, a defamation on the coming judgement of man."

"Well, I didn't think the spelling was all that bad." From experience, Stone knew that humour was the only weapon he had against zealots. He couldn't counter their arguments with logic or research, because the true believers had their own reality to console them. Stone was also comforted by the fact that two security guards had appeared at the back of the room and were making their way down to where the stranger was still standing. From past events, the venues that hosted him knew to take such precautions.

"Mock me all you want, but I have seen the signs. For there will be great distress upon the earth and wrath against the people. They will fall by the edge of the sword and be led captive among all nations, and Jerusalem will be trampled underfoot by the Gentiles, until the times of the Gentiles are fulfilled." One of the security guards reached the thin man and roughly grabbed him.

"Alright then, that's enough of that."

"My voice will not be silenced."

"You can shout and rave all you like," the other guard said. "But you will be doing it outside." What had at first been considered shocking by those present was now seen as laughable. *At the least, it will get me some YouTube hits*, thought Stone. He watched, somewhat relieved, as the man was dragged out.

"Where were we before I was so rudely interrupted?" Stone asked.

"Does that happen often?" Someone two rows from the front asked.

"More often than I would like." Stone looked at his laptop, navigating himself back to where he was in his talk. "Okay, the Antichrist. Many people living today, especially those on the Christian right, believe that now is the time of the second coming. But if the Bible is a work of prophecy, it contains nothing to confirm now is the time when the Antichrist will rise. To think such is, quite frankly, preposterous. And what is the identity of the Antichrist? The Bible doesn't really give us many clues about that, which tends to happen with these vague prophetic works. The Revelation of John states that the Antichrist is the *Beast from the Abyss* and the *Beast from the Sea*. That doesn't really pin it down to any great degree. I'm sure you will agree."

Stone looked out at his audience and saw they were still with him. Sometimes, after such an interruption, you could lose the crowd to the intoxication of social media. Whilst he would have personally preferred that his audience leave their phones at home, he knew that wasn't realistic, especially with the younger attendees. Phones were part of us, a vital connection to an invisible world that didn't actually matter.

"Because of the lack of detail, a lot of what we supposedly know about the Antichrist was added later. Adso of Montier-en-Der, a tenth century monk, integrated the work of several biblical commentators in his treatise, which became the standard medieval reference work on the Antichrist. This was then superseded by Hugh Ripelin's Compendium of Theological Truth. It is from these writings that we get the notion that the Antichrist is the mirror opposite of Jesus Christ. They are exact opposites. Jesus good, the Antichrist bad. Jesus born of a virgin, and the Antichrist will thus be born of a whore. All trite and predictable, and yet it has endured through fiction and has made Hollywood billions." Another chuckle from the audience.

Hopefully, by the end of his talk, the interruption would be forgotten. Unfortunately for Stone, an enraged Christian would be the least of his problems.

13.

Rome, Italy

To his neighbours, Aharon was a hard-working office clerk. He was pleasant, polite and kept himself pretty much to himself. Occasionally, he would disappear for a week or two, ostensibly to go on holiday, but there was nothing remarkable about the man who would often hold the door open for those who lived in his apartment building.

The truth was, his name wasn't Aharon, it was Mohammed. As an agent of the VAJA, the Islamic Republic of Iran's Intelligence ministry, he was a committed and supposedly merciless sleeper agent who had been inserted into Rome nearly seven years earlier. His documents and his history, though forged, were the best the Iranians could produce.

He was not placed there to steal secrets, but to be ready to strike against the infidels if the time was ever deemed right. That time was now.

When he had first been chosen for this mission, Mohammed had despised the Italians and their flawed God. His disdain was so great that he knew he would willingly volunteer his life if it became necessary.

Mohammed knew there was a real chance that he would one day be called upon to sacrifice himself. His chances of surviving and once again returning to his family in Iran were slim, and he had reconciled himself to the fact that he would likely die a martyr for Allah and his holy prophet.

Time passed, and, if he was honest with himself, he knew he had almost been corrupted. Living amongst the westerners had rocked his belief in the cause. Despite his training, he had not expected to find normality in Rome. His indoctrination had not prepared him for the reality of inserting himself into a community filled with normal, everyday people. Some might pray to a different God, but Mohammed struggled to get past the fact that the evil he expected to find wasn't as pervasive as he had been led to believe.

If anything, those who lived in Rome were no different from the people he knew back in Tehran.

As the years progressed, Mohammed developed friends, a network, even the occasional love interest. He knew it was all potentially a distraction from his mission, but he told himself that it was all part of the cover he needed to establish. His trainers had encouraged him to settle into the role, to become what the Italians expected to see. By becoming bland and ordinary, he became invisible, all in the service of Allah.

The Italian External Intelligence and Security Agency was good at routing out the insurgents in its midst, but it couldn't find all of them. So deep was Mohammed's cover that only three people knew of his real identity, and they all resided in Iran. Despite that, he wasn't technically alone in his mission. There were half a dozen other sleepers who had managed to secure safe, meaningless positions of employment and stability. Two of his fellow agents were married to wives who didn't know the secrets their husbands carried in their hearts. By not trying to infiltrate sections of the government or military, Mohammed and his ilk were able to go unnoticed, ready to be called upon at a later date.

The worst mistake would have been for them to try to infiltrate the Vatican itself. His training wasn't up to that task. Those guarding the Holy City state were too good at what they did and would have uncovered his deception in an instant.

Every week, Mohammed would take a walk in the Villa Borghese. A pleasant stroll through the park, a way to unwind at the end of a hectic work week. And every week Mohammed would walk past the same innocuous tree. As long as that tree remained unmarked, he was to continue his imposter's life, free to do whatever his fellow Italians did. For so long he did this, as the weeks passed into months, the months into years. It got to the point where he began to suspect he was forgotten, and that he should accept his new life as permanent. Secretly, in his heart, he was pleased by this prospect. Despite his religious convictions, it was difficult to deny that he enjoyed his time in Rome.

The city was a good place to live. He started to think about the prospect of settling down and starting a family.

Then, two days ago, his heart sank when he witnessed the pink symbol sprayed onto the tree's bark. To most people meandering past, the symbol was just random graffiti, but to Mohammed, it had signalled the end of a life that he had started to cherish.

When he saw the symbol, a part of him wanted to reject the mission he had been sent here for. But that part had to be ignored, even admonished. There was no escaping the destiny he had been given, no way to prevent the inevitable that was forced upon him. If he failed to go ahead with the mission, he would be killed by his own side. If he turned himself into the Italians, he would be interrogated and, at best, locked away for the rest of his life. More probably, they would put a bullet in his head. There was no love for terrorists in this part of the world. At least, that was the fear his handlers had instilled in him.

The illusion he had lived ended that day and the holy warrior was reborn.

Upon leaving the park, he made his way to the nearest internet cafe. He didn't rush, wandering almost in a daze. These were his last moments of freedom. He had known what his mission entailed and the personal risk. In front of the anonymous computer, he logged into an email account that he had never before accessed. The account was filled with spam, as one would expect from an average, everyday free email account. Plenty of email traffic went in, but none ever went out. Instead, in the Draft folder was a single unfinished message. He opened it and read the address he would be expected to visit.

It wasn't hard for him to decipher the hidden message, even though the draft was in code. With the address memorised, he deleted the email and shut down the browser.

That night, Mohammed reluctantly turned up at an isolated building and let himself in. He had known where the key was stashed. The inside of the building was run down, as if nobody had lived there for years. It was secured against squatters, whilst being unappealing to those intent on burglary. To any casual external inspection, the property held nothing of any value. Not to a thief at least, with bars covering its dirty windows. No furniture was visible to anyone who might be standing outside.

Making his way into one of the smaller rooms, he entered a walk-in closet and pushed aside the hidden panel there. How long this property had been in the possession of the Iranians was unknown to him, but behind the panel, Mohammed discovered the parcel he was dreading to find. He knew that his life had been for this sole moment, but still there was regret that he would end things so early. The name Aharon no longer had a place in the world.

Within five minutes of entering, Mohammed had retreated from the property, the fear that he would be grabbed by agents of the Italian police retreating with every metre he put between himself and the drop site. He made it home and timidly placed the package he had acquired on the kitchen table. There had been nothing suspicious about him carrying the large package wrapped in brown paper under his arm from his car to the apartment he rented.

Mohammed carefully opened the box. He was surprised by what he found inside. The contents must have been smuggled in perhaps weeks before. Packaging discarded, he looked at the drone that would bring death to so many. It appeared so innocent, with this technology available on a host of websites. Why the capitalists had invented such a vulnerability to their way of life was beyond Mohammed, but he guessed it was all down to the will of Allah.

The encrypted instructions told him what he needed to do. For hours he battled with himself, worried that he couldn't go through with what was expected of him. His duty won out in the end.

The drone was big enough to carry two one-kilogram containers underneath. Although the containers were opaque, Mohammed knew what they contained. One would be full of a fine white powder, ideal for dispersion in the arid environment of the dry Roman morning. The other would contain a blueish grey metallic powder that would never dissolve. Both, when released, would be breathed in by the unwary and innocent alike.

Anthrax powder and Cobalt 60. It was hard to determine which was the deadlier of the two concoctions. The release mechanism would rain almost invisible death along the pre-planned route. Not only would the mixture kill, it would also act as an area denial weapon that could prevent people living in the region for years.

The timing of this couldn't have been better planned. Tomorrow was Sunday, and the ailing Pope would be on the balcony preaching to the faithful who always gathered. Mohammed would make the most of that opportunity.

Mohammed's job was relatively easy to perform, but his mind still struggled with what was being asked. Fly the drone back and forth over those travelling to St Peter's Square, where Catholic worshippers would be standing in awe as they listened to the lies about their false God. Mohammed's fellow agents would target other areas of Rome, the drones unlikely to raise any kind of alarm so long as they didn't venture over the Vatican's restricted airspace. Once his payload was delivered, the drone would be flown out over the Tiber, where it would fall to its doom.

Hopefully, those who saw it dropping its invisible payload would think nothing of it. Drones were frequently used by the news media, internet bloggers and those with more money than sense.

Anyone who inhaled the anthrax would be fine, initially. As the days progressed, however, they would develop flu-like symptoms with nausea and shortness of breath. Many would venture to their doctors, and the health system would be rapidly flooded by cases. Whilst it was unlikely that the anthrax would spread to medical personnel, the radiation from the bodies contaminated by the Cobalt 60 would cause many of the doctors and nurses to also fall ill. The hospitals themselves would become no-go areas. Tens of thousands would die, and whole swathes of the Italian capital would become uninhabitable for years to come.

How long before the Italians knew they had been attacked? It was hoped that footfall and the prevailing winds would blow the destructive dust into the Vatican itself, contaminating the holiest of Catholic sites.

That would be an added bonus.

By then, Mohammed would be long gone. When his job was complete, his instructions stated he would board an international flight to Canada. There was work that needed doing there as well. That night, by the time Mohammed had managed to get to sleep, he had once again become committed to the cause that his God demanded of him.

If only Mohammed had known that his attack had not been officially sanctioned by the Iranian regime, but by the forces of Hell intent on turning the world's religions against one another.

Once again, mankind was being manipulated by forces beyond their control.

14.

Boston, USA

The problem with evening lectures was the annoying fact that they tended to drag on towards midnight. As much as he was thrilled to indoctrinate young minds with his version of the truth, Stone knew he wasn't getting any younger. He had never been a night owl, preferring to wake and work in the early hours. His body also didn't appreciate being in a different time zone, and it seemed to take longer to acclimatise as his years advanced. At some point, he knew he would need to abandon the marvels of nation-wide and international travel, but at the moment, his reputation and his book sales demanded it. He might have once been on the *New York Times* bestseller list, but such fame was often fleeting and dependent on the fickle whims of the audience that bought his books.

Stone was yet to discover the luxury of being wealthy enough that he no longer *had* to write. What a day that would be, should it ever occur.

Fortunately, the hotel in which he was staying was less than ten minutes' walk away from the lecture hall that had been chosen for him. Chosen because he really had no say in such things. Stone didn't bother with the finer points of organising his talks. He had an agent to arrange all that, someone who took a hefty chunk of his royalties in return. Sometimes that worked, other times not so much.

It was past eleven, and the streets were subdued. He could have caught a taxi, but Stone was well aware he spent too much time behind a computer to take such luxury. Any opportunity to get some form of exercise was advisable, according to his doctor at least. Whilst there was nothing stopping him putting a fitness regime into his normal schedule, when he got into the meat of his writing it tended to sweep him away so that the hours disappeared in a blur of creative passion. And as he tried to write every day, his obsession usually became all-consuming.

Some would say he was disciplined in his ability to put words down in such a religious fashion, but that discipline didn't extend to the rest of his life. Writing was a necessity, for when he couldn't get those often-perilous words out of his soul, they seemed to sit inside him, festering. If he wasn't writing, Stone felt somehow incomplete, as if there was a vital aspect of his existence being kept from him. It was a level of passion that was undoubtedly addictive, but Stone really wouldn't have it any other way.

There was no room for him in a conventional job.

No marriage could survive such a consuming obsession, which was why Stone, at the age of forty-nine, was blissfully single. He also had few friends, despite the outgoing and friendly nature that he painted onto the surface. His life was his work, and with the research it often involved, friends could be forgotten. Through his life, there were those who accepted this and made the required allowances, but often the people he encountered drifted away. As his father had said with tedious regularity, people were either there for a season, a reason or a lifetime.

Stone rarely regretted losing those friendships that needed work to maintain.

Ahead of him, three revellers exited a bar, and he felt the draw that he knew he could never again succumb to. That had been the other thing that had almost engulfed him, an addiction to alcohol that had been more about a stubborn, self-delusional streak than the slow death that so many chose. In his earlier years as a writer, he had used alcohol as a psychological crutch, believing it was a necessity to get the words onto paper. Stone had been mistaken, his own self-doubts like demons that constantly plagued his thoughts. If anything, his writing was better without the influence of the demon drink.

Alcohol had almost killed him, so he could never again allow himself to partake in the intoxicating brew. To do so would see him descend into a chaotic and angry beast that would often lash out at the world, which sometimes made his writing seem vitriolic and, as a very vocal critic had once said, unnecessarily preachy. Away from the word processor, the intoxication often left him violent and unpredictable. Imagine such behaviour in a world of camera phones and social media. Especially now that he was more well known by the public.

Resisting the siren song, Stone turned down a side street and put the temptation behind him.

The street lighting wasn't particularly impressive, the street more an alley that could perhaps allow the passage of one vehicle if it wasn't for the retractable bollards at one end. Despite his rational mind, the pace of his step increased in case whatever dangers lurked in the darkness might suddenly want to claim him. Any danger here would be human in nature. Even with the Satanic and supernatural field he relentlessly wrote about, there was no fear of the paranormal, not in Stone's world. Just as someone who wrote about the horrors of World War One did not fear the prospect of the trenches and mustard gas, so Stone held no regard for the dangers of demons and the other monsters that might dwell in the shadows.

This was a mistake he was to shortly realise.

There was the scuff of a shoe behind him, and glancing behind, Stone saw the ominous figure following. The light was too bad to see the identity of the pursuer, so he stepped off the pavement into the road itself. The end of the alley beckoned, safety mere metres away. If he was to be the victim of some random assault, the criminal was going to end up being disappointed. He had left his wallet in the hotel safe and had less than twenty dollars in his pocket. When you visited as many cities as he did, you learnt the necessary precautions to protect yourself from the human scum that sometimes crept out of the blackness.

Like perhaps taking a taxi instead of walking like a bloody idiot.

"Professor, wait."

The person knew him, and against his better judgement, Stone slowed, turning slightly. The man behind came closer, his identity becoming clearer. The voice wasn't in any way familiar. He had briefly feared it was the man from the lecture, a stalker perhaps intent on converting him to some religious cause. Despite this interloper also being thin, the stranger shared no resemblance to the man who had rudely interrupted Stone's lecture.

"Look, I don't want any trouble," Stone insisted with authority. He faced his foe but continued to back up, careful to not trip himself. How long had this person been lying in wait for him?

From behind, Stone barely registered the sound of a vehicle stopping.

"I would like to apologise for what is about to happen," the thin man demanded. "There are things you don't understand."

"I understand plenty," said Stone. "I understand that you are going to get hurt." So long as the thin man didn't have some sort of weapon, any altercation would be an uneven contest. Despite his lack of prowess in the gym, Stone was a stocky man, and he still held some of the muscle memory from his early years of doing Judo. Whilst nowhere close to being fighting fit, Stone reckoned he could put this stranger on his backside quite easily if need demanded such desperate action.

"You will be coming with me," the thin man advised. "Best you not put up a struggle. That would only see you get hurt. We would prefer to avoid that." So now there were threats, propelling Stone into a situation he had never had to deal with before. How does a mind cope with such a random threat of abduction? The thin man had stopped walking, his hands held passively at his sides, allowing Stone to open up the distance. Curiosity, more than anything, caused Stone to stop.

"Why? You shouldn't be stalking me like this."

"I do what I am told. You will learn to do the same." Suddenly, strong hands grabbed Stone from behind, both arms trapped. Thrashing his head to try to see his abductors, he barely managed to get a glimpse of them. Both of his assailants wore hooded black ski masks.

"Let go of me," Stone demanded, his voice rising. If he shouted, if he caused merry hell, would anyone come to his aid? He doubted it, and he cursed at them, the thin man stepping forward. "I said let go of me."

The thin man thrust something into Stone's face. Despite his efforts, there was no way he could escape the chemical-soaked rag being forced upon him.

"That's it," the thin man said. "Breathe it in. It really is for the best." Stone tried to hold his breath, but it was a foolish gesture of defiance. Held as he was, he had no choice but to let the volatile gas descend into his lungs and allow unconsciousness to take him. Before his lights went out completely, the thin man said one more thing.

"You really don't realise what an honour you are being given. But you will."

15.

Inquisitor training camp, 18 years ago

Two of their number were already gone. One day they had been there, the next their beds were empty, the mattresses stripped leaving cold metal frames. Nobody talked about the missing, for what was there to say? It was better to imagine that the absent were mere figments of one's imagination, a phantom to distract you from the harshness that life in the training camp represented.

There was only one fate that could have befallen them, a penance for their failure to meet the expected requirements. With what was to come over the coming years, it could perhaps be argued that the dead were the lucky ones. At least they were with God now, spared the reality and the brutality of living in the physical world. Those who were stripped from the ranks were not to be mourned. They were to be envied.

The missing certainly hadn't been friends of Lilith. That was one of the first lessons, beaten into her with ruthless repetition. Friendship was a weakness, a luxury that could never be afforded, something to be avoided at all costs. Inquisitors might have allies, they might have mentors, but they did not have friends. There was no room for anything but unflinching loyalty and duty in the life of an Inquisitor. Friends tended to get in the way of that.

That was what today's lesson was all about.

Father stood before them, solemn and unyielding. His face showed no emotion, but his mere presence still filled Lilith with apprehension. There was a long way for her to go before that feeling of dread was extinguished. It would come as the years of training moulded her character into an assassin that could survive in the world most people did not know existed. For now, she knew she had to feel the fear and do what was asked of her, anyway. It was the only way for her to survive. The training was designed to burn everything out of her. Everything except utter devotion.

Compassion, empathy, humanity. These were not traits of an inquisitor. Inquisitors were the iron fist of God. They were his holy vengeance and had to be ruthless in their merciless nature.

The nuns were long gone, returned to their subterranean bunker to help raise the newly born children, who would one day stand where Lilith now stood. The nuns' replacements were harsher, if that was possible. They stood around awaiting any and all commands from Father. The three priests were a terrifying shadow over the lives of Lilith and the other children. Any and all infractions were punished, lessons that often took days to recover from.

Children had to learn discipline, they said, for it was not wise to relent and spoil the child. This was not done out of sadism, but mercy. To be able to fight the armies of Satan, there could be no hesitation, no crack in one's dedication. If the flesh was weak, then the Lord would find his soldiers wanting. Better to fail now than to be allowed to put the most holy of work in peril. The Devil had his ways to worm doubt and disloyalty into those who were frail of flesh and mind.

"We do not crave friendship," Father said, loud enough for them all to hear. The air was warm today, a blessing that was also a curse, for the sun would soon rise enough to beat down upon them. Standing in the open courtyard, there was no shade, no water to quench the thirst that would grow. It did not matter the season, there was always a harshness to be found and endured. "We do not crave acceptance, nor do we desire recognition. Whilst you will all be rewarded on your death, there are to be no treasures or trinkets in your lives. Your only purpose is to serve God and be thankful for his ultimate mercy. Do you understand?"

"Yes Father," they all said, Lilith loudest of all. Already some of the boys in her group were growing stronger than her, faster. That didn't matter. The skills learned were the key, and Lilith seemed to have no equal in that regard.

"Today you will fight. You will fight while the sun is high in the sky. You will fight until half of you submit. There is no failure to be felt here. If you fall at the hands of your fellow students, take that as a lesson to be learnt."

"Yes Father," they said again. This was not a competition. This was a judgement, something that would be repeated many times over the coming weeks and months. They would learn to battle each other, their skin and bones becoming hardened by the repeated traumas inflicted. By the end of the day, they would be bruised and broken, some of them suffering fractures that would take months to heal. Whilst they were not to resort to lethality, there was always the chance that one or more of them could die.

If that happened, then it was due to God's will.

"Why do we fight?" Father asked.

"So that we might live," came the response.

"Why do we live?"

"So that we might serve." Lilith had forgotten how many times she had repeated the mantra.

"Why do we serve?"

"Because our Lord on high commands it." There it was, the essence of what it was to be an inquisitor. Sacrificing yourself for the greater good was the noblest purpose. To do anything else reeked of selfishness.

"Look around you," Father said. "Some of you are strong, others fast. You each have an advantage over your opponent. Find their weakness and never reveal your own. Only through your dedication and commitment can you defeat the dreaded foe. If you feel fear, use it to guide you. The things you dread are to be embraced. They are to be owned and transformed into your ally." Father stepped closer, his eye searching for any hint of doubt or hesitation. He found none which clearly pleased him.

Of all the children he had trained, this group was the most promising. They might only be nine years of age, but already he could see the steel developing in their hearts. The forces of darkness would quiver before those who made it through the training.

Father only had one regret in his life. So many inquisitors had died doing their duty, and yet here he was still alive. There was no pleasure to be had in life, his existence almost as tormented as those of these vulnerable children. And yet he persisted because it was deemed that he was more worthy alive than resting at God's right hand. The limp caused by the injury that ended his usefulness in the field of battle was his mark to bear, his arm painful and limited in its motion. None of the children ever asked him about the injuries, his scarred flesh a constant reminder to them of the dangers they would face.

He had barely made it out alive. Whilst most would have been dispatched to the greater beyond, it had been deemed necessary to keep Father around despite the shattered body he had been left with. His skills were legendary, and at that time the Order had need of a new trainer for the cadets.

Although many of his injuries had healed, he was a mere fragment of the warrior he had once been. He did not complain, despite the agony that wracked his body on a daily basis. Father had been deemed worthy to train those who would follow in his footsteps, a replacement for the Father who had come before him. He had no right or inclination to complain about his own suffering, never mind that of the children he counselled.

"Out there, in the world you may one day have to endure, they say that whatever doesn't kill you makes you stronger. There is a truth to this, but also a lie. Your strength is given to you by God to use, but he also gives you free will to abandon yourself. If you fail, if you fall in the face of your enemy, know that you will receive no mercy from the one we fight. Thus, you must give none. You must never relent. Some of you know this already," Father added.

For the briefest of moments, his eyes settled on Lilith, who did not look away. There was a message there perhaps, an unspoken word that Lilith couldn't decipher. Then the thought evaporated as Father looked away first. "You are no longer children, remember that. You are soldiers of Christ. Christ died brutally for your sins, and now you fight to show your worthiness and to give thanks for his ultimate sacrifice." Father looked at the three priests and nodded to each in turn. In response, they stepped forward.

The children were paired up. Lilith found herself facing a lithe boy who she knew only as Abaddon. The name meant ruin and destruction, which was what she would need to rain down upon him. One of the priests grabbed her left wrist, the manacle he placed there cold and chaffing. By the end of the day, the skin would be blistered and raw.

The other end of the manacle the priest placed on Abaddon's left wrist. Facing each other was now mandatory, making a direct assault problematic. It was all part of the test.

"You will stand here for two hours. You will face your opponent, look into their eyes and try to find the truth about who they are. Learn to feel who your enemy is, discover what there is inside them that you can use." Lilith knew the rules. When those two hours were up, they would fight, hampered as they were. In the two hours that followed, Lilith never looked away once, but Abaddon did.

By the time the battle was allowed to commence, Lilith knew she had already won. Abaddon left the field with a dislocated jaw, Lilith victorious, but with more bruises than she could count. But she had won against a stronger opponent.

The next time she fought, it was Lilith who came away the loser, bested by a boy called Lucien. And so it continued, for weeks and months, the bruises merging with one another. With their injuries, they were forced to fight.

At the end of that period of their training, two of the children were too broken to carry on.

16.

Boston, USA. Present Day

For a brief instance, Stone drifted out of unconsciousness, but his head was too weary to fully acknowledge his surroundings. It caused him physical pain just to open his eyelids, and he did so regardless, the need for self-preservation within telling him that he needed to fight whatever had been done to him.

He felt restricted, his arms and legs tightly bound. The ground beneath him rocked and vibrated, the floor of the van he was lying on covered by a fresh smelling carpet. Coarse fibres irritated the skin of his cheeks. The back of the van was well lit, a burly masked man sitting on a bench, a boot resting on Stone's stomach as if he was some kind of foot rest. Words wanted to form on Stone's lips, but they were sealed by what must have been tape, his breathing laboured and difficult.

There was a burning in his lungs that threatened to make him cough, but Stone resisted that as best he could.

His rousing brought a response from the masked guard, who extracted something from a plastic case beside him. Stone saw the needle from the corner of one eye, and although he wanted to struggle, he really didn't have the energy or the means. The sharpness punctured the side of his thigh. Whoever this man was, he treated Stone like some unavoidable irritation.

Blackness took Stone once again.

Only it wasn't blackness this time, but a realm of dreams. Once more, the images of hellfire and apocalypse assaulted him, though this time they seemed to lack the power that his bad dreams normally held. Whereas before he would be in the heart of the nightmare, feeling the intensity of the traumas that were happening to the world, this time he felt detached, as if he was merely an observer watching a film. To see himself so vividly was an unnerving experience, but he latched onto it, fascination rather than terror filling his veins.

Even the words of the voice sounded disjointed and distant, muffled by the sweet sedative that had driven Stone down into himself. He was able to watch the end of man and he found he didn't care.

Some of what he saw made more sense to him from this perspective, the burning city recognisable, landmarks and buildings still standing despite the sky hurtling down upon the vastness of the ancient human structures. He had been to Rome several times for research, and despite his best efforts, he had never once been allowed into the hallowed caverns of the Vatican archives. If he had been a proper academic, rather than an author of so-called dubious fiction, perhaps that might have been different. It no longer mattered, for here, much of the Vatican had been flattened.

Then the voice came, breaking through the wall of whatever drug held Stone captive from the conscious world.

"*Fear not; I am the first and the last.*"

Through the smoke that swelled the air, Stone witnessed a huge form come into view, towering over what was left of the city and its people. In the few unshattered streets, thousands of people ran, their screams barely audible despite the vast numbers. Whatever this creature was, Stone was unable to distinguish its form. It seemed to swell and gyrate, arms appearing and blending with others, the heads too numerous to make sense. It was a beast of pure chaos.

In the sky above, the blackness was ripped open in a huge tear, seven menacing stars the only things visible in that ungodly rent.

Before his eyes, the city changed. The landscape flattened, the seven hills disappearing as the desert came onto the horizon. The beast was still there though, its identity an enigma to tax the whole intellect of man. This was a place he had never visited, but the secret of it was whispered into his ear.

Stone felt his feet leave the earth, his view changing as he rose rapidly into the red and burning sky. There, at the centre of it all, the Great Mosque became visible, the Ka'bah a shattered and glowing ruin. The walls of the mosque were trembling as the fires surrounding it surged inwards. If the faithful left down there were praying for forgiveness or deliverance, Stone couldn't hear them.

All he could hear were their howls of anguish, unbelievable torture inflicted upon those damned to this slaughter. And the dead? One by one, they began to rise up and attack what was left of the living.

"This can never be real," Stone insisted. He rejected it, renounced what he saw as a hallucination.

"*You defy your own eyes? Repent, or else I will come unto thee quickly*." The voice sounded as if it was in his head now, loud and thunderous, but strangely free of discomfort. As hot as the surrounding air was, Stone knew he couldn't be harmed. This was a dream. How could one be harmed in a dream? "*Come up hither*," the voice demanded as Stone rose further into the air. "*And I will show you things which must be hereafter.*"

Once again, the scene changed, this time structures thrust high into the sky, great skyscrapers that marked the false greatness of mankind. There was no denying the place at the centre of an empire. New York.

"But why?" Stone begged. "There are no religious sites here."

"*Is money not now your God*?" the voice asked sadly.

"Not like this. It doesn't deserve this." As Stone watched, a burning mist fell upon the city. Out of the mist, the creature began to take shape, its fists smashing into the strongest and the tallest of the buildings.

"*You can stop this*," the voice insisted. "*All you have to do is believe.*"

"Believe in what?" Stone implored. "I don't know what you want."

"*You will. For soon you will meet the one who shall reign on the Earth. You are going to learn what he has planned for you pathetic creatures…Dude, it's going to be biblical.*"

"I don't want to see this." Stone closed his eyes, but found he could still see.

"*You are here to bear witness*," the voice insisted. "*You will watch and you will learn. Here, let me show you how it all began.*"

The whole scene changed once again. There was no city now, the space around Stone a seemingly endless void full of light and possibility. In the light, celestial figures clashed, a great thunderous roar cascading into his ears. It was too much for his senses, pain soaring through Stone's body.

How can I feel pain in a dream?

The largest of the figures suddenly took shape, the head of a great dragon, bloodied and toothless, drooped to one side, the body falling, others falling with it.

"*The great dragon was hurled down, the ancient serpent called Lucifer. He was hurled to below the earth and his traitorous archangels with him. He now leads the whole world astray.*"

The war. I'm seeing the war in Heaven.

"What does it mean?"

"*Lucifer thought he could rebel; thought he could take the place of the one on high. Such pride. Such hubris. It makes me smile to think of it.*" The air around Stone stilled, the light dimming, the figures and shapes disappearing from his view. "*Lucifer forgets that it was the Lord who put the thought of rebellion into his head.*"

Although the thought would be lost when he finally awakened, in that instant, Stone realised he understood the true nature of what he was seeing.

No human mind should be forced to carry that curse.

17.

London, UK

Detective Inspector Hargreaves sat in his office and listened once again to the interview with the voice that called itself Legion. He was no psychiatrist, but who could deny the person they had in custody was clinically insane? Either that, or he was an incredible actor. Whilst the jackals demanding justice would want this man locked away in prison for life, Hargreaves strongly suspected that the Broadmoor high security hospital would become Damien's permanent home.

Hargreaves could live with that. What mattered most was getting this maniac off the streets. Locked away with the insane and medicated by force was no light sentence. If anything, it could be worse than prison incarceration. The drugs administered could sometimes strip a person of their being.

When he had witnessed the change in eye colour, Hargreaves first thought that Damien had cunningly discarded some contact lenses he was wearing. But that was dispelled later when the colour had changed back. Nobody had imagined it, and the events of the interrogation were all the talk of the station. Hargreaves was not unfamiliar with the phenomena. There was plenty of anecdotal evidence in the literature he had read over his career of this colour change happening. But to see it, to actually see it…

Even the voice had altered. It had been difficult to pin down Damien's accent, but the one taken up by Legion was definitely from Eastern Europe.

"*You can call me Legion.*"

"*That's a bit biblical.*" Hargreaves hated listening to his own voice. It sounded wrong to him, disjointed.

"*You want to know about the murders,*" Damien's alter ego said.

"*Very much so.*" Hargreaves had briefly looked at his sergeant then, and could still picture the look of utter confusion that was painted on Black's face.

"*I suppose you want to know why? I am happy to tell you.*"

"*Firstly, why don't you tell me how many you have killed.*" Thinking back to the interview, Hargreaves wasn't confident they could rely on what was being said. Time would tell on that.

"*So many, and yet not enough.*"

"*A number,*" Hargreaves heard himself demand.

"*Forty-seven. You found me before I could really get my teeth into it.*" The medium Hargreaves was listening to also had video, but the inspector had his eyes closed to try to detect any nuances in what was being said. He didn't need the video aspect to tell him that Legion had been seated ramrod straight all through this recording. Those eyes had bored into him, never wavering. There was no doubt in Legion, no remorse. If anything, the man seemed proud of the atrocities he had committed.

"*That's more bodies than we've uncovered so far.*" If Legion was telling the truth, then that meant there would be eleven more corpses for the tabloids to eventually go ballistic over.

"*Some of them I hid, to reveal later. Sometimes it did not feel right to let the world see my creations. At the beginning I was learning, discovering my art. I've been at this a long time.*"

"*Are you willing to share the locations of those bodies now?*" That would be a lot of work for the forensic teams. At least the killing spree would be over. Several teams were presently at the first of the locations Legion eventually gave.

"*I will consider it. But I will need something from you first.*"

"*We don't make deals with killers.*" That was Black, letting his emotions through again. The sergeant was new to Hargreaves' team, and the inspector wasn't sure he was the right fit. Black didn't have the correct temperament in his opinion. A bit too volatile, a bit too ready to show his emotions. Sometimes that was an asset in this job, but not with maniacs like Damien/Legion. Twenty years ago, men like Black would have been at ease throwing their suspects down the stairs.

"*But it is such a small request. Barely worth mentioning.*"

"*Go on.*" Hargreaves had thought it better to invite the man to keep talking. Criminals baring their souls to him was far from unusual, but the speed of the confession had been a bit of a surprise.

"*A cherry coke.*"

"*A what?*" Black again.

"*A cherry coke. I drink it every day.*" Hargreaves fast-forwarded.

"*...and to why I did it. The answer is simple, but you are unlikely to believe it.*" There was the sound of Legion slurping his newly acquired drink. Hargreaves reckoned that was deliberate, for the benefit of the recording.

"*Everyone has their own reasons for the things they do. We will listen to yours. Help us to understand.*" That didn't mean that Hargreaves would accept those reasons as valid, especially with nearly fifty people dead.

"*Well, it is simple really. I killed them because of the horror they represented.*"

"*You will forgive me if I say you sound a little vague there.*" The horror they represented? The guy they had in custody was a show-off, someone who took pride in what he did. Hargreaves had met his kind before, and it was always their own arrogance that was their undoing.

What still troubled him, though, was the anonymous tip-off that had led them to Damien in the first place. Nobody had been able to identify who the informer was. Damien didn't seem the type to talk casually about the things he did, and with no real way to identify the man with multiple personalities, the police had yet to establish who his peer group or family were.

"*I killed them because we all shared the same father.*"

"*I find that hard to believe.*" Hargreaves couldn't see how that was possible.

"*I can see your doubt,*" the voice of Legion said. "*You are still trapped in your own mortal beliefs. The father I refer to wasn't the one I killed when I was still young.*"

"*This is preposterous.*" Yes, Hargreaves knew he was going to have to do something about Black.

"*So, is it jealousy? Sibling rivalry?*"

"*Nothing so petty, my dear inspector. I kill them to rid the world of their taint. I do what I can to save the world from imperfection.*" There had been such conviction in Legion's voice that Hargreaves had almost believed him.

"*I hope you aren't going to tell me you are spawned from Satan.*"

"*Of course not. That would be ridiculous. That truly would be a curse.*" Legion had laughed then. "*Damien's true father, the one from outside this earthly realm, is Lucifer.*" Hargreaves stopped the tape. The psychiatrists were going to have a field day with this one.

***

Damien sat cross-legged on the floor in the middle of his holding cell. He'd been alone for about two hours, the surveillance camera in the corner his only companion. Once again, he was as nature intended; the clothing provided chaffed and was therefore unacceptable. He knew he would wear them again, but for now, he was free of their restrictions.

The coolness of the cell did not concern him.

His mind was still, deep in meditation. It was something he had learnt at a young age, a way to protect the brain from the horrors that had been inflicted on him. The meditation also helped purge him of the memories that could have ravaged him, images of what his father had done with the belt, with the fists, and with other parts of him. His mother also shared the blame for that, with Damien the sole recipient of the violence in that household.

Once, at the age of eight, his earthly father had dragged him outside. The decrepit house they inhabited was blessed with a square front lawn that his father had been obsessed about. Thinking back, Damien could not understand why the grass was so important. He didn't realise that it was the only symbol of achievement his father felt he had. Being the father of the odious little boy was no great accomplishment.

His unkempt and unwashed hair had felt like it was being pulled out of his scalp as his earthly father dragged him, hurling the boy, who would grow up to be Damien, onto the front lawn. If there was anyone on the street who could have helped him that day, they didn't make themselves known. Likely they didn't see him, the high hedge at the front of the property making an effective barrier.

"I want you to cut my grass, you little shit," his father had insisted in a measured tone. "You have all afternoon to make a good job of it. Make me proud to call you my son." Damien had looked down at the lawn, wondering how he was supposed to perform such a task, only to have a pair of small scissors hurled at his feet. "You deserve to spend your life on your knees, so this will be good practice." He had seen his mother then, standing behind his father in the doorway, a look of disgust on her face. The disgust was for Damien, not the act he was being forced into.

He had tried, he really had, snipping at individual blades of grass to try to get some sort of conformity with them, but it was a deliberately impossible task, made worse by the rain that started to fall an hour after his toils had started. It hadn't been a heavy rain, but it soon soaked through the rags Damien had been wearing.

By the time the light was failing, Damien was in tears. The cold had eaten through him, his small body shivering as he tried desperately to find some sanity in what he was enduring.

"Let's see how my little shit has done," the voice had said. His father had knelt down next to him, caring not for the moisture that soaked through the knees of his jeans.

"I tried, father, I really did." The words had been hampered by the sobs that had been impossible to hold back. Damien's tears had always seemed to bring his father such joy.

Damien always wondered what would have happened if he had run away that day. The garden gate had been right there. He could have been through and onto the street before his parents had a chance to react. Fear had prevented him. Fear, and the love that he foolishly held. Despite the abuse and the beatings, they were still his parents, and surely they only did such things because Damien himself was to blame.

"You're useless," had come the response. "You can't even cut grass." His father had stood, turning his attention to the woman who should have been out there protecting Damien. "He missed some."

"Pitiful," had been the only reply. Without looking at Damien, she had turned and walked back into the house.

Damien didn't try to resist when his father had then grabbed him because he knew it would only make his fate worse. The beating he received that night had taken days to recover from. At the beginning, Damien had hoped his punishment would be quick, only to hear his mother in the background telling his father to "*stop pissing around and show the boy what real punishment is*". There was no remorse after, as sometimes occurred in such child abuse, no attempt to seek forgiveness. The house he had lived in had been toxic and violent, the authorities barely aware that Damien was alive.

His mother had never hit him, but she did have a tendency to put her cigarettes out on his skin. Sometimes she forced him to sacrifice the tender flesh of his tongue.

Those memories tried to force themselves upon his thoughts, but Damien cast them aside. They held no power anymore, mere pebbles on the long road to where he now found himself. Being arrested seemed like a setback, but Damien knew enough to accept that time would tell on that. For the moment he would be prevented from killing, so Legion would remain docile, only occasionally to make an appearance to keep those who kept him captive on their toes.

Legion had come forth to explain the reasons for the killings to the police, and then the phantom companion had retreated. Did the police see how protective Legion was? Maybe Legion should have shown them other things, like the strength that came with his manifestation. If Legion had willed it, those handcuffs and the necks of those officers would have been left broken.

It was likely only the guns that had prevented Legion's appearance upon Damien's arrest.

There was another aspect of Legion's protection. Damien didn't remember the majority of the murders, his alter ego spared him from that. He could see the bodies in his thoughts, but not the stripping of those lives. The bodies were just meat once the spark of essence had been stripped from them.

Damien could remember the first time Legion appeared to him. It had been during the beating after the grass cutting. A calming voice whispering to him.

"You don't have to fear any more. You no longer have to suffer. Let me take the pain from you." Still young and not understanding how his mind was fracturing, Damien had listened to the voice, blackness taking him as a fragment of him took over. It was like sleeping, only without the dreams.

Legion began to appear and take some of the punishment after that, Damien often awakening to skin that was broken, buttocks that were bruised and, on more than one occasion, broken fingers. The aftermath he could deal with, now that he was spared the actual ordeal. The more of the brunt Legion took, the more frequently the beatings seemed to happen. Damien didn't know it, but his split personality took the trauma without a sound escaping him. Damien was never there to see the desperate look in his earthly father's eye when the older man realised he could no longer break the child. He wasn't there when his mother stepped in and held back his father's hand, fearing that one more strike would kill the kid whose immortal soul they were trying to somehow save. Even *she* couldn't accept murder.

That was the moment the power dynamic in that household changed.

By the age of thirteen, Legion barely needed to be present at all, both his parents deathly afraid of the child they were raising. Damien himself had changed, as if moulded on an anvil into something predatory and dangerous. As for why the beatings and the torments happened, it was years before Damien truly understood their meaning. That came with the realisation of who he really was, and of how he came to be in this world.

His earthly father had beaten him because Damien had been a symbol of betrayal. His mother allowed it because of the images of that night when Damien had been conceived. It had been her husband on top of her, but he had been feral, enraged. Although she tried to forget it, there was no way to deny the face she had seen at the moment of ejaculation. It had not been the face of her husband.

The creature on top of her had not been from this world.

Being highly religious, his mother had become obsessed that the devil had been inside her that night. She was right in a way, but she just got the wrong fallen angel. Not really understanding the forces she was up against, her own sanity had slipped, and she began to see Damien as someone who needed to be punished. Her husband hadn't needed much persuading; the sick sadistic streak was already there.

Then came the night Damien once more stepped aside so that Legion could take his first victims. Both his parents were killed in their marital bed, the father first, the knife plunged deep into his chinless neck. Despite Legion being in command, there was a rare memory of clarity that night, Legion allowing Damien to share in the victory and the revenge.

Deep in meditation, it was like he was there now. His mother sat naked in the bed, the body of her husband in its death throes, the knife free and dripping from the wound it had inflicted.

"*I knew it would come to this.*"

"*And yet you still had me,*" Legion had said.

"*You were my son. I didn't understand.*"

"*So, you beat me instead?*"

"*We thought it was the only way. We thought we could beat what was in you into submission.*"

"*No, you made me. You forged what you now see.*"

"*I should never have had you.*" Those were the last words his mother had uttered before her screams filled the night. With her mother's blood still spurting, Legion had begun what he would do to so many others.

Damien didn't agree with those last words. Damien being in the world was the best thing that could have happened. For without him, Legion would never have been born. And who else was there to kill what needed to be killed?

18.

Inquisitor training camp, 17 years earlier

"You learn the face of your enemies." Today they were inside, a rare treat to escape the elements. Seventeen children remained, the one called Jeremiah having died in front of them at the hands of one of the priests. Sometimes the body could not withstand the punishment demanded by the faithful.

The priest involved had received no reprimand and no sanction. Jeremiah had not been inquisitor material.

They were in a room without windows, the harsh halogens above providing more than enough light. In the centre of the room, a hooded and naked man was bound down to a metal chair. Despite the man's squirming, there was no way for him to escape his restraints. The chair itself stayed rigid, its legs bolted firmly to the spotless white laminated floor.

It wouldn't stay spotless for long.

Already, Lilith was able to tell things about the man and the environment she was in. Despite never having seen this room before, she knew its pristine nature was designed to be kept spotless, the whiteness of the walls and floor there to reveal any lingering impurity. The single tap on the far wall told her the purpose of the strategically placed drains that were spread across the floor. This room was designed to be easily cleaned, the surfaces smooth, impervious and seamless.

This captured man—this prisoner—was not going to enjoy his time here.

"Your enemy will try to hide amongst the very people we are here to protect. There are ways to find them, which you will learn. There are tactics to uncover their places of concealment and methods that are best used to despatch them. By the end of today, you will know all this."

Lilith and the rest of the children were gathered in a group at one end of the room. Behind them, a huge mirror filled the wall, most likely a portal to a viewing room behind it. Sometimes those who came here wished to stay concealed to those trapped. No such extravagance was offered to Lilith and her fellow trainees. They had nothing to fear from the man in the chair.

Father stepped forward and pulled the hood off the man. At first glance, Lilith didn't think he looked particularly unusual. His face was slightly bruised, the upper lip cut from where he had been struck. He didn't look strong or athletic, an average man trapped in a less-than-average situation.

"It could be anyone," Lilith said. The children had no fear of speaking or asking questions, so long as they had something to actually say. Lilith had already learnt enough to not give such a creature a human identity. The children all knew what this thing was from their previous tuitions. This was the first time they would see one in the flesh.

"And that is their strength. This is why you cannot fear killing what appears to be the innocent or those you might consider a victim. God welcomes all those sent before him. The lives you take will either help gather his flock to his loving side, or send the wicked to the hot place where they belong."

"Is it worthy of suffering?" another child asked.

"Oh yes," Father replied. "This one will suffer greatly. You will all see to that."

“Please,” the bound man begged, “you can’t do this. I have a wife; I have a family.” Father struck him with the back of his hand and leaned in close to the man’s face.

“Desist with your lies. You aren’t fooling anyone.” For a moment, the frightened, desperate face persisted on the man, only to be replaced by one of arrogance and defiance.

“Hell, you can’t blame a man for trying.”

“Indeed,” Father admitted. “But then you are not a man. I would have you show your true face for me now.”

“What, and frighten these little children? Where is your compassion?”

“I have no compassion for the likes of you,” said Father. As if to prove this, he stuck his thumb under the bound man’s rib cage and pressed, causing a cry of pain.

“It doesn’t matter what you do to me. You might as well kill me and get this over with.”

“Oh, death is inevitable, but trust me when I say it will be a long time coming.” Father turned back towards the children. “What do we need to defeat our enemy?”

“Faith,” the children said in unison.

“Who gives us that faith?”

“The Lord on high.”

“Your God is dead,” the bound man spat. Father ignored the comment.

“Who are the ones who get to defend that faith?” Father enquired.

“Only the worthy,” the children answered.

“Who are the worthy?”

“Those who are chosen through pain and suffering.”

“Fucking inquisitors,” the bound man shouted. He was enraged. Lilith could see the fear that was masked by the bound man’s bravado. For the briefest of moments, she saw something, almost as if a dark halo had surrounded the man. Her eyes must have shown the truth of it, as Father stepped over to her. She gazed up at the giant.

“Did you see it?” There was almost excitement in his voice. If she had, Father had never known an initiate see the truth of them so soon.

“I saw something,” she answered, “like a dark cloud around him.”

“Yes,” Father exclaimed. He turned and pointed at the bound man. “Demon, I would have your name.”

“Go screw yourself,” came the response.

“Your name, demon. The Lord commands it.”

“Maybe you didn’t hear me. Get fucked.” Father turned back to the children.

“They are as stubborn as they are deadly. To know a demon’s name gives you great power, which is why this one is so reluctant. There are ways, however. And in the end, they always speak it.” A door to the right opened and one of the priests walked in. He carried an open bag over his shoulder, and, stepping before each child, the priest reached in and extracted a small knife that he gave over to small, eager hands.

“Do demons feel pain like we do?” one of the children asked.

“No, it can be worse for them.” Father answered. “Their perception is different. Although they have lived an eternity in the fire, that was without this human flesh they like to wear. Trust me when I say, the demonic do not enjoy being tortured at our hands. They have little tolerance for the torments you can inflict.”

"Why do they come here?" Lilith asked.

"It is like an addiction," Father answered. It would be years before Lilith was allowed to understand the finer details of how demonic possession occurred. Then she would learn that only a proportion of the human population could fall victim to possession based on a deficiency in their genetic code. "They feel compelled, spurred on by their vile, traitorous master."

"I'm not telling you my name," the bound man insisted. The priest handed the last knife to Father, the blade so tiny in his shovel-like hand. These knives were meant for initiates, but the edges were as sharp as conventional weapons. The stronger the demon, the more they could resist revealing themselves, should they choose to.

"Why do you persist in this foolishness?" Father enquired. Lilith thought he sounded genuinely curious. "You know you only delay the inevitable."

Stepping forward, Father held the man's head with one strong hand so that he could remove the bound man's left eye. The flesh wielded easily to the knife. Lilith felt no horror witnessing this, for she had seen far worse. Through gritted teeth, the demon hurled out a tirade of abuse.

"Who needs eyes?" the demon blustered.

"You do, to see the fate that awaits you. Turn off the lights," Father instructed. The priest did, the room not falling into darkness. On the ceiling glowed a host of shapes and symbols that Lilith could barely decipher. She knew some of them, but most were a mystery. These were arcane symbols, meant to trap a demon in the physical plane.

"You can't," the demon insisted. "You daren't."

"I am an inquisitor," Father replied. "I can do as I please."

"You are a broken old man who probably likes to fondle little boys." That brought a laugh from the demon's lips.

"Well," Father retorted, "at least five minutes from now, I will still have fingers."

"This is against all the laws," the demon insisted.

"God's laws do not concern the likes of you," Lilith found herself saying.

"You see," Father proclaimed. "Even a child knows. Your name, demon? I won't ask again. You know what I can do to you." The bound man sighed, finally resigned to his fate. Inside its host, the demon knew it had no choice. "We are not exorcists. We have no time for words or rituals. Your name, scum?"

"Ashmedai," the demon whispered.

"Good," Father said. "That will spare you some pain. When your host dies, we will let you descend instead of being trapped here." That was what the symbols were for, Lilith knew. If separated from the host, the demon could only live so long in the material realm. Forbidden from returning to Hell, they would feed upon their own essence until they were no more. Demons could be killed, but it took a lot of doing. Such a room as this would never be available to an Inquisitor in the real world.

What would happen to a demon trapped in a dead body?

"I hope to see you down there one day," Ashmedai insisted. "You think your God loves you, but I have met many an inquisitor being feasted on by the beasts of the pit."

"Then, if that day arises, I hope I give you indigestion." Father stood tall. "Lilith, step forward." She did as commanded, eager to prove her worth. Father pointed at the bowed head of the broken demon. "Remove its lips."

By the time the children were done, the demon was a shaking, pleading figment of the man it had possessed. Despite the grievous injuries, Father was there to make sure they did nothing lethal. This was one of many lessons in torture the children were to receive. The training was not only to know how to inflict pain whilst keeping the victim alive, but also to withstand the harrowing cries that would often cry forth. Whilst some demons were strong enough to almost ignore what was being done to their bound forms, others were chaotic enough to give voice to their pain.

It would be a rare day that Lilith would ever need to use these skills, but better to have them and not need them.

DI.P.Hargreaves@metpoliceuk.gov.uk

Re: Request for information

To: [UK Europol International Police Liaison Officer] communication@nca.x.gsi.gov.uk

Keith

We have apprehended an individual who we believe may have been involved in multiple homicides. We have not as yet been able to identify the individual, and although the NCCU have no record of his fingerprints, I believe there is a strong chance he may be a European National, specifically from one of the Eastern European countries.

I need you to liaise through SIENNA with Europol and Interpol to see if they have this man in their database (fingerprint data is enclosed).

If this serial killer is from the continent, he may have engaged in such activities in multiple countries. We don't think he has been operating here for more than five years. I've enclosed the relevant request and will be able to upload the autopsy reports shortly.

Let me know what you find.

Thanks for this
Paul

Detective Inspector Hargreaves, London Metropolitan Police

METROPOLITAN
POLICE

19.

Isfahan, Iran. Present Day

The Iranian regime had thought they were clever. They were soon to realise how mistaken they were in that assessment. Just like the Saudis, they too were not invulnerable to attacks from the air.

They had numerous sites where they researched the secrets of nuclear weapons, many of them open to inspection to calm the fears of the ludicrous west. But some, like the hidden facility south of Isfahan, were kept a secret from the world. Built mostly underground, this was one of several areas where the Iranians were attempting to create the required quantities of U-235, the fissile isotope of naturally occurring uranium.

The problem was, it was a slow and laborious process. The other major problem that the Iranians were blissfully unaware of was that the hidden facility hadn't been a secret for months. The Israeli Mossad had uncovered its existence, and with the Kingdom of Saudi Arabia burning, the Israelis decided to share that facility's whereabouts with their Saudi counterparts. Whilst Israel was more than capable of taking out the facility, they chose to play a more restrained hand.

The enemy of my enemy is temporarily my friend.

The Saudis were not slow to act. In the early hours of the morning after the suicide attack on their Stock Exchange, twelve recently acquired Chinese-made J-31 stealth fighter jets of the Royal Saudi Air Force took off from Prince Sultan Air Base. Flying low enough to enhance the impressive stealth capabilities, the Iranian air defence network didn't see them coming.

On the ground, Saudi Arabian special forces were already in place, ready to guide in the precision ordinance the planes were carrying. The Americans may have not been willing to sell their Saudi allies stealth jet technology, but they had been more than willing to allow the sale of a wide selection of their country's plane-dropped ordinance. In this instance, eight of the planes were carrying the GBU-28 laser-guided bomb. At five thousand pounds, each bomb was capable of penetrating twenty feet of concrete as well as delivering an explosive impact that would certainly get the Iranian's attention.

In other words, the Saudis could give as good as they got.

The Iranian facility didn't stand a chance, all eight bombs landing with devastating precision. Although not the only uranium enrichment facility, in one blow, the Iranians found they had been set back by years in their laborious creation of that elusive nuclear device.

This was bad, especially as the Saudis had only started in their attacks.

At around the same time, two squadrons of Eurofighter Typhoons carrying AG88_Harm missiles crossed the gulf and, outside Iranian airspace, locked on to the radar emissions from Iran's defensive SAM sights. Within the same minute, over forty of those missiles were launched, each locking on to a radar signal that was there to detect the incursion by foreign and unwelcome aircraft. The AG88 was an air-to-surface anti-radiation missile designed to detect and destroy the site of radar emissions.

Thirty-seven of those missiles struck their targets, destroying much of Iran's air defence capability in the southern half of Iran. Iran found itself blinded. This was followed by more than two hundred cruise missiles raining down on some of Iran's most important oil sites, as well as the launch facility for their beleaguered space program. By the time the Saudis were finished, Iran discovered it was not in a position to profit from the loss of Saudi oil on the world market.

There were many in the Iranian government who could freely admit to themselves that attacking Saudi Arabia had been a strategic blunder of monumental proportions. That opinion would be reinforced when they learnt that the United States carrier strike group twelve, with its aircraft carrier *USS Abraham Lincoln,* had set sail from Norfolk to join the *USS Harry. S. Truman* and carrier strike group eight who were already in the area. So far, the Americans were prepared to sit back and watch the firework show, but events would soon set that aspiration to the flame.

The world was heading for a war it would likely never recover from. The Iranians should have learnt from the lesson inflicted on them. Instead, they decided to double down.

And all the while, the forces guiding this madness chuckled under their demonic breath.

20.

London, UK

For most of the residents of the Pit, the chance to venture into the green pastures of the mortal world was a haphazard affair, driven more by chance than anything. Occasionally, in the past, a thinning occurred to the barrier between Hell and the place that serviced it with fresh souls. When that rare phenomenon arose, demons could occasionally step through, ready to randomly occupy the unwilling and the unsuspecting. That was when people found themselves in the wrong place at the wrong time, demonic possession the essence of where that saying originally came from. Numerous humans were immune to this kind of possession, but there were always some ready to be claimed.

There were other demons who worked at the barrier, breaking holes in it, chipping away at the defences that had been put in place. This took time though, and again, for the lesser demons, only some of the humans were available to ride. God hadn't designed his creatures to be taken easily.

Some demons were drawn through the ancient rites practiced by the unwary. Those foolish enough to partake in those rituals thought they would be brought fame and riches, instead only to suffer anguish and torment as the demons claimed them. They opened their souls and allowed the blackness in, and in doing so, cursed themselves for all eternity.

This was how the innumerable lesser demons used to make their way to the human realm. Luck, persistence and human stupidity. These were the vermin that engaged most of the inquisitors' time.

Unfortunately, being close to the end times, things were becoming easier in that regard. With each passing day, the barriers separating the Earth from Hell were becoming weaker. More and more of the creatures from the Pit were being given the chance to claim their prize.

There were higher demons as well, created by the Fallen, who had the power to force their way through to the realm of man. This was through the power of their own will, or sometimes with the help of those more knowledgeable on the other side who acted on the Dark Lord's behalf. The Fallen had their human emissaries who thought their service would gain them power. It never did. The fallen archangels liked nothing more than tricking the gullible into damning themselves.

These more powerful dark forces could overpower any without the restrictive genetic trait, and it was rare for the human form to be able to withstand a higher echelon demon for long. Whilst there were select genetic bloodlines that could carry such a powerful demon, most human bodies ate themselves alive trying to reject the invader. The Fallen would sometimes send one of their emissaries, dispatching one of the Kings of Hell to earth on some specific mission. Those trips were often of a limited duration.

That was how the great and powerful demon Baal found herself once again on earth.

The body Baal claimed had surprisingly tried to fight back, but over countless nights of attrition, Baal had wormed her way in, the host not understanding the satanic forces he was up against. It was just nightmares, he had told himself, the result of too much stress. His own denial of what was happening had worked against him until, ultimately, Baal had claimed her prize.

"*You are mine. Fighting me will only extend your suffering.*"

The body she claimed as her own was a politician, a man of reportedly low morals and a weak constitution. Overweight, with high blood pressure, the body was only a decade from its ultimate demise due to neglect and high living. Still, its resistance was annoying. It was also too frail to hold a being as powerful as Baal for long. It would do for what was required, though.

The man's physical appearance meant nothing to Baal. The meat was merely a suit she wore to exist in this realm. It chafed at her essence, but being here was a pleasure compared to the torments suffered down in the Pit. Being a King of Hell did not spare her the vengeance of the almighty and the force that ultimately ruled the underworld. The Fallen might have created them, but the spawn were always treated harshly, no matter their rank.

Her host had some intelligence and a degree of charisma, which was good. By now, the mind of the man would be pushed aside and locked away, able to observe everything done in his name, but incapable of intervening. He was now nothing but a passenger, a spectator who would bear witness to the foul deeds Baal would do in his name. And yet, he always seemed to be there in her thoughts, nibbling at her patience.

"*Be still,*" she told the human mind. "*You are only hurting yourself.*" She didn't remember humans being this tenacious.

In the times before technology and literacy, Baal had only been allowed to possess the insane or those with rare genetic traits that left them vulnerable, and only then on rare occasions. She was a King of Hell, her place was to serve in the Pit, to do the bidding of her Masters and to command her battalions. When she was allowed out, she took what she could get. She and those like her possessed who they could, committing acts so heinous and so despicable nobody in those times spoke of them. Whereas the insane and the downtrodden were usually removed from any chance of conceiving offspring, the Kings, Dukes and Princes of Hell made sure that rape was used to propagate the better gene pools.

The proportion of humanity that could easily be claimed by those in the Underworld began to grow. Still, the number one law of the Fallen had to be upheld. Those who venture to earth must never reveal the true nature of what so many religions preached. The Fallen had worked hard to fool the world into believing they were a story in a book. It would not do for their existence to be realised until they were ready. The faithful thought they believed in him, but really, they had no concept of what Hell really was, just as the faithful could never comprehend the true nature of God.

They were told stories of Satan, but had no idea the reported thing ruler of Hell was merely a figment meant to distract them. The greatest trick the Fallen ever played was to make the world think Satan existed.

The veil between worlds had grown thin of late, the seals that held the gate clenched shut, brittle and close to failure. Gradually, over hundreds of years, it had become easier for demons to slip through. And as mankind expanded its intelligence, so more of them developed and learnt the arcane knowledge that allowed the unwise to tear small holes through the veil. Hell had been designed to contain Baal's kind, but things had been getting interesting of late. The bulk of the demonic possessions were still random affairs. That would change. And when the wall separating realities finally fell…

Now was the time of prophecy. The first Seal was close to breaking.

Baal had access to the host's memories and was able to mimic his personality. She would have to be careful, though, as those close to the man would be able to see the change that would inevitably seep out.

He was a man of power, so she would use that and the knowledge she had already gained from him to steer her way through the mission on which she had been sent.

His essence within her was an irritation. And Baal only had so much time before her presence started to corrupt the flesh. She was too powerful to be contained for long in a random human; another reason why the Kings rarely ventured up here. As for the Fallen, they were trapped, despite their power. Hell was their domain, but also their prison.

The time for their rise would soon be at hand. Once again, the Fallen would walk the land they coveted. Then the demons would finally be free of their prison.

For a time, at least.

Standing before the door of her new home, Baal prepared to step out into the freshness of the air. It had been so long since she had used lungs, the sensation of breathing feeling alien. Humanity claimed to have advanced so much since then. If this man she rode in was anything to go by, they were still just monkeys driven by their basest desires and animalistic urgings. With their technology, they believed they were gods, which many thought was why the Creator was tiring of them. If the time of the Great Tribulation truly was at hand, Baal was determined to make the most of her time here.

She would help pave the way for the Antichrist and have some fun in the bargain. Still, she couldn't quite get over her unease at how stubborn she found this host. Even locked away in his own mind, Baal could see he was going to be a constant pest.

"*You should accept your place*," she told him. She got a silent scream of defiance in response.

Gripping the door handle, Baal opened the door, the cold slamming into the flesh she wore. Outside, a small melee of police and press waited for him, cameras flashing away as Baal made herself known to the world.

"Home Secretary, what is your response to the crisis in Saudi Arabia?" one of the reporters asked.

"You know better than to ask me that, Neil," Baal responded. "You will need to wait for my official statement to the House." Inside the brain she shared, a second scream of frustration and despair momentarily distracted her. *I will have to keep an eye on this human I now own*, Baal thought. Sometimes humans can be such a frightful nuisance. It would be so much better when there were less of them.

21.

Los Angeles, USA

"Get your fucking hands off my car," the annoyed Hispanic voice said. Cliff looked out of his repo truck at the overweight man running towards him. It was too late for the poor guy, Cliff already having hooked the towing apparatus in place. For a brief moment, he contemplated having a unique and in-depth conversation about the benefits of keeping up with your car payments, but instead he simply drove off, the forty-thousand-dollar vehicle with four missed payments dragging easily behind.

The Hispanic gentleman chased after him for about ten metres, before giving up. It wasn't wise to run in this heat, especially when you were that out of shape. In the three years he'd been doing this job, Cliff had only been stopped from taking a car twice, both times by idiots wielding guns. Didn't they understand how ridiculous that was? One call to the cops had seen them arrested, as well as losing their cars. Usually, he was in and gone before the hapless motorist even realised.

That was the way he preferred it.

This was Cliff's second repossession of the day. He absolutely loved this job, and preferred to start early because that way he could catch people at home when they were off guard. It was rare for people to actually park their cars in the garages they owned, driveways and streets making it easy for him to do what he was paid for. The GTM he had snatched reared up in his rear-view mirror, Cliff's GPS Satnav showing exactly where he was to deliver it. This one was going to give him a handsome bonus.

He loved this country. It was filled with so much opportunity.

Cliff would never make that delivery. He was on the 10 where it crossed over the 110 when the catastrophic earthquake struck. The impact was swift and violent, the road beneath him shaking and cracking, causing the surrounding cars to swerve as drivers panicked. To his left, a black Ford Ranger slammed on the brakes. The semi-trailer behind it, unable to stop, slammed into the truck and jack-knifed across the carriageway. This naturally led to more collisions, with drivers travelling too fast to react in time.

As accidents went, that was bad enough, but it would barely register when the death toll of the morning's disaster was tallied up.

Cliff slowed, concrete dust exploding into the air as parts of the freeway fractured. Unbeknownst to him, the support pillars under him were devastated by the suddenness of the earth's revolt, and almost in unison, they shattered. The road collapsed in on itself, Cliff's truck falling down, the vehicle he was dragging crunching loose. Before he impacted the road below, his whole world rushed into his throat as gravity claimed him.

Like hundreds of people that day, Cliff didn't get to recount his experiences of the greatest earthquake to hit California in recorded history. It was 7.6 in magnitude, damaging most of downtown LA, as well as setting parts of the city on fire as gas lines fractured. Most of the hospitals in the impacted area became inundated by the thousands who were injured by falling debris and flying glass, and the emergency services were too swamped to make any kind of impact.

As natural disasters went, it wasn't the worst thing to hit the United States of America in its recorded history. That would come later. Not just for America, but for the world.

22.

Silicon Valley, USA

Horn had felt the tremors, the concrete floor below him vibrating slightly with the effects of the earthquake. Fortunately, his facility was far enough away from the epicentre that, to him, the disaster would only be experienced by what he saw on the news. It was all a sign that the world was heading towards the brink that had long ago been foreseen.

He couldn't deny that he was rather looking forward to it.

And it was empowering to know that he was the key to it all. Although many of the events happening in the world that marked the end times were out of his control, Horn's role in the coming apocalypse was pivotal.

There had always been something special about him. Horn had felt it from his earliest days. Even as a child, he didn't seem to relate to his peers. They had seemed so bland, so lacking in ambition, petty and filled with pointless fears and doubts. Hanging around with rich kids, he had witnessed how most of them had things handed to them, without any comprehension of the way the majority of people on the planet struggled to make ends meet.

That taught him the dangers of greed and also showed him how mesmerising shiny things were to the human mind.

Horn might well have been chosen, but he had needed to work tirelessly at every stage to keep the imagined future a reality. When you thought about it, growing up in a rich family had as many disadvantages as it did advantages. Whilst it put him on a firm footing to forge forward, it also gave him ample opportunity to reject his calling. That was all part of the test.

With the money he had, Horn could have easily retreated to an island and lived the life of most people's dreams. That was part of the trial he knew he needed to pass. Whilst Horn had grown up in a home of privilege, he hadn't let it corrupt him. He knew that wealth, on its own, was a pointless pursuit that turned those who craved it into their own kind of slaves. Instead, he learnt that money was a tool for his greater purpose.

What mattered was the power it could bring.

Horn had also learnt, at a young age, why he was here, the truth blossoming in his head one fateful day. There was no doubt in his mind that he was being guided and shaped, the environment around him manipulated to create the character he needed to be to change the destiny of the planet. In the rare moments when he would reminisce about his life, he could identify the turning points that had been needed to build the intellect and the type of personality willing to sacrifice the lives of billions to fulfil his potential. Every experience was a building block to the creation of the man he was right now. Every failure was a teacher, every setback a moment of growth. Without those lessons, he might have taken a different life, rejecting his calling altogether.

He knew he was chosen and spawned for the man he was meant to be. And yet, at times, he still had doubts in his abilities, which couldn't be silenced by his innate genius.

Distrusting one's abilities was only natural, given that the epic finale he was overseeing was so monumental in scope. Despite the countless prophecies of his coming deeds, he also knew he was just a man. Although he was protected by the likes of Kane, he could fail and die as easily as anyone. He may have believed he had been sired by the Lord of the Pit, but he was still inherently a weak and pitiful human being.

That fact of his own mortality was only a problem for Horn. Those who waited in the darkness had been building to this moment for centuries. If he failed, there would always be another to take his place. That was the beauty of prophecies. Most of them were so deliciously vague they could mean almost anything. If the gates to Hell weren't flung wide this time, then the demonic would wait and try again. Hell was known for its persistence and its patience.

Satan, his true Father. Wasn't that why he was here?

When you thought about it, it explained his mother's collapse into alcoholism. Somehow a mother always knows the truth about her child, and to realise you have given birth to the Antichrist would put a dampener on any mother's love for her son. The mortal mind could be fractured and ruined by the things it didn't understand about the world.

Serves her right for being so unfaithful to the man she so frequently cuckolded, which was another reason he held little respect for the man whose name rested on his birth certificate. If she had been loyal to the man she married, Horn had no doubt that Satan wouldn't have wanted anything to do with her. It wasn't right that the son should know of the mother's transgressions, but Horn knew everything about his parents. You couldn't understand who you were if you didn't know why you came into being.

When those doubts manifested, Horn did one of two things. He either indulged in his other passions, or he ventured down here to where the secrets of his corporation were hidden from the world. Most of his business empire was exposed for the world to see, but beneath the ground, in the parts that required ludicrous levels of security to access, the truth about Abaddon Industries would forever remain covert.

He had a whole army to protect it.

The deepest part of his corporate headquarters housed the laboratories where they grew and experimented on biologicals. That was where Horn was, looking through a reinforced window as three of his most trusted scientists conducted trials on their most lethal creation. For once, Horn had not been the originator of this asset. When you had no morals in business, you soon found yourself collecting those minds that were prepared to break all conventions. Out there amongst the sheep, there were geniuses to match Horn's intellect, some with the same willingness to abandon scientific morals. When he had gained control over the business, Horn had started collecting those geniuses.

Some people wanted to create the end of all things just to see if they could. Those people were a great asset to Horn. Others could be *persuaded* to do the work he demanded of them.

He didn't interrupt the scientists' work. Instead, he watched their tireless dedication. It helped with the doubts, Horn's mind calming at the prospect of what the laboratory's contents could do. When it was complete and when Horn was ready, the terrible organisms being created in these sterile rooms would be released to devastating, but necessary, effect. It was all for the greater good, the death of billions a small price to pay for changing the fate of man. The human race was reckless, driven by greed and a self-obsession that bordered on the suicidal. Horn would see an end to that. He would help make his race finally complete.

The coordinated release of several viruses would be one of the key moves in the secret battle he now waged—the battle to save humanity from itself.

Inside, one of the biohazard suit-clad men turned to look at Horn. They locked eyes for a moment, no real warmth shared between them. This was a business relationship, a partnership of mutual respect and trust. They didn't have to like each other. The scientists would make the organism and they would be rewarded handsomely. No doubt they would use that money to secrete themselves away from the world. Most of the mayhem that was soon to be unleashed would occur in the key population centres where humanity had gathered itself. There would be a chance for a select few to escape most of the madness, at least in the beginning.

The vaccine was another key ingredient to the great recipe of chaos that was building. To control a thing, you had to be able to defeat a thing and the vaccine would be instrumental in that. Horn's goal wasn't eradication, but modification.

The scientists were days away from being ready, a week at most. Once they had both aspects of the virus perfected, then it could be put into mass production and stored away until it was needed. That would come later when the signs were clearer. There were other things that needed to be readied first.

If Kane's brothers and sisters were to be finally freed from the prison that held them, there were a few changes that needed to be made to the world. As evil as they were, they too were only a means to an end.

Horn thought he knew his place in the great scheme of things. The denizens of Hell, as feral as they were, would all bow down before Horn, and wouldn't that be a sight to behold. They had no choice, for he was Satan's son.

How could anyone deny that?

Horn left the laboratory and made his way through the almost deserted corridors to the one and only lift that serviced this part of his vast empire. The few employees he met stepped aside respectfully, their heads bowed in sign of their submission. They knew not to speak to Horn unless he first engaged them. Horn had no inclination to distract himself with such pleasantries, as there were few people on this planet worthy of his time.

He was twenty floors below ground, the subterranean fortress built to withstand the worst that nature and mankind could throw at it. Each floor was segregated from the one above it, with the security clearance needed increasing the further below the earth one descended. The surface was guarded by an army, with Kane there to oversee any and all defence that might be needed. Such an assault would never occur, of course, but it paid to take precautions.

The people who were allowed access to the lowest level—the one he was presently on—were those who either showed the utmost devotion or were gifted with a level of genius to rival that of Horn. Some of them knew of Horn's true identity, and they worked tirelessly to try to win favour in his eyes and in the eyes of the one who was making this all come to pass. Horn's true father, the one with the infernal names.

Some of those here worked just to stay alive.

There were no rituals needed here, no black rites. That sort of thing was practiced haphazardly by those who didn't understand the nature of the universe. There were ways to open up a porthole to Hell, but only fools engaged in them. Rarely could those brought forth be controlled. That knowledge was put on earth by the prince of lies, to entice the unwary into corrosive acts.

In truth, it was Horn's belief that Satan didn't care if you prayed to him. Unlike his demons, he demanded no sacrifices or a promise to surrender one's immortal soul. All Satan asked was that you believed, and in that belief came your commitment to serve. This wasn't Hollywood, the depiction of Satanists a deliberate travesty to confuse and bamboozle the world. The mere contemplation to call on the devil was often enough to damn your immortal soul.

You didn't choose to be one with the Pit and the fallen sons. They chose you.

Horn knew there were more of his true father's offspring out there, some oblivious to their true lineage, others mentally crippled by the revelation of how they came to be. It was said that Satan worked by corruption, by inserting his ethereal spirit into the thousands that were viable. He was said to be an angelic being, tainted, poisoning the world. But those who believed knew that Satan was so much more than that. And although he wasn't alone, Horn knew he was the best candidate for the role that would soon be handed to him.

There were texts that were said to prove Satan had known his rebellion against God would see him cast out, and yet he did it anyway. None of the Fallen had any say in the feckless games the almighty chose to play. Those who prayed to their gods thought they were serving an all-powerful being of love and blissful omnipotence. But to Horn, God was a spoilt child who liked to break his toys.

For those who saw the darkness in the light, there was no other option but to serve Satan. When you saw the lies that the various religions told, you understood how humanity had been led astray. Horn thought he could see it clearly; thought he could see the villainy and the torture that had been done in the name of humanity's obsession with a greater power. If they didn't believe in God, then they created their own gods, all in an attempt to control and condemn their fellow man. All to provide the justification to slaughter millions.

Man had been given free will, only to not understand the torment that free will represented.

Horn would see an end to all that. Through blood and sacrifice, he would see humanity shaped anew. It would be spared the hypocrisy of the priests and the various churches. Horn would become the light and the way, and would usher in the new world order. And God would sit back and let it happen, probably because it amused him.

By the time he was done, Horn knew the world would be a very different place. He would save humanity from itself, dragging it back from the ecological and moral abyss it presently teetered on. Many wouldn't understand, thinking he represented evil. They wouldn't understand that those who served the dark lord in the Pit would only ever reveal the truth that dwelled in the heart of men.

Hell was a mirror to the world.

The selfless would always be immune to possession by demonic spawn. He'd learnt that right at the beginning, as if God himself was protecting them. But such people were rare because there was an evil that dwelled in the core of the human race, a vileness for which Horn would see brought to fruition. Demons, as sickening as they were, had a purpose in all this. As loathsome as they acted, they were no worse than humanity. Horn would use them willingly.

Then there were others, genetically resistant to the strongest demon. But conversely, there were genetic traits that allowed the powerful to claim a human form easily. That was why Horn's mega corporation owned three of the world's largest genetic testing companies. People thought it novel to pay a few dollars to find out who their ancestors were, never realising they were giving a madman the genetic map to engineer demonic domination.

When the seals were finally broken and the gates of Hell swung open, the whole world would be there for the taking. Horn saw himself at the centre of everything, not realising his entire existence was a lie.

And Horn was merely a tool being used and manipulated due to the naivety that dwelled within him.

He thought he had power. He thought he was the son of Satan. What a surprise Horn would suffer when he finally learnt the truth.

23.

Soumetande, Guinea

Despite an abundance of mineral wealth, the people of Guinea were some of the poorest in Africa. Without the help of international organisations like Médecins Sans Frontières, many of its people wouldn't have access to basic medical care. Doctor Xavier Bisset was there to help provide access to the healthcare they desperately needed.

He could have been back home in France living the easy life, but he hadn't become a doctor to take things easy. He was dedicated to helping those who could not help themselves. Volunteering for Médecins Sans Frontières seemed like the logical thing to do.

It helped him sleep better at night.

The problem was, standing in a village that reeked of death, he was kind of regretting it. Xavier had been to this village the month before, and as far as he'd been able to tell, the people had been healthy. Well, they weren't healthy anymore. The only evidence of life he could see were the animals and insects that found this human devastation so appealing.

There was still smoke hanging over the village, shrouding it, a sign of the panicked burnings that had been enacted. Some of the huts still smouldered, the stench coming off them caught in the prevailing breeze.

"Go, we must leave this place." That was his driver. A good man all told, but sometimes vulnerable to superstition.

"We have to find out what happened here," Xavier insisted. If it was what he feared, the world would need to know. "Radio in and let base camp know the situation." It was a four-hour drive from this village to anywhere resembling civilisation, the ground uneven and lacking any paved roads. There were other villages around, most constructed from mud and wood, just as this one had been.

"I do that, yes," the driver agreed, the interior of the Jeep far preferable to whatever had been set free in this place. They were far from the border, so it was unlikely whatever had happened here had been down to some kind of incursion. Xavier reckoned that would have resulted in bodies being strewn all around. Instead, the dirt paths between the huts were free of any evidence of the dead.

Most likely, the people here had fled, which was the worst thing that could have happened.

From the pouch on his belt, Xavier took out his protective gear. Mask, gloves and safety goggles. It would be enough for him to safely investigate, he told himself, but already he could feel the adrenaline kicking in and his heart rate rising. He'd witnessed scenes like this before. When you ruled out human violence as a cause, the next thing that sprung to mind was Ebola.

Leaving his driver, Xavier made his way to the first hut. They knew him here, the people often grateful for his appearance. He had saved lives, vaccinated the children against a host of disease and earned the respect of the village elders. It was so easy to be confused as to why the villagers hadn't radioed for help, but Ebola broke all the rules. The virus was so deadly and so feared it tended to mutate not only itself but any semblance of rational behaviour.

There had been cases of health workers being attacked and killed by people who couldn't understand what Ebola was. Sometimes, those trying to cure it got the blame. That was why his driver was armed.

The first two huts he tried were empty. The third wasn't, the smell breaking through his mask even before he opened the door. Three bodies lay inside, a woman and two young children. Dead for several days at least, the bodies bloated from the heat, food for the battalions of flies that already feasted greedily.

That pattern repeated itself throughout the village. Xavier didn't find anyone alive, which he was strangely thankful for. He wasn't equipped to go anywhere near a viral carrier, and yet he would have felt compelled to put his own safety in peril. The burnt-out huts didn't get a visit. There was no point. Xavier knew what would be inside them. Why only some of the huts had been cremated, he didn't know. Surviving family members maybe doing the only thing they could.

Where were those family members now?

Whatever this thing was, he reckoned it had killed a third of the villagers. Which meant there were others out there likely carrying the disease. Some would die out in the dry savannah, but if any made it to the surrounding villages, the disease they were carrying would spread.

Hell, it probably already had.

Xavier returned to his driver, the native Guinean standing nervously by the Jeep.

"Relax," he said, "it's time to go." Whilst he wouldn't know for sure until a team arrived and the bodies had been tested, Xavier was pretty certain. Ebola was back.

That was the problem with the apocalypse. Old forgotten diseases had a habit of blossoming once more into the light. It was a sign that the planet was getting ready for humanity's final act.

24.

Hendon, London, UK

It was inevitable that Baal, now holding one of the great offices of state, would have the dubious delights of meeting with the head of the Security Services, MI5.

Baal found herself in an impressive room, the likes of which she had never seen before. Truly, it was apparent that humans were getting way ahead of where they should have been allowed to progress, but she hoped this technology would all help with her mission here. The room had seating for at least fifty people, a vast array of monitors of varying sizes scattered at individual workstations and on the main wall in front of her. To those who worked here, this was not the first time the Home Secretary had come to visit them.

It was a first for Baal, though.

This was the Metropolitan Police's Operational Command Unit in Hendon, one of three that serviced the capital. It monitored and recorded all that was captured by the city's array of street cameras, as well as acting as a headquarters for any major operations. From here, everything that was recorded was further sent on to GCHQ, the government's listening headquarters.

It also happened to be close to where the three bodies had been found the day before. Unfortunately, with regards to preventing and detecting the culprit of that crime, the unit had failed in its purpose.

"We have not been able to identify the assassin," the man standing beside her confirmed. His accent to some spoke of superior breeding, but to Baal, he was just another fool for her to use. He was taller than the body she possessed, with a full head of hair combed neatly into place.

"That is unacceptable, Sir David," Baal said. Her host was renowned for being obstinate and unforgiving of failure. She was happy to play the part.

What had surprised her was the lack of any information about the Inquisition in the head of the Home Secretary. Had the inquisitors really been able to keep themselves so secret, even to this day? How could they not be known to the world? Baal would be happy to correct that. It was one of the reasons she was here, to expose the inquisitors to the world.

"Unfortunately, it is the best we can do at present," the MI5 man, Sir David Middleton, said defensively. "Whoever this person was, they knew what they were doing. The murders were enacted well away from popular areas. We have no surveillance covering the murder scene."

"Are you telling me that, with all this equipment, you didn't capture one image of the person who perpetrated this atrocity?" Was atrocity the right word to use? She thought so, and the investigation the humans were doing was still ongoing.

"That's not technically what I'm saying."

"Perhaps you could enlighten me. I would like to know why a dead MI5 agent was found with his fingerprints all over the car containing a mutilated child."

"So would I, Home Secretary." Sir David shifted uncomfortably on his feet. This was difficult for him, the embarrassment to both the Met and MI5 unquestionable.

"We need to get to the bottom of this," Baal said. "Which is why I persuaded the PM to issue a blanket D notice. If the press report on this, it will only be after we get all the information we need." Baal had plans for the press. They would be another tool for her to use.

"What I am trying to allude to is that if the cameras picked up the image of our assassin, that image was not recorded."

"How is that even possible?" Baal searched through the memories she had acquired from the mind that was locked away and could find no precedent for such. "The system is supposed to be able to track anyone across the city."

"Paul, pull the map up on the big screen," Sir David said. Paul was the minion at the computer monitor before them. Several areas of the map were highlighted. "We've pinpointed where someone would likely be able to escape the area. Based on the estimated time of death and the time of the text we received, we can calculate when the assassin fled the scene. We were able to triangulate in where the text was sent from, but even then, nothing was picked up by surveillance."

"So, what are you saying?"

"According to our cameras, nobody left this area in that timeframe, Home Secretary. At least, nobody who was captured on CCTV."

"Are you sure? There's a lot of ground to cover there."

"It's also secluded, Home Secretary, with limited entry points. Mainly abandoned industrial wasteland. It's not the first time we've found bodies dumped there."

Which was why the foolish demons had taken the boy there, thought Baal. A good place for disposal. From the corner of her eye, Baal noticed a heavyset man enter the command room.

"We need to find this man," Baal insisted.

"We will." Sir David seemed convincing in his confidence. "That's why I invited Detective Inspector Cooke to join us." The heavyset man came closer. He was obviously the Inspector.

"Sir David. Home Secretary," Cooke said. He waited for hands to be offered, but none were.

"What can you tell us?" Baal demanded. She found that she was getting impatient. Part of that was due to the itch that had started in the centre of her back. Already the body was beginning to reject her presence in it. Then there was the body's owner, who persisted in his attempts to be heard. To her, this world was one of irritation. Baal even had a headache, an experience new to her.

"Your killer? Whoever it is, they've killed before." Cooke stood before them, clearly proud to be sharing his knowledge.

"How certain are you of this?" Baal tried to stare the policeman down, only to have her gaze matched. Impressive. The last person to have tried that had lost both eyes. A different time and a different place. Baal doubted if Cooke would have been so formidable had he been aware he was facing a Great King of Hell.

"I won't know for certain until the forensics are back, but the similarities to several cases I'm investigating seem pretty clear." Good, thought Baal. With any luck, this unsuspecting police officer would be the final piece in the puzzle that would let Baal complete her mission before the body she had stolen rejected her entirely. "Knife wound to the back of the neck between the vertebrae, followed by forced asphyxiation. It's not every day you see that, and I've got two unsolved murders that show a similar pattern. I've linked multiple unsolved murders countrywide, some showing other aspects not visible in this case. I'm betting the bullets used will be of the same calibre and have the same rifling as those in previous crimes." Baal knew the paralysis technique well and had heard the returned tell of it.

Some of the inquisitors enjoyed their work, it seemed.

"If that's the case, then these killings are likely to continue," Sir David added.

"I agree," Cooke said. "Whoever this is, they are professional in the way they go about it. To overpower three armed and trained individuals with knives shows an impressive level of skill and commitment. It might even be more than one individual. Our first opinion was that of a serial killer, but yesterday's discovery reinforced my opinion that we are dealing with something else."

"Meaning?" Baal demanded.

"I'd rather not say at present. It would be conjecture," Cooke admitted.

"Why don't you humour us?" Sir David insisted. Cooke looked at them reluctantly, then shrugged.

"This is a trained professional," Cooke said. Baal smiled at that, the door opening wider on the game she was playing. "I hate to use the word assassin, but I can think of no other that works in this scenario. If there is more than one, then this represents an organisation we aren't so far familiar with."

"This reminds me of something I'm sure I read in a briefing paper once." Baal knew that her host had no notion of the Inquisition, but perhaps the head of MI5 did. Now was the time to start sowing seeds. "I seem to remember there was talk of a secret Order of Catholic assassins working in the shadows. Does that mean anything to you, Sir David?"

"I can't say it does."

"Perhaps you could ask around. I'm sure everything that happens in the world doesn't come across your desk."

"Catholic order of assassins?" Cooke repeated. Both his superiors ignored him.

“I would like to ask GCHQ to assist in this investigation.” Sir David wasn’t going to reveal the true powers of the government’s cyber and security agency in front of a mere Detective Inspector. He wouldn’t have to, because the Home Secretary would know of GCHQ’s significant abilities.

“I will approve that,” Baal said. Anything to help with the mission. She wanted to be away from this planet as soon as possible. She would return, but when she did, it would be into the accepting body of a more suitable host. This one was taken out of necessity.

Her mission was paramount. Find and capture an inquisitor. Then the true inquisition could begin. She wanted to see what made her enemy tick and hopefully uncover them to the world. Baal wanted to know what it took to break those who called themselves inquisitors, and she was sure she could persuade Sir David to help with that. It would be the end of the inquisitors if they had to combat both the damned and the law enforcement agencies of the world.

Baal, despite her power, knew only a small piece of what was now being manifested in the world. She would do her part, for no matter her discomfort, her fear of the Fallen archangels that lorded over Hell was paramount and all-consuming.

25.

London, UK

There were many things Hargreaves didn't like about the career he'd chosen. The endless paperwork, the long hours and the tedious bureaucracy were all part of it. But worst of all were the bodies he invariably ended up confronted with. It was part of the job and he accepted that. Still, when he eventually retired, it wouldn't be something he would ever miss. His mental wellbeing could only be improved by being removed from such tragedy.

The two bodies that had been discovered at Damien's lair lay in cold storage, the autopsy on one already done. Hargreaves had seen them first hand in the field. That was enough for him, although there was an array of photographs to give him a second chance at gazing across Damien's magnificence. Those photographs were neatly filed in the folder Hargreaves was clutching, a faint pain threatening to fill his gullet.

It was the sort of thing you needed a stiff drink to cope with, but that was a fool's plan. If you let it, alcohol would gladly comfort you initially, only to drag you down into your own personal hell. Hargreaves had long ago made a conscious effort to stay away from the chemical crutch, because he knew one day he would end up depending on it. He'd seen too many good men go down like that.

"Your boy really went to town," Phillip Hodges, the Home Office pathologist, stated somewhat obviously. Hodges' reputation for competence was well earned, although there were some who found his manner brusque, sometimes callous. It could be argued that his was the ideal personality to deal with the dead.

They were both in Hodges' office, the smell of death thankfully left in the adjoining mortuary. "He did most of my job for me."

“Same as the others?” There had been so many corpses left behind by Damien that it was amazing the killer hadn’t attracted more notoriety. For some reason though, the press hadn’t latched onto it like they had with other serial killers. Hargreaves preferred that. It invariably made his life easier.

“Not exactly, but that’s probably because you interrupted him before he had time to finish. It was also unusual that there were two bodies. The pattern in the past has been one at a time.” Hodges had been involved in several autopsies of the victims. The antics of this particular serial killer were ideal for entry into the book Hodges one day planned to write. There weren’t many killers who went to such brutal extremes as the man who called himself Damien.

Or should that be Legion?

“The guy is a freak of nature.” Damien might have been a curiosity to the officers in the custody suite that presently held him, but to the men and women who had been there to see his handiwork at first hand, Damien was an abomination. To see those bodies displayed like hanging cuts of meat would haunt the strongest of minds.

“So I heard,” Hodges admitted. “Did his eyes really change colour?”

“Yeah, right in front of me. Totally hit me for six, if I’m honest.” Hargreaves wouldn’t admit it, but he had dreamt about that last night. The essence of the dream was forgotten, but he had awoken feeling more disturbed than he could ever remember.

Hargreaves turned the page and continued to read the autopsy report. There wasn’t anything new.

INTERNAL EXAMINATION

EVISCERATION OF THE BODY: Much of this had already been done. What areas were left were eviscerated by the pathologist PH.

ORAL CAVITY: The tongue and all the teeth have been removed. Panoral radiographs show no root fragments left behind.

BRAIN: The brain weighed 1300 grams. Unusually, the surface of all lobes had a fluorescent green appearance, as did the whole of the brain stem, which was confirmed by incision. We have not been able to find an explanation for this appearance.

BODY CAVITIES: The right and left pleural cavities contain 10ml of clear fluids with no adhesions. The pericardial sac and peritoneal cavity were both absent.

HEART: The heart was absent, having been removed via the opening in the abdominal cavity. Most of the associated blood vessels were also absent. Remnants of the pulmonary artery and the superior vena cava were still present. The heart was found at the scene. It appeared withered and showed definite signs of coronary disease.

The heart was damaged, evidence that it had been bitten into. We will need to establish, via forensic odontology, if the bite marks match that of the suspect's teeth.

AORTA: The entirety of the aorta was missing from the body.

LUNGS: The right lung weighed in at 640 grams, the left weighed 710 grams. The lung parenchyma is pink without evidence of congestion or haemorrhage. No unusual pathology was found associated with the lungs.

GASTROINTESTINAL SYSTEM: The oesophagus was intact without evidence of ulcers or varices. However, the oesophagus was found to be clogged halfway down by a folded piece of cloth. There are vertical scratches down the length of the oesophageal epidermis, which suggests something was used to shove the cloth down the throat whilst the victim was still alive. See the appendix for a description of the cloth. The stomach, liver, gallbladder, pancreas, duodenum, ileum, jejunum, colon and appendix are all missing, although they were recovered at the crime scene. Like the heart, they appeared aged and withered. We are still awaiting genetic matching to ensure these recovered organs belong to this individual.

RETICULOENDOTHELIAL SYSTEM: The spleen was found free in the abdominal cavity, unattached to any blood or nerve supply. It weighed 350 grams. It was already showing signs of marked decomposition, which strongly suggests it is from another body. DNA tests are pending.

GENITOURINARY SYSTEM: Both kidneys were absent. The external genitalia were absent, with no abnormalities detected. The prostate and seminal vessels were intact and were cut, revealing normal-appearing tissue without evidence of embolus or inflammation.

ENDOCRINE SYSTEM: The adrenal glands were missing.

EXTREMITIES: All the digits on both hands and feet were missing. Both legs and calves were found to be of similar circumference. There was no blood found in the venous system of the arms and little was produced on milking the venous system of the legs.

CAUSE OF DEATH: Due to the nature of the body as it presented to us, we have been unable to determine a definitive cause of death.

"Why do you think he does it?" Hodges asked. In all his twenty years at this, he'd probably never seen anything like it. Most of the bodies recovered hadn't been in such good shape, so these weren't the most unpleasant corpses he'd dealt with. But that arguably made it worse, more clinical. It was almost as if what Damien was doing was a mockery of Hodges' profession.

"It's clear to me the man is insane. Whatever drives him is his own private Hell." Hargreaves wasn't expressing sympathy. "Hell being the appropriate word. Guy says he's Lucifer's son."

"Normally they just hear the voices," Hodges pointed out.

"Not this one. Full-blown delusion to go with his killing frenzy."

"Strangely, he has some skill in what he does. His ritual is so methodical, almost surgical in nature." Hodges had noted in his reports, on more than one occasion, that it almost seemed like the killer had surgical training. The knife used had been found at the scene, and when Damien had wielded it, the wounds created had been precise, without hesitation. It was a steady hand that created such atrocities.

"We still don't know who he is. We've turned to Europol, because my gut tells me he is from the Continent." It was the accent Legion had spoken in. Hargreaves had dealt with enough Eastern European criminals to know it was legitimate. If he had to guess, he would say that if anything, it was Damien's accent that was the acquired one.

"At least you finally caught him."

"And we still don't know who turned him in." There was so much about this case that confused Hargreaves. Well, it was up to the courts now. Hopefully, the judge would decide to lock him up for the rest of his miserable life.

"Looks like we solved the mystery of the missing hearts, though." All the previous bodies had been missing the hearts, even amongst the organs that had been removed and placed on display. Not this corpse.

"You really think he eats his victim's hearts?"

"I don't think there can be any other explanation, do you?" That would be a first in Hodges' career.

"This is one sick fucker. And you still don't know why the brains are the colour they are?"

"No," Hodges admitted. "It's got me stumped. I've run every test I can think of. What about you? Any closer to determining a pattern in the people he selected?"

"If there is one, we can't find it. I would say it's random, but I've a feeling I'm missing something. It's unusual for a killer like this to choose his prey over such a wide age range. At least he's consistent to the same sex. But then he does seem to think he's slaughtering his half-brothers."

"The papers are going to love that." Hodges reminded him. And there were still plenty of bodies out there yet to be unearthed.

Experience told Hargreaves there was something about this case that had yet to reveal itself.

He didn't know how right he was.

26.

Inquisitor training camp 17 years earlier

"To defeat your enemy, you must know your enemy."

They sat at pristine wooden desks in an underground classroom, the air pleasantly warm around them. Unlike school children the world over, Lilith and her cohorts did not scratch at the wood of their desks, for they did not deface property that wasn't theirs. Their minds were concentrated on the teacher before them, a man with a sad face and stooped frame. They knew him only as The Librarian, the scholar who tutored them in the ways of the underworld. Some people, like the inquisitors, fought the demonic hordes with their bodies. The Librarian, slender in stature and diseased by his advanced years, battled their enemies with his formidable mind.

The knowledge the Librarian contained within his head was said to be worth a dozen inquisitors. What would he have said if the true nature of Hell had been revealed?

"Demons seek chaos. Whereas the Catholic Church tries to bring order, those from the dark place wish to see that order destroyed."

"Why?" one of the children asked.

"A good question."

Unlike the priests that guarded them, The Librarian never beat them and never scolded them. He encouraged questions because he knew that was how some people learned. With a class as well trained as this one, he had no fear of any disruptive elements. Any interruption would be purely for the benefit of all.

"Demons are rejects, a creation of those who fell. They look upon our world and are filled with envy. This is a world with such potential, whereas the Hell they know will only ever be a place of suffering. In my view, they come here to vent their fury."

Lilith shifted slightly in her seat, the hard wood uncomfortable beneath her buttocks. Comfort was not something an inquisitor should ever have to suffer.

The Librarian continued.

"What we know about the demon hierarchy has been derived mainly through guesswork and the interrogation of the few demonic forms the Order has been able to capture. We have to remember that demons lie. They are tricksters, deceivers, bent on warping the best that humanity has spawned." Lilith had heard this before, had spent the last three days reading many of the demonic encyclopaedias that had taken centuries to put together. This was done via the computer tablets they had all been given, for the original texts were locked away deep in the most secret alcoves of the Vatican archives, their pages fragile and decaying. Lilith had access to ancient manuscripts that academics the world over didn't believe existed.

"Of course, before we talk about Demons, we need to consider those that rule over them. The Fallen Ones, those who went against the will of our Lord." The defacers, thought Lilith, the scum that corrupted a world that shouldn't need inquisitors.

"Traitors," her young lips whispered. Nobody heard her.

"Popular culture will tell you that it is Lucifer that rules the underworld. This is not actually correct. He is only one of several of the fallen who help rule over the Pit. By our understanding, Satan is the true Lord, never to be confused with the Morningstar."

"Why did the Fallen defy the will of God?" Lilith asked.

"I would claim they didn't," The Librarian said. "Everything occurs according to God's plan. Like man, angels were designed to be imperfect, to be susceptible to temptation. That some fell was no surprise to God, and those that did were essential for the great tribulation to come. It is my belief that God let them think they were rebelling, when in fact they were doing exactly what our Lord wanted."

"But why?" another student asked. There was an electricity in the room, the origins of the greatest story ever told about to be understood.

"Man has been allowed to drift through the ages based on his own independent thought. We are here to suffer so that we can be tested. Even with our advancements in technology, the world is still designed to rip any stability out from under us. Our greatest pleasures are fraught with dangers and unwanted consequences. When we grow too numerous, we are held back by disease. When we become too self-assured, we are beset by war. And all the while, the voices from the darkness are whispering in our ears, taunting and tempting us with illusions that can never be real."

That made sense to Lilith. She had once been a happy child, but that happiness had been ripped from her. With both of her parents dead, the Order was her new home. It would be nearly a decade before she copied the actions of the inquisitor who saved her.

"This is God's way of finding the best of us. The trials of life are merely a selection process for the bliss of the afterlife. Only the noblest and the best of us can ever be allowed entry."

"Why did God make us this way, though?"

"I do not know for sure," The Librarian answered. Unlike other factions in the Catholic Church, those who served the Order of Tyron were not arrogant enough to think they knew every answer. It was, in fact, quite the opposite. "Remember that I am just a man. Despite my professed learning, I am flawed and no more important than a speck of dust. I would be a fool to proclaim I understood the will of God. All I can tell you is what I believe and understand from the righteous verses he had blessed us with over the centuries. Are such limitations acceptable to you all?" Everyone in the windowless classroom nodded. "Very well. Let us learn about the first of the Fallen. The book of Enoch gives us some glimpse into why the angels fell. Head of the defilers was Lucifer, sometimes called Samyaza, the leader of the renegades who became consumed with lust for the mortal women they gazed down upon from their heavenly loft. Do you see the dangers of lust, children?"

"Yes, Librarian," they answered together.

"If it can corrupt those that were deemed to be pure, imagine the dangers it means for such weak flesh as ours." The Librarian had a little chuckle at that, perhaps remembering a time from his past, thought Lilith. "But I am getting side-tracked. Perhaps I am being subtly influenced so as not to reveal to you the truth."

"You are too noble," one of the children insisted, not understanding that The Librarian was merely teasing.

"I am as naïve and vulnerable as anyone," The Librarian informed them. "Perhaps I am able to withstand the ultimate temptations, but I will never know, for I have not been subjected to them. Unlike inquisitors who must have hearts of iron, I am merely a man who reads too many books." He saw that the message he was trying to impart to them had broken through the cracks of their own innocence.

As the years progressed, he would tell them more about the frailties of those they would be charged with protecting. "So, back to the fallen. Although Shemyaza was the initial leader of the fallen, it was the angel Azazel who wreaked the most havoc. In Enoch 10:12 we are told that all the earth has been corrupted by the effect of the teachings of Azazel. It is Azazel that taught the world the pleasures of sin."

Sin, the one thing inquisitors were taught to avoid above all things.

"What happened to the Fallen?" Lilith asked.

"They now serve Satan. Many people consider Satan a being of immense power, but that is not my understanding."

"Is Satan one of the Fallen?" Lucien asked.

"In the more popular biblical texts, yes, but many of those were written out of ignorance. To me, Satan is an idea, just as evil is a concept created by the minds of man. When Eve took a bite from the apple, it was not on the urging of Satan. That is a false translation, deliberately left in by the earlier corruption that was prevalent in the church. Satan could even be a creation of human consciousness. There is no way for us to know for sure, but if you ask me, Satan was created by God to give him a worthy adversary. Satan's presence is within us all, and it manifests as the overlord of the place we call Hell. The Fallen Ones and the demons serve him. With God's blessing, of course."

"But why?" Lilith demanded. Her young mind couldn't understand why the Lord would be so cruel.

"Because of us. The Lord gave humanity the chance to be free of suffering, but mankind rejected that. We chose to forge our own path rather than being loyal servants of God. Sometimes I think that might have pissed him off."

"I do not understand, Librarian," one of the children said. There were several nods of agreement that this was beyond their understanding. The Librarian smiled.

"I know, but you will. By the time you are done with my tedious lessons, you will have a deep knowledge of why mankind faces such an enemy. Just know it is an enemy from within, a force of our own doing. The Fallen may serve it, and the demons may be spawned from it, but Satan is more than a single entity. It is a collection of everything that makes humanity impure. But Satan is real and is your ultimate enemy. Pray you never have to face him."

27.

New York City, USA. Present Day

"It's difficult. I don't sleep well, and when I do, I'm woken by the terrors." Paul Jackson resisted the temptation to hide his mouth behind his hands. The nine faces in the sharing circle were here for him, and he didn't have to try to hide away from them.

"We've all been there," Jerry said. Jerry was larger than life, with a belly to match. They all knew Jerry's story. He'd lost both legs in Fallujah and had formed this veteran's group to help those who'd been through the shit. "You taking your medication and staying off the booze?"

"I try to, Jerry," Paul admitted. "But it's hard, you know? Some days it feels like the whole world is collapsing in on me." Paul had fallen into alcoholism and a dependence on pain medication. Those two monkeys rode his back relentlessly, although recently he'd found he could get the better of them. These meeting helped with that. It was good that there were people he could talk to, who could understand the way it was so easy to feel abandoned.

"Then you call me," Jerry insisted. "You all know that, right?"

There were nods from around the sharing circle. There were no new faces today, which was disappointing to Jerry. He had wanted as many people present as possible for when he shared his news.

"We should never have been sent over there in the first place," one of the others stated.

"Whilst that might be true," Jerry pointed out, "pointing fingers isn't going to get any of us anywhere. We have to take responsibility for where we are at if we are going to pull ourselves out of this."

"They could still help us more," Paul pointed out.

"Yes, they could, but then you would be even more dependent on the government. And I can tell none of you really want that. We have to learn to look after ourselves." Jerry had a way of getting that message across, although tonight he seemed irritable to Paul, as if Jerry was eager to get this meeting over with. That was strange because their organiser was always the last one to leave.

"I think I'm ready, Jerry," Paul suddenly said. This was the third meeting he'd been to, and as yet, he hadn't shared what had happened to him. They all got around to that sooner or later.

"I think you are, too," Jerry said.

"Ironically, I came out of it pretty much unscathed, or at least I thought I did. We were on patrol outside Tikrit a few years back. Seemed like just another ordinary day. One second, the Humvee is part of a four-vehicle convoy, the next it is on its side and I'm covered in other people's blood."

"IED?" Jerry asked.

"Yeah. They ambushed us, killed half a dozen of my unit. We hit them hard in response, made the bastards regret picking that fight. But I missed most of that. I was trapped in the burning wreckage. They ended up cutting me free."

"And you feel guilty about that?" Jerry asked.

"Guilty? I don't think…"

"Well, you weren't there when your friends needed you." There was an uneasy stillness that suddenly filled the room.

"Hey man, it wasn't like that."

"Really? Sounds like that's exactly what it was. Sounds like you sat there in your own piss whilst better men did the fighting for you."

"Hey Jerry…" one of the other group members tried to interject, but his words were cut off by the withering glare Jerry cast him.

"What the hell's wrong with you?" Paul almost begged. His hands were shaking, the skin pale from the palpitations the unexpected confrontation had brought on.

"What's wrong with me? I'm sick of your bullshit. You need to own your failure."

"I didn't fail," Paul insisted. There were supportive voices to back him up. Jerry had lost the room, nobody understanding why their group leader was suddenly being so vicious.

"It's the same with all of you," Jerry pointed out, looking each individual in the eye. "You come here with your sob stories and your tales of woe, instead of growing a pair and making something of your lives."

"Fuck you, Jerry," the oldest member of the group said.

"Truth hurts, does it?"

"I'm not sitting here to listen to this," Paul insisted, standing up, ready to storm off. The Sig Sauer P320-M18 that Jerry seemed to pull out of his ass quickly changed that plan.

"Sit down, Paul. I won't tell you twice." Paul did, his anxiety reaching new heights.

"This isn't you, Jerry," someone pointed out.

"You don't know how right you are," Jerry said. It was only then that Paul noticed their group leader wasn't in his usual position. Jerry's chair was set back from the circle, instead of being part of it. Nobody was going to get the jump on him.

"Why are you doing this?" Paul begged.

"Ah, the thousand-dollar question. Why do any of us do anything?"

"Are we supposed to frigging answer that?" one of the group said defiantly. Jerry shot that man in the forehead in response.

“Jesus,” Paul exclaimed. As the dead body slumped to the floor, Jerry pulled himself up onto his fake legs. Nobody saw the black specks that briefly floated across his eyes. The children of New York were fortunate that this demon was interested only in the body count he could create, rather than selecting individual targets.

“We are going to play a little game. I’ve got sixteen bullets left in this baby. If you play your cards right, some of you might get to live through the night.” Nobody was willing to argue with him.

“What kind of game?” Paul demanded.

“Well, it’s quite simple. I want to see who has the greatest will to live. You’ve all been through the wringer, and some of you are ready to just curl up and die. I want you to prove me wrong.”

“How?”

“By fighting, of course. There are eight of you, so it should be easy for you to pair up. Just know, only two of you will survive this night.” Jerry was lying, of course.

Despite being surprised by how ferociously some of them fought, he didn’t let any of them walk out that night. When the police finally arrived, Jerry went down, gun blazing, taking one of the officers with him.

Just another bit of chaos and violence added to the world. Jerry had been possessed, but the world had been driving him slowly mad anyway.

There seemed to be a lot of that, recently.

28.

London, UK

"*Tell me, Father, will the world ever end*?"

Those had been some of the last words she had said to her teacher. In the final year of Lilith's training, Father had fallen sick. At first, he had defied it, the pain he experienced mingling with the other aches that plagued him. But as the days and weeks passed, the pain became a world unto its own, standing out as an agony that no amount of prayer or self-denial could ignore.

When he found he could no longer hide the discomfort he was in, Father had reluctantly asked the Order to send him a doctor. Lilith had known something was wrong, perhaps before Father had himself.

"*Cancer. Pancreatic. Untreatable. You will be dead within months.*"

Father had accepted the words given to him by the doctor, who seemed to possess the bedside manner of a Waffen SS death camp guard.

"*I can give you something for the pain,*" the doctor had added.

"*Why?*" Father had asked. "*God feels I am worthy of this punishment. Who am I to defy his judgement*?"

By the end, Father's flesh had been emaciated, the muscle stripped from him, his face a constant grimace. Every breath was a torture and yet Father refused to complain. He also refused to give up, clinging on to what was left of life. There were saints who had suffered more than this. It was enough to know his time on this planet was finally at an end.

"*Yes,*" Father had said finally, the words laboured. "*There will come a time when the world will end. We do what we do to try to hold back that day, but when it comes, it will be because the Lord commands it.*" A cough had ripped through him, blood exploding onto the once pristine sheets that covered his frail and broken body. "*Everything happens because of his design. Everything.*"

Lilith remembered those words. Deep in her meditation, she found herself once again wondering what that design was. There were things about it that didn't make sense, and until recently, she had not let her mind wander there. Despite the completeness of her training, she was struggling with the inconsistencies that kept cropping up.

Her Order proclaimed to be the protector of mankind, the guardian at the gate, and yet they failed to pay heed to the evidence set before them. She was a mere foot soldier on the ground. If she could see how the enemy was coordinating, why couldn't her superiors? Lilith had tried to set these doubts aside, knowing them for the heresy they were, but she couldn't help herself. Her training had taught her to trust her intuition.

She had to stay faithful to her Order, and yet her inner voice was screaming at her that the Order was failing in its duty. But if Father's teaching was to be believed, that failing was part of some otherworldly plan. Did that mean her doubts were, too?

Was she in control of the thoughts that were rampaging through her mind? She suddenly felt like a pawn, a disposable piece being used for somebody else's ultimate benefit. Opening her eyes, Lilith cursed under her breath. She knew who she had to talk to. Picking up the phone, she dialled the number that was burned into her memory.

"The library is about to close," were the first words she heard.

"But I have an overdue book," Lilith said, the code technically unnecessary because the man she was speaking with knew her voice.

"Oh, and what mighty tome have you kept from us?" There was humour in the voice, the man on the other end enjoying the chance at conversation. Lilith knew he rarely got to speak to people these days, having retired from the inquisitor teaching. He sounded every bit as old as his ninety years on this planet.

"The Pilgrim's Progress." That completed the code. There was no chance that this conversation was being intercepted by outside ears, the phone using the same secure network as before.

"Are you riddled with temptation then, Lilith?" She knew he was having fun at her expense, and she couldn't admonish him for it. The man she still knew only as the Librarian had watched her grow from a child into a woman. Much of what she knew about the world had come from his lips.

"I am riddled with doubt," she said honestly. You didn't lie to those for whom you had the utmost respect.

"Doubt is a dangerous path for an inquisitor. It leads to a dark path too many of your kind have wandered onto."

"My doubt is about my Order," Lilith added.

"Ouch," the Librarian replied, humour still in his words. He had been a welcome relief from the harshness of the priests' and Father's reign. Although humour was not something to be embraced, it was something inquisitors needed to understand if they were to blend into a world that often used humour to cover the horrors that existed there. "It happens to most of you, eventually."

"Really?" Lilith was shocked by this. She had thought herself alone with such doubts.

"You think your training ended when you left the camp? I thought we taught you better than that." There was no humour now, just genuine disappointment. She didn't seek his forgiveness, because she knew she could never offend this man.

"I've seen things in the field that contradict my training." Lilith hesitated. If she couldn't trust the Librarian, then the concept of trust was a lie. But should she tell him these things?

"It has been that way for centuries. Why don't you tell me what is troubling you?"

"The demons. It seems that they are working together."

"And I take it your superiors disagree with you?"

"Yes," Lilith agreed. "They think I am imagining things."

"What is your job, Lilith?" the Librarian asked. Lilith was in for another lesson.

"To serve mankind and protect him from the forces of darkness."

"And can you do that alone?"

"No, that would be suicide." To go out into the world without the resources of the Order would be foolhardy.

"So, you need the Order behind you?"

"Yes, always."

"May I therefore suggest that bashing your head up against the bureaucratic brick wall is not the way to go." He sounded stern, something that had rarely occurred in his lectures. It was the Librarian who had taught them to laugh, but who had also instructed them in the dangers of laughter. Whereas the priests would beat them for showing pleasure in humour, the Librarian would patiently explain why laughter was seeded into the world by Satan himself.

"But how am I to persuade them otherwise?" She could see a glimmer of what was coming, but she wanted to hear it from his own lips.

"You know how," the Librarian stated. "I taught you the ways of persuasion myself. The willow bends in the wind and adapts to the forces against it. What do you think would happen if it were to stand defiantly against the mighty breath of God?"

"The tree would fall."

"Do you want to fall, Lilith?"

"No, Librarian. I want to help my Order." She was well aware that her doubt was her own failing. If there was one thing her training had taught her that applied to this situation, it was that to find a failing, one first had to look within.

"Then do your damned job." Lilith could almost see the twinkle that was likely in her mentor's eye. He had a way of hitting home with the truth.

"I will still have doubts," she said.

"What do you do when your muscles ache when you run?"

"I keep on running."

"Then let your doubts wash over you, as other emotions do. You resist the normal human pleasures that surround you, and you can resist this." He sounded so sure of himself.

"That's what I'm worried about," Lilith admitted.

"Ah, and now we come to the meat of it. It is not the doubts of your purpose in all things. You doubt yourself to fulfil your mission. Do you no longer believe in yourself?" *Was that the key to it*? Could she ignore what was so obviously a failing of those in command? "Have you thought that maybe, just maybe, your superiors aren't telling you everything for a reason?"

"Most of my life." The realisation hit her with such clarity it caused her head to ache.

"Did Caesar tell his Legionaries the intricacies of his strategy?"

"No, Librarian."

"Did Napoleon sit down with the lowly privates of his Grande Armée and tell them how he was going to defeat his enemies?"

"Of course not, Librarian. I have been a fool."

"I am glad I could remind you of that. We are all fools in the eyes of God."

"The greatest lesson you ever taught me," Lilith agreed. She felt lighter inside.

"I'm pleased you think so." The mirth was back. "I'm glad you called, Lilith. This old man doesn't have much in the way of company these days." It had been nearly a year since Lilith had spoken to him.

"I will call again soon," she promised, both of them knowing she wouldn't. It was with regret that she ended the call and once again placed the phone down on the ground before her. She ended the call because she had nothing more to say.

She should have felt reassured. But with the truth in the Librarian's words, she still had the strongest feeling that something wasn't right with the world she defended.

The surrounding room suddenly felt stifling. She needed to be out there on the streets, doing the one thing for which she had few equals. Rising, she walked over to the walk-in closet this room was blessed with. Inside were several items of the same coloured clothing. This was what she wore to hunt and to move amongst the sheep. It allowed her to blend in, whilst hiding her features from the cameras that watched vigil over the streets. The surveillance cameras had been programmed not to see her, but there was no reason to take the risk.

Unknown to the world, the Vatican had some of the world's most accomplished computer hackers under its protection. They existed to do the Lord's work in the dark and dismal world of cyber space. To the countries they operated in, the inquisitors were invisible to watching eyes. Their faces weren't seen, the assassins immune to detection via the biometric gait analysis that many systems now incorporated, because their presence on the streets was never recorded.

First, she donned the black trousers with their anti-ballistic and stab proof weave, followed by boots with reinforced soles. They felt heavy on her feet, but she was used to that. The belt she draped around her waist, its various knives hidden away by its special design. Her hand hesitated over the shoulder harness that held the Glock 43. Lilith preferred this smaller Glock for street patrol. It had a Six round capacity with a short barrel, and was reliable with the stopping power she needed, especially with the armour-piercing rounds fitted. There was also a fitted silencer, an essential on the London streets. She would prefer the dull slapping sound the silencer would allow rather than the highly detectable report that electronic ears listening to London's street could identify.

Whilst a larger gun with a larger magazine would have been preferable, she had to weigh up concealment as the main factor.

Withdrawing the weapon, she ejected the magazine and loaded it with the bullets that sat patiently on a dust-free shelf. Lilith meticulously loaded two further magazines and slipped them home into the slots in the harness. She kept only two loaded guns on these premises, swapping the magazines regularly, for she didn't want the spring mechanism weakening, which could cause the gun to jam when she was depending on it the most.

Suitably armed, she slid on the leather jacket, also lined with protective weave, enough to save her from a knife and anything up to a 9mm round. The impact would leave her bruised, might break a bone if the shot was a lucky one, but only a higher calibre had any chance of penetrating. Unless she was faced with someone using armour-piercing rounds, but the chances of that were slim on the streets of London.

Most of the demons she had dealt with in the past weren't expecting her and generally didn't have access to anything more exotic than a kitchen knife.

The jacket was a stylish cut, to hide the bulge of her gun, and also to blend with the people around her. It wasn't figure hugging, instead giving the appearance that it was designed to promote warmth rather than admiring glances. It draped loosely below her thighs, hiding the belt whilst allowing quick access to the delights that were held there.

With her perpetually short crew cut, the wig slipped over her scalp easily, the artificial hair designed to hang over her face. Even with night nearly here, she finished her look with the mirrored sunglasses that allowed perfect vision. Everything she wore was designed to make her look like someone else. She could fool most of the government owned and run surveillance cameras in this country, but not the human eyes that would often witness her murderous deeds.

She did these random hunts occasionally, the urge to find the demonic spawn sometimes overwhelming. Her Order preferred her to act on its specific instructions, but what they didn't know wouldn't hurt them. It had been by this type of direct street patrol, through the rich and the powerful of the City of London, that she had discovered the last demon she had killed. His black aura had been unmistakable amongst the clueless people she had been there to protect.

Tonight, she would walk the streets of London again, the memory of her own abduction a constant motivator to rid the world of her enemy. She did this because it was all she knew.

29.

Slough, UK

Emily knew her mother was going to say something about how quiet she had been since being picked up from school. Normally Emily would regale her mum about what she had learnt and the crazy antics that Lucy often got up to. Not today. The whole car ride had been in silence, Emily staring worried out of the window.

Now at the kitchen table, Emily played with the sandwich that had been made for her. No appetite either.

"What's wrong, peanut?"

"Simon wasn't in school today," Emily said gravely. She was hesitant to speak.

"Who's Simon?"

"One of the boys in my class. I overheard one of the teachers saying he had gone missing." A little jolt of alarm jumped into her chest. She didn't want her mum to worry. What could be worse for a parent than a child going missing? There were so many predators out there. "Miss Jones asked us all if we knew where he might have gone, but nobody did."

"I'm sure he's okay."

"What if he's not?" Emily had never mentioned Simon's name before. She was surprised by the emotion welling in her own words. "What if Mrs Rawlinson has taken him and done things?"

"Emily, enough of that."

The adults couldn't see it. They couldn't see what was right in front of them. They would all wonder why Emily was so obsessed about her teacher in this way.

"Mrs Rawlinson would never do that."

"You don't know," Emily insisted, wiping tears from her eyes. "You don't see how she looks at us." They were across the kitchen table from each other and Vicky pulled her chair round to be next to her daughter. Emily saw the look that said, *what has got into this kid*? "You weren't there when…"

"When what?"

"I just know Mrs Rawlinson is involved."

"And when Simon turns up unharmed?"

"He won't," Emily insisted. Fear permeated her every word.

"Do you want me to have a talk with your teacher?"

"No," Emily begged. "You can't because then she'll know."

"Know what?" Her mother was clearly wondering what was going on here. Emily knew this wasn't like her. And whilst she knew her mum would like to trust what she was saying, there was no denying how it all sounded so crazy.

Emily once asked her mum what she did for a living. "*I help people who have sick minds.*" Was that the category Emily had fallen into? Would her mum's intuition tell her there was more to this, for these fears to have come on so suddenly? Was Emily already being analysed?

Vicky had always said how proud she had been at how her daughter had dealt with the loss of her father. She'd been the rock Vicky herself had grabbed onto. Well, she wasn't a rock anymore. Emily wanted to bottle this all away, hide her fears from the world. But she was just a kid.

"She'll know that I see her," Emily whispered. "She'll know that I see the blackness."

"Oh, honey."

"Please, I don't want to go to school tomorrow." The plea was said with such desperation that Emily knew her mum couldn't deny the request.

"Well, okay. But you can't stay off school for long. Can I at least talk to your headmistress?" She would have to do that anyway, Emily knew. At least her mum was asking permission.

"Do you have to?"

"Afraid so, peanut." Emily nodded, but there was no certainty there. Emily's education was important, but so was her safety. She didn't want to be around people who could hurt her. What worried Emily most of all was not being believed by someone she was so dependent on. *Could there actually be something wrong with her teacher, like Emily was saying*? Her mother would ask that. What if she then came to the conclusion that no, such accusations were ridiculous? What happened then?

But still… Emily was well aware that children saw things that adults often missed. Usually they kept that to themselves, frightened that they might be rejected, but Vicky had always let it be known that Emily could tell her anything. Would that promise turn out to be a lie?

"Can I stay with you tomorrow?"

"No peanut, mummy has to work. So, it looks like you will be having a sick day with Grandad." Emily brightened at that.

"Can I have ice cream?"

"I don't see why not," Vicky said.

What if this fear of her teacher didn't go away? How would her mum, and the school, manage that?

30.

Cheltenham, UK

GCHQ calls itself a world leading cyber and security agency whose mission is to keep the United Kingdom safe. But it is much more than that, for it monitors the people it protects, as well as intercepting and analysing a range of electronic data from across the globe.

Although it claims to work under Parliamentary oversight, much of its activities are kept secret and out of the scrutiny of the public eye. It is part of the Echelon network, so is linked to its American cousin, the National Security Agency. The people it answers to are more than happy for it to act as the country's digital guardian despite the civil liberties it might sometimes infringe upon.

The question as to who watches over the watcher is rarely answered to anyone's ultimate satisfaction.

Under the *Tempora* program, it buffers most internet communication extracted from the backbone fibre-optic cables across the UK and overseas. This allows the data transmitted to be stored and searched at a later date by computers with vast processing power, and ultimately, if necessary, humans.

There's more to this. There always is with such secretive organisations. MTI, or *Mastering the Internet*, is a mass surveillance project with a one-billion-pound annual budget. The system is capable of copying signals from up to two hundred fibre-optic cables at their physical points of entry into Great Britain. Ultimately, anything that travels through those cables is filtered and scanned.

Basically, this allows the UK government, through GCHQ, to keep a record of every website a UK citizen visits, for up to a year, although most of this data is kept longer. It also allows GCHQ to be a central hub for government CCTV feeds, which helps the police and the security services monitor the country for those it deems undesirable. The goal was for the police and security services, namely MI5, to be able to follow an individual in real time from one city to another if need be. It was hoped, one day, that every citizen of the country would be under constant never-ending surveillance as soon as they stepped out of their homes. For those who thought this was impossible, they really needed to expand their horizons. It was already being done.

GCHQ watches and detects incursions by the country's many enemies. And it was suspected that this protection had been breached and compromised. That was not only embarrassing, but potentially damaging to the country. If terrorists could go about undetected, there was no telling what chaos could be created.

"You are asking me to find another ghost?" Rashid Khan was incredulous. He had been instrumental in protecting the network from such weaknesses in the past. Years ago, the Russians had tried it and almost succeeded. To counter that Russian threat, it had been Rashid and his team that had spent countless hours searching through lines of code to find the malicious virus that had made its way into the heart of GCHQ. They had soon uncovered the mole who had managed to smuggle that virus in, a high-level analyst who had decided that money was more important that national loyalty.

That analyst was presently living a world of regret.

Rashid had closed those holes in the system, or at least he thought he had. Now his supervisor stood over him, stating there was a chance another virus had slipped in.

"I'm asking you to do what you do so well," the supervisor said. False flattery never worked with Rashid, because he was not one to accept any kind of bullshit, even from those above him. What Rashid couldn't understand was how this man, his intellectual inferior, was in a position to give Rashid orders. Organisations like GCHQ were supposed to be meritocracies. His supervisor was evidence that perhaps that wasn't strictly the case.

"Do we have any proof that there even is a virus?"

"No, it's just theory at the moment."

"Well, come back to me when it's proven. You know how long such an investigation would take." Months, if it was possible. Searching through lines of code, thousands of them. Although he was happy to accept the praise from last time, he knew he had been lucky rather than skilful.

"But you love it," the supervisor said. He was one of those passive-aggressive types who never outright told you what to do, but instead used false praise and sarcasm.

"Like a hole in the head."

"Doesn't matter, mate, it comes from the top. The Home Secretary himself."

Shit. Where was he supposed to start?

"Can I at least finish what I'm working on?"

"No can do, buckaroo. The director wants you straight on it."

"Okay, but I want the request in writing," Rashid insisted. He didn't want to be responsible should this all turn out to be a wild goose chase.

"What? My say so not good enough?"

"What do you think?" came Rashid's answer.

31.

Vatican City, Italy

Cardinal Valentina Esposito had no complaints about waiting. His holiness the Pope was, after all, infallible, so if you had to sit around for an hour before he was prepared to see you, then the failing was obviously yours. Besides, it wasn't unpleasant to rest here, the open window allowing a faint breeze to enter in from St Peter's Square. It was a chance to meditate and reflect on the recent information he had been given.

He didn't notice the faint dust that had already settled on his robes.

Unlike many who held positions of power in the world, Cardinal Esposito was ruthlessly competent, which would have been a surprise to Lilith. As the unofficial head of the Order of Tyron, he couldn't really be anything else. He had risen to prominence seven years previously, and he liked to think he had overseen changes that had made his Order more efficient in the fight against the Satanic hordes.

He was well aware of the dangers facing the world, the constant reports from his inquisitors frequently crossing his desk. That was one of the reasons he had requested an audience with the Pope.

When the Pope's private secretary finally appeared to tell him that His Holiness was ready, Esposito rose wearily, his old bones complaining about the years of abuse they had suffered. The Pope's emissary didn't follow Esposito into the room, for he wouldn't be needed for this most secret of conversations.

The meeting was informal, as such meeting always were. There would be no risk of eavesdropping, not with the security precautions taken by the Swiss Guard. The room he entered was dominated by the roaring fireplace, two chairs set far enough away to gain the benefit of the heat without any of the potential discomfort. The Pope sat in one of the chairs, eyes closed, head cocked as if he was listening to some distant whispering. Esposito waited for permission to approach.

"Cardinal, you stand there like a frightened rabbit," the Pope finally said.

"These are frightening times, your Holiness." Esposito remembered a time when he would be expected to bow down and kiss the Pope's ring before having such a conversation, but not this Pope. This Pope was known for his humility, rejecting many of the outdated norms that so many of his predecessors had enjoyed.

"This is why we meet like this? In secret like conspirators?"

"Yes, your Holiness."

"You'd better sit down, then," the Pope said with a sweep of his hand.

"I'm afraid I bring troubling news," Esposito said as he sat down. The chair was comfortable, more comfortable than he would have liked. Men weren't supposed to enjoy such luxuries in this life.

"You always have troubling news. Every time I see you my heart sinks with the knowledge that Esposito has troubling news." Esposito could appreciate the Pope's light-hearted manner. So many of those before him had been too serious, almost too afraid to hear what the delegate from the Order of Tyron had to discuss.

"I crave your forgiveness, Holy Father."

"There is nothing to forgive, Valentina. If you deem something important, I would be a fool not to trust your judgement. So?"

"I received a report yesterday. The person who made the report did so reluctantly, as if not believing the message himself." Esposito looked briefly at the flames, his mind trying to find the best way to break the news to Christ's emissary on earth. The Pope stood suddenly, putting a hand on Esposito's shoulder.

"You will find the words when they are ready to appear," the Pope said, brushing the faint dust off the subordinate's shoulder. It was not like Esposito to not have noticed such a blemish.

"I find this troubling, because of what it might represent." He watched the Pope move away, grateful that they had a Pope who was of such formidable character. They would need a man like that in the times to come.

"I presume you still drink," the Pope asked as he approached an ornate cabinet.

"Of course, your Holiness."

"Good. There are too many in these walls who have renounced such delights lately." Esposito watched as the most powerful man in the Catholic Church poured two glasses of red wine. No doubt it would be an excellent vintage. When the Pope returned to his seat, Esposito accepted the drink gladly, taking the smallest sip.

"The Seals are weakening." Esposito could have said it in so many ways.

"Go on."

"We have multiple confirmed reports that demon spawn are working together, coordinating their approach. I fear my Order alone can no longer keep the equilibrium."

"That is indeed grave news," said the Pope. He had shared a secret with Esposito years ago. When the conclave of the Cardinals had made their decision, the most shocking moment of the elected Pope's life was when he had learnt of the true reality about Hell. Demons were not a thing of myth and legend. They were a very real threat to the stability of the human race. "So, what do we do about it?"

"That is why I am here, Holy Father. We have less than two hundred Inquisitors on active duty. If the Seals break, we will not be able to stop the deluge."

"You have concocted something. I can see the cogs in your brain ticking over."

"For years we have worked in secrecy, to keep the truth about Hell hidden from those whose minds would crumble at such knowledge. If the people of the world knew that demons walked amongst them, there would be mass panic. Neighbours would turn on each other, governments would fall."

"Which is why your Order, and your Order alone, has furnished the soldiers to fight this battle," the Pope noted. He took a sip himself, wiping the moisture away from his lip. This was a fine wine, just a shame the Pope had smeared contamination across his mouth.

"Yes, your Holiness."

"So, how do we tell the world without ripping it apart?"

"Perhaps it is time to tell the leaders we can trust," Esposito offered.

"That doesn't leave us many options." Despite the wry smile, Esposito knew the Pope was being serious for once. Many of those who ran the countries of the world were not fit for the jobs they held.

"I have collated a list, your Holiness."

"Of course you have. Always prepared and ready, eh Valentina?"

"Yes, your Holiness." Esposito reached into his robes and pulled out an envelope sealed with wax. He handed it across, the Pope taking it gravely.

"I always hoped I would never have to do this."

“So did I, your Holiness.” The Pope opened the envelope and frowned at what he saw.

There were only twenty-three names there, half of them not even world leaders.

“You depress me, Valentina. I will need to sleep on this.”

“As you wish, your Holiness.”

Esposito trusted his pontiff explicitly. That didn’t mean he wasn’t able to get the jump on things. There was one name on that list, to whom Esposito could talk directly.

32.

Silicon Valley, USA

Kane stood outside the room, a solemn look on his face. That was no reflection on the present situation. He always looked like that.

"How is our guest?" Horn asked. They were on the third sub floor, the surrounding corridor an opulent combination of polished wood, marble floors and chrome. There was no point being worth billions if you couldn't shape your environment to your own image. Although the great tribulation was coming, Horn would not sacrifice the comfort he enjoyed.

"He came to about an hour ago. I don't think he's too happy."

"I'm sure we can persuade him that this is all for the best." Horn would find the motivation to make this man do his bidding. And if not, then Kane would get to have his fun. Horn could see that Kane was long overdue the relief he so desperately craved.

"I don't like him," Kane advised. "He doesn't smell right. He feels like a threat. Let me remove that threat."

"You don't like anyone and I need him. Besides, he doesn't have to be liked. He just has to do what we tell him."

"I hope he doesn't. I hope he disappoints you."

"Kane, you should calm down. Go and torture some kittens or something." Horn had noticed that Kane never let any of his master's jibes bother him. Kane had suffered for millennia in the Pit; mere words were thus inconsequential. Demons didn't have a problem with ego. The lower ones were base emotion, consumed by the need to inflict pain and misery. Those from the higher orders, the Kings and Princes of Hell, still had cravings, but they were able to resist such obsessions.

Kane stepped aside to allow Horn entry to the room. The door was polished oak with an internal steel reinforcement. If you didn't have the access biometrics, you weren't getting in, or out. The person trapped inside would be there until Horn decided he wasn't needed any more. If Ari Stone could do what Horn asked of him, then the author could still have a long and happy life. Disappointment, however, would mean the unleashing of Kane.

Beyond the door was a large living space with two further doors off it. One would lead to sleeping quarters, the other to a bathroom. The living space was the height of luxury, but it was still a prison. The centre of the room was recessed into the floor, an L-shaped leather sofa presently occupied by Stone. All around the walls were bookshelves filled to overflowing.

The captive still looked groggy, Stone's face pale from the effects of the sedative that had kept him compliant during his transfer from Boston. Some would say snatching a world-renowned author off the streets was a risk, but apart from a few days of intrigue, Stone's disappearance would soon be forgotten. With the exception of a small number of chat rooms and the odd newspaper article, the disappearance of Stone would have remarkably little impact on the world.

People went missing all the time. With what was presently happening in the universe, Stone wouldn't be missed. There were far more exciting things to keep the news anchors busy.

"Who are you?" Stone demanded. "Why have I been brought here?" Horn closed the door behind him, leaving Kane outside. His Chief of Security wouldn't be needed for this.

"Mr Stone, it's a pleasure to meet you." Horn stepped further into the room. He had designed its layout himself, personally choosing each and every book and manuscript that adorned the many bookshelves that surrounded him. When you had considerable wealth, you could easily accumulate things. This was his own personal collection that, for the first time in his life, he was willing to let another individual read.

"Cut the shit and tell me what you want." The fury in Stone was understandable, although it was notable that he didn't possess the skills to back up any anger he brought forth. In physical combat, Horn would have the man at his mercy within mere seconds. The writer was long past his prime and, although big, much of his mass was excess fat. Horn was a prime physical specimen who had been trained to fight by the best. Stone's previous martial arts experience wouldn't stand a chance with what Horn brought to the table. When you were as committed and driven to excellence as Horn, you tended to do everything to extremes.

And besides, a man like Horn had others to do his dirty work. Imagine what Kane could do to the man if provoked.

"You're angry. I can understand that."

"Damn right I'm angry."

"Your abduction was necessary. You have something I need."

"Well, it's clear this isn't about money," Stone said, looking around. Despite the indignity of his abduction and drugging, Horn could see the intrigue the library held for his captive.

"No, it isn't about the money. I need you for what you have in your mind."

"What does that even mean?" Instead of answering directly, Horn stepped over to one of the bookcases, his finger trailing over several volumes until he found the one he wanted. Carefully, Horn pulled the book free, its surface worn with evident age. It was so big that Horn needed both hands to carry it.

"I've spent a lifetime collecting these books. Some of them I have read, many still remain unexplored." He hoped one day to read them all, but he knew that was one of the few things he would likely fail at.

"Why do you think I care?" Stone had remained sitting, obviously not yet trusting his own legs. When he had come round, he had briefly explored his surroundings, only to be driven back to the sofa to rest and allow his body to recover. Horn had seen it all thanks to the surveillance cameras scattered about the room.

"I should imagine you would care a great deal, given the nature of these many volumes." Horn walked over to where Stone sat, and carefully placed the huge book down on the glass table in front of him. Horn was glad to see Stone couldn't hide his surprise.

"Is that…?"

"The Codex Gigas? Yes." The Codex Gigas, otherwise known as the Devil's Bible. "There are some interesting illustrations inside, none of them particularly accurate."

"How the hell did you get it? Last I heard, it was in the National Library of Sweden."

"It still is. You don't honestly think only one copy was made, do you?" Horn let the book sit there, Stone clearly struggling to resist the temptation to delve into it. *You can't help yourself,* Horn thought. *You were brought here against your will and yet your obsession drives you.* "Many of these books were supposed to have been destroyed, but it's amazing what you can find when you know where to look."

"I still don't understand what you want."

"I thought it was obvious."

"Not to me," Stone insisted. Horn had gone to the effort of dragging Stone halfway across the world. Now was the time to explain why. Horn sat down.

"I have a proposition."

"You could have just called my agent." Stone couldn't hide the intrigue that was welling inside him. If this man could get a copy of such a book, what else did he have on these shelves? Wasn't that what the writer was thinking?

"No. The project I have in mind needs complete secrecy and complete focus." Horn had instructed a team of researchers to find the man fit for the task required. He needed to have a writing style that appealed to the greater masses, as well as being free of any religious indoctrination. Stone, being a bestselling author and a self-proclaimed atheist, had been deemed the best selection for what Horn needed. The fact he was also without strong family ties helped. It would not do for the man tasked with writing this great work to be distracted by concerns for his wife and children.

"Okay, I'm listening."

"I am sure you are familiar with the notion of the Great Tribulation?"

"If you had read any of my books, you would know not to ask that."

"What if I told you the time of the Great Tribulation was at hand?" Horn noticed the look of scorn that came over his prisoner.

"Don't be ridiculous. Is that what this is all about?" The captive's face communicated his thoughts clearly. Seriously, had he really been kidnapped by a bunch of end-of-days fanatics?

"I can assure you it's quite real."

“I’ve heard many people say the same,” Stone said. “Usually when they were ranting at me from their self-proclaimed pulpit.”

“I am not here to convince you. I believe you will convince yourself.”

“I’d advise you not to hold your breath,” Stone insisted. “Look, why don’t you tell me what it is you want?” Horn smiled at that, sitting forward on his seat, the excitement building.

“I want you to write a book. It will be a definitive work.” *It would indeed.*

“A book about?”

“Why, the end of days.”

“But I’ve already written countless volumes on that topic,” Stone insisted.

“Not like this. Look around you. Have you ever had such resources at your disposal?” Stone’s eyes wandered. He shook his head in obviously reluctant admission that what was on display here was certainly impressive. “And these are only the physical volumes. I have thousands more available to you in digital format.”

“I still don’t understand.”

“That much is clear, but it doesn’t matter. All that concerns me now is that you will write the book I desire. If you do this, I will see that you are handsomely rewarded.”

“You expect me to believe that? You expect me to buy that you will just let me go once I have done what you ask?”

“Of course, I do,” Horn insisted. “Because when you have finished your work, when you have seen what only I can show you, I have every faith you will come to my way of thinking.”

“You hope to make me a believer?”

“I do.” Horn stood. “Not that you really have much choice. The only way you are getting out of here is if you do as I instruct. Do as I ask, and you will live the rest of your days in luxury, free from all cares of the world. Defy me and I will have you killed in a manner so horrific that you presently can’t imagine.” The paleness in Stone's face worsened. Any bluster he had left had been struck from him. “But don’t make your decision now. Take a few hours and think about it. Peruse the shelves and see what we have here. Most of the books are first editions, some supposedly lost centuries ago.”

“Who the hell are you anyway?” Stone demanded. Ah, the question Horn had been waiting for.

“My dear fellow, I’m the man you are going to be writing about.” Horn leaned in so that the writer could see what Horn wanted to show. Pulling his lower lip out, he exposed the inner mucosa.

There, just visible, was the birthmark that so few had seen. Three sixes, joined together by their tails. Horn winked then, before letting his lip flop back.

There, I have shown you who I am. Now let’s see what you make of it.

33.

London, UK

Baal sat behind her new desk, regretting her presence here. This really wasn't what she was about. She had taken this man because of the power the Home Secretary supposedly wielded, misunderstanding the complexities humans lived in. When Baal had last ventured into the mortal world, things had been a lot different. Back then, she could order the deaths of hundreds with the nod of her head.

That wasn't the case anymore, humanity becoming civilised. How Baal detested them for that. She'd spent most of the afternoon meeting with people who called themselves lawyers. The world of man was a peculiar place, these hairless apes thinking themselves so special that they swamped their own lives with rules and regulations. They thought themselves gods, able to shape the world around them, but they were too naïve to understand their own stupidity. Baal would help them in that regard. When the Seals began to break, they would quickly revert to the barbarians they truly were.

For now, they were an annoyance, like the spreading rash on her back.

Baal was already tired of this body, but she would stay because she had no choice in the matter. She wasn't idiotic enough to believe she had free will. Baal would leave those stupid notions to the pitiful humans. The Fallen had sent her here, and you didn't defy those sons of bitches.

She'd also had to restrain herself. Severely. Being such a prominent figure, she couldn't come and go as she pleased, a whole army of bureaucrats and security personnel seemingly there to keep her under constant watch. They were guardians, there to keep the Home Secretary safe, but Baal also suspected they were there to ensure the man who held such an important position of state didn't do something that would be ultimately disastrous for government.

If only they knew who their boss really was. They would bow down in the terror of Baal's presence. Such adulation wasn't why she was here and would ultimately be counterproductive. It would be nice to go back to the way things used to be, though.

This was the first moment she had been able to sit alone since leaving the house this morning, her demon mind reeling from the banality of what this host body was supposed to do. She was a King of Hell, so she was more than up to the task. But damned if it wasn't tedious.

Things would change when the Great Tribulation came. Then the evil within men and women would be unleashed, this mask of civility stripped forever. Baal wasn't a fool; she knew what the apocalypse would ultimately represent. The reign of the new Lords over this world would only last so long, and then Hell would be sealed for the rest of eternity, all evil purged from the planet and locked away.

They all had to play their part in God's fetid schemes.

She could have come up here and let herself loose upon the world, but she would avoid such cheap thrills. Taking this human host had weakened her, its resistance constant and more draining than she could remember from her previous experiences. These meat suits used to accept their place in the world, but the constant prodding by the trapped irritated her. No matter, it was something she would be able to endure.

The phone on the desk in front of Baal rang. Such a curious device.

"Home Secretary," the female voice announced when she answered it. "The person you asked me to contact earlier is on the other line."

"Thank you, Christine," Baal said pleasantly, although her mind was filled with the perversions she could force upon the frail, middle-aged receptionist. Ooh, how she would like to really go to town on her, but there would be no way for Baal to cover that up. To her knowledge, there were only a few of her kind in these great offices of state, all lesser demons of no great note. That would change as the time of the apocalypse grew near, the mesh separating the world of man from the Pit growing frail. Though the higher demons would struggle to exist here, the mission couldn't be left in the hands of lesser creatures of chaos.

As it was, there were still too few of her rank who had made it through. Whilst there were thousands of demons out on the streets of the cities their prey walked, they were mostly random possessions, intent on pleasure and murder rather than forging ahead to the great plan. There were six Great Kings loose on the world apart from herself, three in the Middle East, creating the spark that would see the world burn. The other three had been here for decades, preparing the way for what was to come.

"Home Secretary," the voice of Sir David said.

"You have news for me?"

"Yes. Because of the nature of yesterday's incident, we were able to expedite the forensics examination of the bodies. As Detective Inspector Cooke suspected, the person we seek has killed before."

"Are we any closer to learning their identity?"

"Maybe," said Sir David. "Do you remember the Russian Prizrak program?" Prizrak, meaning ghost. The Russians had managed to infiltrate western systems to make their agents invisible. It was a crude affair, uncovered after several high-ranking Russian defectors had been slaughtered on British streets. The images of Russian agents were scrubbed from all surveillance recordings. As the video feeds were being written to storage, a virus altered the images it was programmed to scrub, writing over the pixels with an approximation based on the available background data. It left blotchy images on occasion, which was how it had been spotted.

"You think our assassin is using similar?"

"My analysts seem to think so. We have them hunting through the systems, trying to find the code that could allow this to occur."

"When do you expect to have a breakthrough?"

"Well, it took us three months to uncover the Russian code that had been hacked into our system."

"I don't have three months, Sir David." Her frustrations were breaking through. She knew it. Maybe she would need to find some way to relieve the pressure that was building after all.

"You also asked me to look into that rumour."

"Good. What did you find?"

"Nothing. I checked with SIS, and they have no knowledge of such a religious organisation. I don't know where you remember seeing such information, Home Secretary, but it wasn't from us."

Fuck.

"That's disappointing. Still, I'm more certain than ever that my memory isn't playing tricks on me. Could you put a request in with our allies? See if they know anything."

"As you wish, Home Secretary." Baal knew it would be more important than ever now to capture one of the Inquisition. If they could be made to talk…

"Thank you," Baal said, almost choking on the words. Such pointless formalities these monkeys went through.

"I've asked GCHQ to work on the virus problem."

"You don't sound hopeful, Sir David."

I want to rip your heart out.

"It's just a matter of time. If there is a program similar to the one the Russians infected our system with, we'll find it." Yes, but not in time, Baal seethed. How the hell was she going to be able to capture an Inquisitor if they were ghosts?

***

Lilith walked the streets, blending in with the world around her. The air was crisp, the side alleys dark and filled with the hidden malice that could so easily be lurking. Even with her skill, there was no need to take unnecessary risk. It would be painfully ironic for her to survive the demonic hordes, only to become the victim of criminal violence.

There were those amongst the people she worked to protect who weren't worthy of that protection. Lilith had long ago accepted that. They were all God's creatures, nonetheless.

She went to where the people were, because she knew the possessed would be drawn there as well. Lilith's advantage was that she could remain invisible to their eyes whilst the enemy would let itself be known to her through the nature of its infection.

Some demons liked to stalk their prey, toying with it, building up to the act of slaughter. Others acted impulsively, murdering those around them. Humans were more than capable of committing acts of savagery and barbarity, but more and more, Lilith sensed the manipulation of those from the Pit. There was a certain pattern left by those the demons killed. Many were children, prolonged torture being a particular favourite of these depraved beings.

They killed adults as well, usually in a way that created maximum emotional impact on the world.

Several of the recent terrorist attacks were good examples. Those who proclaimed to be acting on the will of whatever God drove them had demons whispering in their ears. That was another way the unclean influenced the world. Some they could possess. Others they could drive to acts that the majority would think insane. All supposedly random.

Or was it? Lilith still felt much of the recent activity was coordinated, planned, almost surgical in its application.

The more she thought this, the more she became obsessed with the hunt. The streets drew her, a religious vigilante forever on the lookout for those who threatened humanity. There was the risk of addiction as well, her growing craving to send this scourge back to where they came from. In her moments of meditation, she would admit that she enjoyed the battle against the Beast a little too much.

She didn't see it as a problem, though.

Maybe she should have.

Despite it being late, the Queens Walk was still busy, tourists drawn to the river with its restaurants and bars that stayed open to fulfil their mindless cravings. Most of the people here were too consumed with their own lives to see the threats presented to them. And there were many threats. Before she saw the demon, Lilith had clocked the members of the gang picking bags and pockets. Many a tourist would later uncover the horrifying realisation that their purse or wallet had been lifted.

There were other dangers here, too. Up on Westminster Bridge, the pair on the moped that had passed her on the road earlier were clearly looking for something more substantial to steal, the police spread too thin to have any chance of stopping them. Down side streets, away from the glare of the ever-present cameras, were the drug peddlers concealed in doorways, ready to slip a plastic wrap into the hand carrying the right amount of cash. Death often waited in those tiny envelopes, the promised pleasure defiled by chemicals human physiology was never designed to imbibe.

Cockroaches of humanity slipping through the cracks. All would suffer in the eternal fires when the time came.

The civility this pedestrian area displayed was a lie, a veneer over the sickness that permeated the lives of so many. Lilith saw it all and knew that she remained invulnerable to it. As long as she kept her wits about her, the sheep and the wolves were no threat to her.

Out here in the open like this, the criminals would not bother her. They knew who to go for, their acquired sixth sense keeping them clear of someone who walked with such purpose, whose eyes scanned the surroundings so thoroughly. Only the meek and the distracted were targets here. Elsewhere, it would be different. On the lawless estates, and in the lesser travelled areas, those who defied the nation's laws might try their luck. But not here. Here, the criminals needed the mask of normality to exist for them to succeed.

They needed to be the rarity for their actions to be successful. It was the same with the demons. Too many of them spread throughout the herd and they risked fighting amongst themselves. Worse than that, they risked the world becoming aware of them. There would be a time for that, but hopefully now was not that time.

The demon she ultimately spotted was hanging out at the top of the Westminster Bridge steps that led down to the Queen's Walk. She didn't react to his presence. Instead, she walked closer to the base of the steps, watching his aura from the corner of her peripheral vision. To normal folk, he was a well-dressed businessman engaged in a phone conversation, but to Lilith, he was an abomination that needed to be removed from the surface of the planet.

Could she do that here, though? Taking the battle to him in such a large crowd and so publicly might lead to open battle in the streets. It was a risk, but the urge within her tried to convince Lilith to take that risk. Instead, she pressed the small notch on the side of her sunglasses. Inside the frame, the tiny zoom lens video camera began recording. Stopping at a safe distance, she briefly looked directly towards him, capturing the images of his face. If the body he inhabited was on any commercial or government database, she would have that identity within hours of returning to her accommodation. That was her backup, in case what she planned didn't bear fruit.

The demon watched those who wandered past, oblivious to his own danger. He hid the delight well, but she knew he was here to pick a victim, savouring every soul that came within reach. He was the watcher, unaware that the slayer had arrived on the scene.

A woman walked right by him and the demon's blackness reached out to her as if in an invisible caress. A thin smile spread over the demon's face, and, pushing himself off the ancient stonework he had propped himself against, followed his new found prey as she made her way down the steps. Lilith knew if she didn't act, that woman would not survive the night.

It looked like opportunity had presented itself after all, forced by the need to protect the vulnerable. Lilith knew that to wait would mean the death of another innocent. On any other day, she might have been willing to accept that. But not today. She had already failed to save one life, and the thought of another death gnawed at her. Was it really failure that drove her, though? Could it be she was denying the thing she had come to crave?

Whatever the reason, she would take the demon on the steps.

The woman Lilith was about to save descended from Westminster Bridge, the demon about ten metres behind. He had the scent of his prey, and it wasn't likely he would lose her in the crowd. Lilith closed the distance, stepping up to meet the demon without looking at him, the sharpest of her blades slipping into her right hand. The scarf had already been pulled across the lower half of her face, protection against the night's chill.

Lilith had practiced this a thousand times.

She brushed against the demon, who gave her an annoyed glance before the pain in his leg hit him. Her knife had slipped in unseen, penetrating the area of the upper thigh called the femoral triangle, slicing open the femoral artery, her wrist twisting to prevent a clean surgical wound. In this part of the city with first responder response times what they were, it wasn't definite that such an injury would result in death. Paramedics could arrive in time; miracles could happen.

That was why her knife had an extra little bonus. Aqua Tofana, a deadly poison that was slow to work but impossible to cure. Should the demon be unlucky enough to survive the cut she had administered, it could look forward to a slow and excruciating end unless it chose to abandon its host and venture back down to the dark place.

Lilith reached the top of the steps before the demon fell, his body cascading down the steps, doing more damage to the host body.

Screams followed him, those nearby having no idea why such a well-dressed man had suddenly collapsed in their midst. Lilith's only regret was that she wasn't there to see his end.

Her job was once again done and Lilith stalked off into the night. She knew she had no fear of the surveillance cameras monitoring the area. But this was a rare occasion where she had made a mistake. She did not see the two tourists, one with her phone held out in front of her.

The city's eyes might not have spotted her, but that tourist's video recorder did.

34.

Silicon Valley, USA

Tiredness had threatened to take him, but Stone held it at bay. His accommodation was not only a world class library. There were shower and toilet facilities as well as a well-stocked kitchen and a bedroom. He had everything he needed to keep him alive except freedom and the feeling of fresh air on his skin.

Not knowing where he was felt somehow liberating. His imprisonment and pending death had been surprisingly empowering. The everyday things that had been bothering him no longer seemed worthy of his concern. Being here, in this place, took all that away. There was suddenly no worry about his bank balance, or his Amazon sales rank. The fact that he sometimes felt lonely and inadequate around women was stripped from his mind.

As amazing as it was, he felt alive for the first time in years.

What replaced his banal existence was a primal urge to survive, as well as a longing for the knowledge that was contained around him. His kidnapping was a curse, but the scholar in him could also see the blessing and the opportunity. He was about to learn things that had been hidden from him, that would always have been outside his ability to discover. What he had access to made his heart ache.

He was finally free to discover the knowledge he had always craved.

The book he presently read was a first edition published in 1801. Whilst he had come across it before, what he had read had never been the original. He was drawn in by the intricate illustrations, time slipping by unseen. That was the other thing with this room. There were no time pieces, no means for him to tell whether it was night or day. Although he had a computer tablet, that too had been stripped of any indication of the passing of time, its purpose solely to hold the digital version of the books he would need to create his great manuscript. There was nothing else to occupy his time except the fragile contents of his own mind.

Stone didn't need time to think about this. He had already decided to accept Horn's proposal. All he needed to know was exactly what kind of book he was supposed to be writing.

The door to his lavish cell opened, and a man walked in. The fact that people came in here alone highlighted how powerless Stone was to fight his circumstances. The people who had captured him were rich, powerful and totally confident. Stone had a vague awareness of who Horn was, as the billionaire's name occasionally appeared in the news that Stone did his best to ignore. He was one lonely author against the owners of a multinational company that clearly had its own army. Escape wasn't going to be on the cards.

"I trust you are settling in?" the man asked.

"Who the hell are you?"

"My name is Kane. I am here to introduce myself. I hope you have everything you need?"

Stone almost went into a sarcastic tirade, but there was a predatory nature that seemed to lurk below the surface of this person that stopped him. Instinct said this was not a man to antagonise. "I am still unsure as to what my mission is here."

"Your mission is to do as my master bids." Kane sat down right next to Stone. Positioned as he was at the end of the luxurious sofa, there was no way for the author to move up any further. Standing would be the only way to escape Kane's proximity, but he knew that would be a mistake. Kane was here to show him something. Likely to further prove how powerless Stone knew he already was. "It is also to keep me happy."

"Do you have to sit so close?"

"Always," Kane said, inhaling deeply. "I can smell the fear on you. But there is something else, an arousal in your soul." A strong hand descended on Stone's shoulder. "Do I have to tell you how unwise it will be to make Mr Horn unhappy?"

"I don't think you do, no."

"This is good," Kane said, giving the shoulder he held a painful squeeze. The fingers felt like iron, working into the flesh. Enough to make Stone wince, but not severe enough to cause any lasting harm. "You are still confused as to why you are here."

"Yes," Stone admitted.

"I shall help with that. It is important to me that Mr Horn gets what he wishes."

"Look, I get it. I'm committed."

"I don't think you *do* get it," Kane advised. He let go of the shoulder, his hand landing on Stone's leg. Stone realised he preferred the pain than what this implied. "I don't think you get it at all."

"You should let me get on with my work," Stone begged. "There is so much I need to read."

"Not until you understand." The hand in Stone's lap didn't move, a dead weight resting on his thigh. "You need to look at me now."

"I'm..."

"I *said*, look at me." The order was matched by Kane's fingers once again finding purchase, digging deep into the meat of Stone's thigh. Though it brought forth a cry, Stone did as he was commanded. At first, he didn't know what he was supposed to be looking at, and then the whites of Kane's eyes turned pitch black.

"My God!"

"Do you understand?"

"No," Stone admitted. "Please, I don't know what you want." *Is he possessed*? The eyes looking at him returned to normal, and Kane rose from where he had sat. Instead of saying anything more, the possessed man wandered over to the furthest reach of the bookcases and, after several seconds of searching, pulled a book free. It looked surprisingly modern.

"You need to be fully committed to the task ahead of you. For now, I advise you to read as many of these great works as you can. Spend your every waking moment devouring what is on these shelves." I was doing that, Stone wanted to say. Kane once again approached, the book held out in front of him. "May I recommend you start with this impressive tome. It will give you an indication of who your new owner truly is."

"This makes no sense," Stone protested. When he didn't take the offered book, Kane placed it carefully down next to him. Surprise caused him to yelp as Kane lightly slapped the author's face.

"Do not fail Mr Horn, or else you will learn what I am truly capable of. You do not want me practicing my art on you." Stone didn't say anything. Instead, panic rising, he watched as the owner of the sometimes-black eyes stood there. Had that been a trick? No, of course it hadn't. Looking down at the book, Stone really wasn't surprised by the title.

The Antichrist, by Nietzsche.

"I don't understand." Maybe that wasn't the truth. Maybe he understood very well, but he tried to hide that fact even from his own mind.

"I think a demonstration is required, then. An expression of what I am willing to do to ensure your compliance." Stone sank back as

Kane fell on him, the skin of his chin burning with the pressure being exerted by the one-handed grip applied. Despite his best efforts, Kane was too strong to fight off, a knee perilously close to ruining Stone's future relationships. They paused like that for several seconds, Stone pinned to the couch with the passive-faced Kane above him.

"Let me go," Stone begged, as Kane's free hand suddenly appeared with a pair of pristine pliers.

"As I said, a demonstration. There should be no doubt as to what you are dealing with." The pliers came closer, pushing their way into Stone's mouth. He tried to move away, but Kane's grip on him kept his head fixed, the mouth forced open. "Hold still. I only want to take one."

When he grabbed Kane's wrist to try to stop what was coming, it was like gripping cold steel.

Then the metal tool was there, crushing down on his front tooth, the searing pain intense as Kane's wrist began to twist. At first the tooth resisted valiantly, but then there was a give as the tissues relented. The pliers turned back and forth, working on the meat that held the tooth in place. Something cracked, and then the tooth was free, the pain replaced by a void as Kane released his captive. With a flick of the wrist, Kane sent the tooth flying towards the door he had come through.

Kane released him.

"Fuck you," Stone managed to mumble through his protective hands. His mouth was already filling with blood, the gap in his dentition exquisitely intriguing to his tongue. He'd never experienced such abject terror.

"Another for my collection," Stone advised. "Your dental records indicate you have thirty-two teeth. You get to keep the rest, so long as you are diligent in your work. Do not test me, because if you run out of teeth, then I will turn to the more vital areas." Stone was sure the pliers pointed at his groin wasn't an accident.

The threat was real. The horror he had seen in Kane's eyes had been real. Any doubt as to who Horn was had been extinguished. Before Kane left the room, he plucked the bloodied tooth from the floor and popped into his pocket.

"I look forward to working with you," Kane said. Then the demon left, leaving Stone to wallow in his misery.

35.

Slough, UK

Vicky opened her eyes to the real possibility that there was something wrong with the world. She found it difficult to breathe, the air somehow thick in her lungs, a noxious smell hinted at. If she inhaled deeply, it seemed to escape her, but it taunted her nostrils with its potential.

Sunlight shone through her window, but the colour was all wrong. It was too red, too malignant. Normally on waking, the thoughts would come, interlopers to display how imperfect and flawed her life was. Today, though, there was no time for such self-pity, for she had other concerns.

Vicky was certain there was someone in the room with her.

Her bedroom wasn't big enough to hold many hiding places, the bed itself free of any cunning space beneath it. Still, she was certain someone was here, and she threw the duvet back to allow her feet access to the floor. If someone was hiding here, she couldn't see them.

Vicky still knew something was wrong.

A hand slammed on the hidden surface of her bedroom door. It wasn't her daughter, the force too strong and too high up on the wood. The impact sent a jolt through her throat, and Vicky found herself on her feet, the carpet beneath her strewn with invisible debris. The fibres felt corrupted, vaguely moist, but in the available light any visual evidence for such was hidden from her.

The hand slammed again, and she retreated away from the door.

"*Vicky, I'm coming in.*" The voice that spoke came from the surrounding air, no direction discernible. There was pain in that voice, and a sadness that had taken generations to reach perfection.

"Who's there?" she demanded, although there was no strength in her words.

"*I have come for you. Let me in. It will be so much easier.*"

"Get out of my house." Vicky searched frantically for some kind of weapon, but there was nothing, and she retreated further, moving onto the boundary of the ensuite bathroom this bedroom was graced with.

"*I'm not in your house,*" the voice stated. "*But I want to be in you. Let me in, or I will hurt the one you love.*" Emily! Where was Emily? She knew she had to protect her daughter, but Vicky's feet moved in the wrong direction, pushed away by the terror behind her door. That was the worst of it, the guilt that she knew she couldn't protect her own daughter.

"Go away."

"*No, never. Not until you let me in.*" What did that mean?

Vicky stepped into the bathroom and closed the door, her fingers frantically slipping the lock closed. She heard it then, the presence entering her sanctuary, the ethereal form moving around where she had been sleeping moments ago.

"*You can't hide from me,*" the voice said, the handle in front of Vicky moving slowly and rhythmically. "*I want you. I will have you. I will have what is mine.*"

It was then that Vicky noticed she was naked. That didn't make sense. She never slept naked, not since she'd given birth. The hair on her arms stood on end despite the warmth that infused the space she was trapped in. She wanted to speak, to at least shout some kind of defiance, but all that escaped was a pathetic keening. Vicky knew there was no way she was getting out of this, the intruder now scraping something along the outer surface of her only defence.

Stepping into the walk-in shower, Vicky knew there was nowhere left to go. If whoever this was got through that door, there would be no chance.

The wood of the door seemed to pulse inwards, the handle and the lock vibrating. The handle began to turn again, faster, more frantic, as if the owner of this display wanted to tear the metal out of the door. Vicky found herself collapsed to the floor, her knees pulled tight into her chest, the cold tile wall almost a blessing against the sweating skin of her back.

"Leave me alone," she managed.

"*No, I will come until you relent. I will take everything you hold dear until you give me what is mine.*"

"You can't have me. You can't have Emily. I won't let you."

"*And how will you stop me*?" the voice questioned. "*You have no hope. You should surrender and let your life have some meaning.*" Surprisingly, anger blossomed in Vicky.

"I have meaning, damn you. I have my daughter."

"*And when I take that? When I cut out her tongue using your hands, what then? What will be left of you except a shattered ruin*?" The wood of the door cracked as something impacted it, the door frame splitting. Two more hits like that, and the beast would be in.

Beast? Vicky had no idea why she used that word except to say that her tormenter wasn't a man. No mere man could perform the spectacle she was witnessing here.

"I won't let you take her."

"*You won't have a choice.*" The red of the rising sun seemed to deepen, casting a glow around her. For the briefest of moments, it seemed to Vicky like the bathroom was on fire. "*I can make this easy for you, or I can make it hard. You like that word, Vicky? Do you like to think about my hardness inside you?"* It was then that Vicky understood what this was. It wasn't real, hadn't been from the start.

"Get out of my mind," she roared.

Her eyes opened, the bed underneath her welcoming, fresh-smelling air infusing her lungs. The dawn was a long way off, but Vicky knew there would be no more sleep for her tonight. Whatever had caused the dream had passed, but its effects lingered, the images she had witnessed failing to diminish.

Although she knew the fear was unwarranted, Vicky crawled from her bed and made the short trip to her daughter's room. The door opened silently, the gloom of the night enough to show the child sleeping peacefully. Emily wasn't snoring so much, but the sounds she made proved that Emily was safe from whatever night terrors had descended.

"You will not have her," Vicky said under her breath, although she didn't understand who she was saying it to.

12.04.2014

To: Professor Ari Stone

Re: Your request to gain access to the Vatican Archives.

Thank you for your request to gain access to the hallowed Vatican Archives. As I am sure you can appreciate, we receive thousands of requests every year, and as such, we must limit access due to the demands such visits would put on us.

I note specifically your request to view the original document that holds the witness statement of Lucia Santos, one of the three Portuguese shepherds who received the apocalyptic visions known as the Three Secrets of Fatima. This is a common request, even though the full text of these visions has been released, usually made by people who do not trust the reported text of the third vision.

I am unable to authorise your request at this time. Quite frankly, we do not feel you meet the strict criteria of an academic that would warrant your inspection of this document. I would include the text in the body of this letter for your interest, but as you know, this is freely available on the internet. You have my assurance that it is an accurate reproduction of the events recorded.

I regret I cannot assist you further in this matter.

Respectfully

Father Alfredo Renaldo, Curator and Chief Librarian, the Holy Vatican Archives.

36.

Yellowstone National Park, USA.

When he felt the stresses of life, Gavin Clay liked to retreat from the world into the wilderness for a few hours. He always came to the same spot on the shore of Lewis Lake. He wasn't much of a hiker, so Gavin picked an area he could drive to.

He liked the beauty of nature, but not the inconvenience of it.

This place wasn't particularly secluded, but it was far enough from the road that there was little chance he would be disturbed. And when he did occasionally see people, they were like him, wanting to be left alone. That was often the draw of this paradise, the chance for solitude and alone time.

There was a chill in the air, the lake water lapping at the shore he sat on. He came here about once a month to unwind and fill his soul with how humans had once lived. He never stayed more than a few hours, because despite the fresh air and the relaxation, he couldn't resist the draw of technology and the conveniences it represented.

The lake was a nice place to visit, but he wouldn't want to spend the night here. Gavin had no illusions that he could survive out here. He was a man of the modern age, born into the benefits of science. If he was stranded out in the wilderness, Gavin would die quickly from the elements or from dehydration. There was no knowledge lurking in his head about how to make the water around him safe to drink, or how to build a shelter. He had no tools, and no desire to carry any.

He came here to get his fix, and then he would return to comfort knowing that the life of his ancestors was a burden he no longer had to carry. Electricity and sanitation made survival skills obsolete. Within minutes, he could be in his car heading back towards the blissful call of civilisation.

Gavin's brother was different, a polar opposite. His brother could hunt and fish, went camping regularly deep into the wilderness. Gavin's wife would often cuttingly say how she had married the wrong brother, usually when their arguments blossomed. That seemed to be more frequent these days, something that Gavin couldn't understand. He provided for her, gave her everything she asked for. And yet she never seemed happy. His brother, on the other hand, lived by the seat of his pants. Gavin had a 401K that would see him sitting comfortably in retirement, whereas it was unlikely his brother had anything as simple as a savings account. What the hell was the appeal of adventure if you didn't have a sound financial base to live off?

Out in the lake, Gavin barely detected the movement. He ignored it at first, not realising what it represented. But as more fish rose to the surface, Gavin finally realised that something was wrong.

"What the hell?"

The direction of the air shifted ever so slightly, the wind blowing inland off the lake, bringing the faint smell that he instantly recognised. Rotting eggs; it was unmistakable. As more fish began to bob up from the depths, Gavin rose to his feet. He didn't have enough experience to realise the peril he was in. The fact that Yellowstone National Park was on a huge volcanic caldera was not known to him. This was the personification of natural beauty; how could there be any real danger here? Okay, there would be the occasional bear, but not here.

The smell grew stronger, and that was when his eyes started to water. On the surface of the water, maybe twenty metres out, bubbles started to rise, the water starting to froth and churn. He rubbed at his eyes, only then noticing that the skin of his hands was starting to itch. Gavin found himself suddenly gagging as a burning spread to his lungs.

The air became thick, toxic, and he scrambled away from the water's edge.

Beneath the lake, something had given way, allowing the poisonous gases stored there to release. Further out, a plume of steam erupted from the lake's surface, then another. The ground under him trembled and, clawing at his neck due to the lack of oxygen, Gavin collapsed to his knees. The steam cloud expanded rapidly, washing over the shore, washing over Gavin. And that was when the pain really started. That was when Gavin's skin began to slough off.

Hydrochloric acid mist floated over him, coating him, filling his lungs, burning and melting his eyes. The pain was unbearable, and he collapsed to the ground, the skin bubbling as it began to disintegrate. All around him, the foliage and the trees began to corrode as the gas attacked them, too. Gavin's lungs gave one last attempt to keep him alive, and instead, he coughed up blood, his throat filling with dissolved lung tissue. Although unpleasant, it was a relatively quick death; the acid sucking all the calcium from his body. His heart stopped beating within a minute of his first exposure.

The gas cloud expanded, spreading across the road, killing half a dozen motorists who were unlucky enough to be passing by that spot. And all the time the ground rumbled, warning of its discontent. There was more to come.

So much more.

37.

Silicon Valley, USA

Stone's eyes opened to see the bare walls of his fully illuminated bedroom. He'd tried to find some way to switch the lights off, but any means eluded him. In every corner of every room, surveillance cameras scrutinised him, and he resisted the temptation to stick his middle finger high in the air. If they wanted to watch his every movement, he had no choice but to go along with that.

He did not wish to antagonise those who held him captive. The simple act of extracting his tooth had proven to him that his kidnappers were deadly serious. If he had any chance of getting out of this in one piece, he knew he had to do what was asked of him. Still, the temptation for rebellion remained. He hoped he could keep it restrained. It would build as the days progressed, the enforced seclusion and the indignity of what he been done to him burning into his ego almost as fast as his hope was evaporating.

If he succumbed to that desire to show some sort of resistance, he knew that Kane would return and, when he did, losing a tooth would seem like a picnic.

"Shouldn't you be doing something more productive, Mr Stone?" He couldn't tell where the voice was coming from, the speakers likely hidden in the walls for all he knew.

"When do I get something to eat?" he asked timidly. Not that he was hungry, as the throbbing gap in his smile was enough to put anyone off their appetite.

"Food will be delivered to you twice a day. Any more questions?" Stone shook his head and got out of bed. He hadn't bothered to get undressed the night before.

The living area had changed slightly since Kane had overpowered him yesterday. On the main table, a single piece of paper had been placed, upon which a list of books had been written. The handwriting was pristine, precise, giving Stone his instructions for today. Despite his predicament, the list piqued his interest as soon as he saw it, especially the first item.

The Three Secrets of Fatima.

The bookshelves came with a rudimentary filing system; the list telling him where the document and books could be found if they were in physical form. In this case, the document was digital, and Stone grabbed the computer tablet, which, to his surprise, was fully charged.

The document on the tablet wasn't easy to find at first, the single computing device containing more ancient texts than half the national libraries in the world. Whoever had compiled this had known what they were doing, writings covering almost every aspect of religious and Satanic teachings. If you had asked Stone if he would surrender a tooth to be given such resources prior to his abduction, he would have agreed eagerly. Now that such an eventuality had occurred, he was committed to make something of this—partly to escape any more mutilation, but also because his own inner curiosity was demanding he comply with what was being imposed.

Didn't they always say that opportunity came wrapped up in an impossible situation? What could be more impossible than being held prisoner by the Antichrist and his minions?

He was well acquainted with *The Three Secrets of Fatima*, but was bemused to see the state of the digital copy of the document. It was a scanned copy, taken from what was most likely a photocopy. In the margins, red notes written in a gentle hand were connected to passages and individual words by arrows and exclamation points. Whoever had done this had tried their best to decipher what the secrets were supposed to mean.

For anyone going down the rabbit hole of apocalyptic prophecy, *The Three Secrets of Fatima* was standard lore. In 1917, three children were said to have received apocalyptic visions after being visited by the Virgin Mary. When you thought about it, the story was preposterous, but it was one of the many tales that had always intrigued Stone. He had always believed that the official transcript of the third secret was false, a ruse released to the world to deceive and deflect.

If he could believe those who had kidnapped him, he was about to have his suspicions put to the test.

The document contained all three secrets, and was signed by Jose Alves Correia da Silva who, in 1942, had been the Bishop of Leiria. The first two secrets were as Stone remembered them:

Our Lady showed us a great sea of fire which seemed to be under the earth. Plunged in this fire were demons and souls in human form, like transparent burning embers, all blackened or burnished bronze, floating about in the conflagration, raised into the air by the flames that issued from within themselves together with great clouds of smoke, now falling back on every side like sparks in a huge fire, without weight or equilibrium, and amid shrieks and groans of pain and despair, which horrified us and made us tremble with fear. The demons could be distinguished by their terrifying and repulsive likeness to frightful and unknown animals, all black and transparent. This vision lasted but an instant.

In capital letters at the side of this, the amateur scribe had written, *FEELS JUST LIKE HOME*. That suggested to Stone that the owner of the impressive penmanship was Kane. A demon would undoubtedly be well acquainted with the realities of Hell. Regarding the likeness to animals, another arrow snaked away, leading to tiny words that needed the tablet's zoom feature to read.

Wait till you see them on earth.

It occurred to Stone that no human mind could comprehend Hell. The old fire and brimstone model that was so popular clearly wasn't close to what one would experience should an individual be unfortunate enough to be cast down into Hades. There was also another aspect of this hanging over him. Despite what he had witnessed, and the fate life had deemed him worthy of, Stone still didn't believe Hell existed. He knew it did logically, but within, where the core of his being resided, there was still doubt.

To believe in the existence of Hell meant inevitably that one was forced to accept the presence of a Heaven with a heavenly host and Stone didn't think he was ready for that yet. He moved to the next secret.

You have seen hell where the souls of poor sinners go. To save them, God wishes to establish in the world devotion to my Immaculate Heart. If what I say to you is done, many souls will be saved and there will be peace. The war is going to end: but if people do not cease offending God, a worse one will break out during the Pontificate of Pope Pius XI. When you see a night illumined by an unknown light, know that this is the great sign given you by God that he is about to punish the world for its crimes, by means of war, famine, and persecutions of the Church and of the Holy Father. To prevent this, I shall come to ask for the Consecration of Russia to my Immaculate Heart, and the Communion of Reparation on the First Saturdays. If my requests are heeded, Russia will be converted, and there will be peace; if not, she will spread her errors throughout the world, causing wars and persecutions of the Church. The good will be martyred; the Holy Father will have much to suffer; various nations will be annihilated. In the end, my Immaculate Heart will triumph. The Holy Father will consecrate Russia to me, and she shall be converted, and a period of peace will be granted to the world.

Stone read the notes which were more numerous for the second secret.

The light is already known.
Wrong Pope.
Russia will be forever lost.
The Immaculate Heart beats in the deepest Pit in Hell.
There will be no peace.

His own intrigue had demanded he move directly to the third secret, but he resisted that. The words that had been written could have been random madness, but Stone expected otherwise. They were clues, hints at what his future writing project would be about. He was being given a puzzle, as if in some kind of elaborate test. His hope was that at some point, the reason for his being chosen would be revealed.

It was something he kept asking himself. Why had those intent on his long-term incarceration chosen him from all the authors in the world? There were plenty of other people who wrote about this topic, some who actually believed in the teachings of Christ and the creatures that lived in the Pit. What terrible crime had he committed to see him condemned to this fate?

Swiping down the document, he came to the third secret.

After the two parts which I have already explained, at the left of Our Lady and a little above, we saw one of the Fallen with a flaming sword in his left hand; flashing, it gave out flames that scorched the earth and set fire to the cities; throughout this, Our Lady smiled thinly, shaking her head at the coming plight of man. Pointing to the earth with his right hand, the Fallen One cried out in a loud voice: 'Penance, Penance, Penance!'. And we saw in an immense light that is God.

Other Bishops, Priests, Religious men and women going up a steep mountain, came before the Fallen and were commanded to kneel so they could take the mark and pay homage to Them who now claimed the world; behind them, the Holy Father passed through a big city half in ruins and half trembling with halting step, afflicted with pain and sorrow and boils, praying for the souls of the corpses he met on his way. Those corpses walked with him, feeding off the cowering and shrivelled masses they encountered.

The Holy Father died from the pestilence that afflicted the faithful. He was replaced by the one they called Peter the Roman, Pope Peter VIII.

Some of the religious ones who knelt before the Fallen renounced their new master and were killed by a group of soldiers who fired bullets and fire at them, and in the same way there died one after another the other Bishops, Priests, men and women Religious, and various lay people of different ranks and positions. More of the Fallen appeared and gathered up the blood of the Martyrs and with it sprinkled the souls that were prevented from making their way to God.

Then the Fallen came and took up the bodies of their chosen.

What the hell did I just read? thought Stone. He read it again, noting what the prophecy was indicating. There were only two annotations on the third secret, this time written by another hand.

Do you see?

This is how it all ends.

Those words had clearly been written for Stone's benefit. Could it really be that the religious texts and their prophetic words were true? That meant he had spent nearly twenty years mocking what was about to come to pass. How does a man respond to that? How does a man react when he learns that everything on which he has chosen to base his life is all a lie?

The other disturbing thought was the timing. The apocalypse was here. Although not said, Stone figured he was here to write some kind of account of the end of days. If that was the case...then the end times had already begun.

And Stone would get to live through it all. Maybe that was a blessing, but more likely, it was a curse. Stone's tongue played with the gap in his teeth, reminding him of what awaited any kind of failure. It was enticement enough to ensure he read the next book on the list that had been left for him.

38.

London, UK

Lilith herself didn't see the broadcast, but then she didn't need to. There were people in her Order who monitored the world's news broadcasts for just such an event. Never before had such a high-profile Western individual been possessed in Lilith's time as an Inquisitor.

Evidence that the UK's Home Secretary is the victim of demonic possession. Await instructions.

She read the phone message again, soaking up its implications. Such a high-level individual was surely not a random occurrence. Whatever name this demon went by, it was here for a reason. This demon was not here to abduct children or to feed on the fear of the weak. There would be no opportunity for such a high-profile figure to engage in brutality.

Lilith sensed the edges of a trap forming around her. She also felt an emotion that hadn't visited her in nearly a decade. *Hopelessness.*

She cast that thought aside, not allowing it a chance to take root.

She felt the need to act, to do something, *anything*. If the denizens of Hell started claiming the leaders of countries as their own, then the battle was lost. Such earthly positions came with power and power came with resources. The inquisitors were too few to fight off demons *and* men. It would also be difficult for her to deal with this threat if such an action was sanctioned. The Home Secretary would be protected, hidden away by a screen of armed security.

There was also the fact that killing such a man would cause an international outcry. If she was to do it, it would have to be planned, coordinated. There were ways of making such deaths seem like an accident, but they were difficult and haphazard. She would need help to plan such an assault, which invariably risked the Inquisition losing a significant number of its agents in the UK. And yet, if their actions were sanctioned, she would be told that the risk was worth it. Lilith had no reservation about giving her life for the cause. What better way was there for an inquisitor to be gathered up unto God than to die in the holiest of fights?

She felt the agitation again, the pull of the streets. As much as she knew she should meditate and calm her mind, there were demons out there that needed purging. This time she resisted, feeling her own agitation. Lilith needed to rid herself of the sins that were always with her.

When you grew up knowing pain, it sometimes became welcome. Pain you could understand, could respect. There was no arguing with it, no denying it, and all you could do was accept and forge through it. Some of the other Orders also believed in mortification, either through fasting or self-flagellation. Such actions, although inviting, would leave her injured and that would impact her abilities. There were other ways to prove her worthiness that would leave her unmarked.

Taking her middle finger, she dug it under the angle of her jaw, the electricity pouring through her as she pressed on the nerve bundle. The nail was cut to the quick, but the pain was still exquisite. Lilith pressed harder, knowing the exact force to apply to get the desired result.

Part of the punishment came with the relief she could give herself. Stopping and starting was part of the torment. The relief would come, but it would be tempered by the knowledge that she would begin her own agony again. Willingly, over and over. There were other parts of her body that she could press, some more painful than others, a cascade of abuse that she could play across her vulnerable flesh.

If mankind was not meant to feel such anguish, the Lord wouldn't have designed them so.

By the time she was done, she was sweating, her head dizzy from the stimulus overload. She would recover quickly, multiple points of her body on fire with the nerve pain she had inflicted. Lilith did this daily to remind herself of her own weakness and her own place in the world. She was an instrument of God, a soldier made to sacrifice everything. Part of her liked the pain, her mind insisting upon it. The sheep she protected spent their lives trying to avoid such discomfort, not realising they were supposed to welcome it and revel in it. That was all part of the test, the ability to withdraw from earthly pleasures to make the flesh pure for the true ecstasy that only enlightenment and ascension to Heaven could bring.

The saints and the holy martyrs had all suffered so for this reason. This was knowledge that had been beaten into Lilith and her kind on an almost daily basis.

Lilith knew to limit herself, though, because there was an addictive quality to this self-abuse. It could take control, wrapping you up in its warm embrace. If you weren't careful, it could become its own corruption. If Lilith lost herself to it, she would become dangerous to herself and to her Order. So, she danced on the edge of her obsession, knowing this, too, was a test of her own self. Still, nothing she did to herself came close to the tortures that had been forced upon her during the decades-long training.

What the priests had done had been horrendous. What the recruits had done to each other had been even worse. Those who had complained, or who had rejected that part of the teaching had either received more of the same, or had been deemed no longer worthy of the role.

They had been the lucky ones. The scars that tarnished Lilith's skin were a mark of her strength and her purgatory. Never once had she seen anyone enjoy the agony inflicted on her, but secretly she wondered if they felt some sort of satisfaction when her teachers wielded the whip or the cane. She supposed some of them had. The best could be seduced by the power to hurt another. Lilith certainly had.

Whoever had designed the training program for the inquisitors must have been a sadistic bastard.

The training took the human body to the edge of physical and mental endurance and then pushed it further. The body and mind had to be broken, shattered, so that it could be rebuilt. Empathy, compassion and basic humanity had to be stripped away. There was no place for such frailty when you were dealing with the outcasts from Hell.

Lilith always felt much calmer after her self-inflicted punishment. It provided her with a much-needed clarity, a reminder of why she was here. That was likely the endorphins flooding her system. Then the answer came to her. Lilith picked up the satellite phone and made the call she thought she would never have to make.

39.

Inquisitor training camp. 15 years earlier

Since Lilith's arrival at the camp, this was the first time any of the children had been allowed outside its boundaries. Up until now, everything in Lilith's world had been contained by the razor-topped wire fences.

She should have been excited to be given a glimpse of how humanity lived, but she knew excitement was an emotion that had to be suppressed. The small coach they were on, driven by one of the priests, stopped outside a huge structure the likes of which many of the children couldn't have imagined. Unlike Lilith, most of those in her class were born to the church, raised in confinement and secrecy. Father sat at the back, silent as he observed the reactions of his students. Some gazed out of the windows with wide-eyed wonder. Others barely lifted their gazes up from the floor. Each reaction was valid and useful, telling Father things he already knew.

To look at the people in the vehicle, you would not be able to guess they came from a religious order. To innocent bystanders, they would be another collection of school kids enjoying the thrills of a day out of the classroom.

What the children didn't realise was that another of them was already marked for termination. It was regrettable, but as each stage of the training progressed, those with irredeemable weaknesses became evident. There might have been some wisdom in allowing age to try to correct the flaws that Father saw, but that was not how inquisitors were trained. Only the strongest and the purest could be allowed into the inquisitor ranks. Not everyone could be an inquisitor, but there were other roles just as important.

None of the children knew why they had been ordered onto the coach. The field trip was a complete surprise. It would be the first of many trips, the world outside a vast puzzle that they would need to decipher. They could not protect a world if they could not understand it.

"Everybody off," Father commanded, the priest leading the small procession out into the bracing air. They huddled together, unsure of what was expected, safe under the glowering stare of the priest. This particular priest was known for his ruthlessness. Out in the normal world, there would be no immediate punishment for any infractions, as that would draw unwelcome attention to the group. No, such remediation would be stored away and dealt out later in the safety of the camp. Lilith was determined not to be one of the ones punished.

She no longer feared punishment despite its obvious harshness. To her, it was becoming tedious. Perhaps that was why she was one of the ones so rarely to feel the brunt of that chastisement.

"Those we protect do not have the passion or the drive of inquisitors. Their lives are often dull, void of true meaning and in need of distractions and entertainment to cancel out the tedium of their existence. This place is where some of them go."

"What is this place, Father?" the boy next to Lilith asked. Lilith knew, because she had memories of such a place from her younger years.

"This is where people go to shop. They work as wage slaves to acquire money that they then use to buy things they often don't need." Father was pleased to see the look of disdain in some of the eyes gazing back at him. "Some people make money their God. Today, you will see how it affects them."

With the priest in front, they marched in twos to the main entrance, Father bringing up the rear, a rare sign of order. It was busy, a prime time for people to be visiting the shopping complex, and it felt strange to be around so many people. Their regimented procession received several curious glances, but mostly the presence of the children was ignored. Lilith took everything in. The clothes the people wore, the way the other children laughed and ran. She had been that carefree once, before her kidnapping, before the murder of those who had brought her into the world.

She found she didn't miss such activities. How could you be wary and protect yourself when enraptured by such obvious delight? The children of the town needed their parents to watch over them because they were oblivious to the horrific danger the world around them represented. Not just the world mind, but also the corrupters from the other place. If Lilith and her fellow students had been ordinary children, they would have needed double the number of adults to keep them under control. As it was, they followed the priest without a word being said, Father hobbling behind them.

For about twenty minutes they wandered around, gazing into shop windows, many of them not really understanding what it was they were seeing. Why was there the need for so much stuff? Why were so many people consumed by the things they were buying? How many shirts did one person need? The attire Lilith wore was functional, jeans and a t-shirt, meant to allow her to blend in. But she could already tell mere clothes weren't an adequate disguise. The way she and the others walked put them apart from everyone else.

That was why they had been brought here.

Eventually, the priest led them to a food court and instructed them to seat themselves together at two tables, Father wearily settling himself down with them. Despite his injuries, Father suffered his discomfort in silence. It would not be right to share his pain with the wider world. His suffering was his own private burden.

With them all seated, the priest went off to buy food. This was not to be a treat, but a lesson.

"Why are we here?" Father asked.

"To learn their ways," Lilith answered.

"That is correct," Father said. "You are dressed like them, but you do not act like them. Now you stand out like tall poppies in a ploughed field. But soon you will all learn the instinct and the secrets that will allow you to disappear in a crowd."

"Why are there cameras?" one of the other children asked.

"You have a keen eye. The cameras are there to watch over the sheep that treat this place as their own. They think the cameras are there to protect them, and whilst to some degree that is the case, mostly the cameras are there as a form of control."

"By being watched, they learn to behave themselves?"

"Some do. Those that don't feel the weight of law enforcement. Fortune smiles on you though, for you will not need worry about surveillance cameras in your future." Lilith expected him to add if you have a future, but the words were not said.

"Why is that?" Lilith asked.

"The cameras will not see you," answered Father. Although cryptic, he would say nothing more.

When the priest returned with the food, the aromas of the offerings regaled Lilith and her mouth watered. The food at the training camp was bland, meant for survival, not enjoyment. She felt emotions flooding her, memories of times past that had still to be scoured from her mind.

"This tastes good," a child said. His face tried to hide the pleasure.

"This is why society is weak and why we are needed," the priest said. Lilith noticed that neither the priest nor Father were eating any of the food. She looked at the offering before her and pushed it away. Seeing her do this, several of the other children did the same.

"No, Lilith," Father admonished, "it is important that you eat."

"Only if you are sure?" Lilith questioned, and Father nodded. The faint semblance of a smile crept onto the priest's lips, but then it was gone. Lilith bit into her food, and it was every bit as good as her mind told her it would be.

"To protect mankind, you must understand mankind. You must know what makes them tick deep down inside. You must feel their yearnings and their desires but have the strength to cast those aside for the greater good." Lilith continued to eat, slowly, savouring each bite, taking in the lesson with each delicious swallow. Two of the children had already finished their food, and Lilith found herself judging them for their gluttony. This was a weakness on her part. She shouldn't have been old enough to hold others in a critical eye, and yet she found herself doing just that with more and more regularity.

They shouldn't be enjoying such treats, but Lilith felt the pull back to her old life. In some ways, she was already ahead of her brothers and sisters due to the remnants of a past that reeked of normality. But that was also a curse, threatening to drown her in sensations that those born purely to the church did not have.

"Tastes good, doesn't it?" Father asked. They all nodded, acknowledging the truth of his words. "And yet, if you eat enough of this shite, it would probably kill you." That surprised Lilith. Not the curse word, Father was not one to hold back in front of children.

"Why do people eat this if it is bad for them?" That was the boy called Lucien. Of all the students, he was the most likely to surpass Lilith. Like her, he was an orphan from the world of weakness. Of all those students present, Lucien was the one she consistently failed to beat. Over the last year, despite herself, she had felt a rivalry developing.

"Men and women, on the whole, are slaves to their base urges. Some are able to control their desires, but they are rare. So, know that the teachings and the practices of our Order are not unique. There are people who can match us in skill, in intellect and in our devotion, but they are rare." As Lilith listened to the words, her eyes strayed, caught by a movement on the periphery. She did not turn her head, for that would betray her.

"I think the enemy is here," said Lilith.

"Undoubtedly. The foe is drawn to places such as this." Father held her with a steely gaze. "What gives it away?" It, a fine word to describe a demon. Although demons were gender specific, it felt wrong to somehow give them such legitimacy.

"The way it skulks. It moves as if it is a lion on the edge of a field of sheep. Plus, it seems to pulse with blackness." When Lilith had first shown this ability, Father seemed surprised. It was rare for that skill to develop so early in the training. Through meditation and a purging of the self, the ability to see the evil riding a human host came to many of the inquisitors, dependent on them having the right genetic trait. Whilst it wasn't an essential skill, it did tend to make the job easier.

"Several children have been abducted in this neighbourhood over the past three weeks," the priest added.

"What do we do?" Lucien asked. He seemed eager, as if he felt he was able to take on such a creature.

"We do nothing," came the answer from Father. "Is there anyone here who has not seen the demon of which we refer to?" Five hands went up, the priest noting those silently. "Fear not, the ability will come with time. And if it does not, well, then we know."

"We should do something," Lucien insisted. There was his weakness, his youthful rashness.

"The matter is in hand," Father said. He didn't tell the children that the demon was being stalked at this very moment, an inquisitor of renown hiding in wait. "Remember, just as the demons keep their presence secret, so must we."

40.

London, UK. Present Day

Lilith sat waiting for the man she hadn't seen in nearly three years. Outside the cafe, she chose her seat purposefully, the wall to her back, the avenues of approach limited. This was a pedestrian area, so there was no way for an assassin to creep up on them via a random car on the street. A sniper shot was more than possible, but she reckoned there was little chance of that. She'd never heard of a demon taking out an inquisitor in such a fashion, and at the moment, it was only demons who would have an interest in her.

That was about to change.

The wig itched her scalp, made worse by the baseball cap she was wearing. Soon the winter days would descend, which would make it easier for her to hide. With the digital anonymity she thought she possessed, it was still wise to hide one's face as much as possible. This was one of the reasons she chose to ride a motorbike to get around the city. That, and the ability to manoeuvre the crammed city streets.

With this choice of venue, it would be impossible for demon or man to approach her unseen on foot. There was also a dearth of surveillance cameras in this particular spot.

The precautions, as they were, shouldn't have been necessary, but she had learnt early on to be cautions as an inquisitor. As Father had always said, *one underestimated the enemy at one's peril.* Things were changing, the balance between dark and light shifting. Lilith could almost taste the venom that was being seeded into the air by the presence of the defiled ones.

She saw his approach from her peripheral vision, the chair next to her free and inviting. Although Lucien walked with purpose, it was as if those meandering through their day never saw him. Inquisitors had a way of deflecting attention, of walking through the world unnoticed. They were bland and grey to the public. Nobody enquired about the inquisitors because to them, inquisitors didn't exist.

They had no friends, took no lovers, and craved no status. The delights of civilisation were denied them, except the one true pleasure of ridding the satanic scum from the streets. Nothing could compare to that.

Lucien sat down next to her, pulling the surgical mask free, a not uncommon sight in a world filled with killer viruses. Especially for someone of Lucien's Asian heritage. His face was not as she remembered it. There was the hint of a scar running down his right cheek, a run in with a particularly formidable demon two years back. A lesser inquisitor might have been bested. Only she saw it, the makeup and the artist's silicone hiding the blemish. Inquisitors knew how to hide themselves in plain sight.

"We shouldn't be meeting like this," Lucien scolded.

"And yet here we are."

"How could I deny your insistent charms?" He was the closest thing Lilith would ever have to a companion.

"You could have said no. You could have refused my request." She turned to look at him, for a moment putting all her concentration on the only man she had ever felt inside her. "You feel it too, don't you? You feel the change in our enemy?"

"Yes," Lucien admitted.

"What have you seen?" They had not discussed this over the phones they used. As encrypted as they were, this was something that needed to be discussed face-to-face.

"I believe they are coordinating."

"Did you inform your handler?"

"Of course," Lucien said. A waiter appeared and Lucien ordered tea, his eyes searching the man who took his order. There was no threat there. "My concerns were apparently dismissed."

"As were mine. I spoke to the Librarian."

Lucien smiled at that. "You always were his favourite. He let you get away with things the priests should have beaten you for."

"I have a loveable personality."

"It's not that. He saw something in you; we all did." A pigeon landed at his feet, pecking away at some morsel that had been previously discarded. Lucien ignored it, a minor distraction sent to interrupt his train of thought.

"And yet he, too, dismissed my concerns. I don't like this. There is something wrong that we aren't seeing."

"Do you really think our Order could be that blind?"

"I think those who control us see what they want to see. They don't have the benefit of being here on the front line. The Librarian said they wouldn't tell us, even if they did know. I'm not sure which option to believe."

"Of any of us, you were the last I would have expected to have such doubts." Lucien had always looked up to her, ever since she had been the first to step forward and take the mark.

The waiter appeared, depositing the steaming cup on the table between them. Lucien didn't touch it. The pigeon at his foot suddenly took flight, several others across the paved area lighting into the sky. "I don't think we should go through with this without further planning."

"I asked for authorisation and it was given. You were always too cautious, Lucien." Lilith was surprised by his hesitation. "The demon that has possessed this country's Home Secretary needs to be vanquished."

"This is no lesser demon. I think you know that."

"Yes, and it will be guarded. Fortunately, such security can be dealt with." Lilith had no hesitation in killing anyone that got in her way.

"Then let us get this done." Lucien still had his reservations, but if he couldn't trust Lilith's judgement then there was something seriously wrong with the world.

"I'm going to rely on you. If I get into trouble, you will be my only backup."

"I won't fail you," Lucien said. "And if I do, we will both be with our Lord."

"We must not fail in this," Lilith said. It felt abnormal to be this vulnerable. The plan she had come up with to rid the land of the demon Home Secretary had been agreed to by her Order faster than Lilith had expected, but it was more than one person could accomplish.

She caught something in the corner of her eyes and scanned the area for the presence of any threats. When she finally looked back at Lucien, he was looking at her intently.

"What?" Lilith demanded.

"Do you ever wonder what lives we could have lived?" Lucien asked.

"No, what would be the point?"

"I see these people we protect," Lucien continued, "and I sometimes wonder what it would be like to live amongst the normal."

"Why would you want to be fodder?"

"It's not that," Lucien corrected. "I just ponder what it would be like to be free of this knowledge." Lucien tapped his left temple.

Lilith stood, her drink long forgotten. "Do not let your mind be corrupted, brother."

“I won’t.” He smiled, a rare event indeed.

“This will take some time to arrange. I will need you to be ready.”

“I will be,” Lucien said. Lilith was satisfied with that answer.

She walked away from the table, not looking back. She took the standard precautions to ensure she was not being observed or followed. The baseball cap was pulled low over her eyes, the fake hair in a ponytail tucked into her jacket. For now, her safeguards were enough.

That would change.

41.

Cheltenham, UK

Rashid was constantly amazed by how luck played a part in uncovering the enemies of the country. When the man had been killed on the steps of Westminster Bridge, two tourists had unwittingly recorded the whole thing on their phone. They had then stayed at the scene, wrapped up in a sense of duty that had surprised the officers who arrived at the place of murder.

Their witness statements and the recording on one of the pair's mobile phones had captured what London's multi-billion-pound surveillance network hadn't been able to. Rashid had that recording, and it was exactly the thing he felt he needed to crack the problem that made this killer invisible to them.

He was presently in the central command hub, GCHQ's main eyes and ears on the world. His section was portioned off by glass screens that could have been made opaque if he wanted to, but none of those with him had given that instruction. Including his supervisor, there were five other people present, two complete strangers to him. He knew of one of the strangers though, for there was no hiding the identity of the country's Home Secretary. They were all here for what Rashid was about to show them. He hadn't been introduced to the strangers, so Rashid kept his arrogance in check, knowing that now was not a time to let his irritation and short temper free. It wouldn't do for someone important to take objection to his usual abrasive manner.

In front of him were two monitors with two separate views of the murder scene. One showed a man clutch his leg and fall down the steps. This was the official copy captured by a lone surveillance camera, the image's manipulation a fine piece of work if Rashid was honest. The person who had written this virus was a master. Rashid was not modest about his own abilities, but he reckoned he was up against a competent enemy here.

The second version, higher in quality due to the expensive nature of the phone used, showed a hooded woman walk past the dead man. Part of her face was clearly captured. There was a brief glint as the polished blade of the knife caught the available light, and then the woman had struck, walking casually away as if she hadn't committed murder. So skilful, and yet Rashid was almost pained by the mistake he had witnessed. To be uncovered by such bad fortune.

Not bad for Rashid and GCHQ, though.

Like everyone else in the room, he was surprised that the killer was a woman.

"If a human operator had been watching this feed at the correct moment, they would have seen the killing. Whatever has been done to our system can't stop the woman's image being displayed live," Rashid pointed out. He wasn't being critical. It was impossible for human eyes to watch every video feed of every camera in a city of ten million people. "Whatever is happening, it's obvious that the video recording is being altered as it is written to storage. That's where this woman's image is being stripped out." He said what others in the room would already know.

"Just like with the Russians," the supervisor said.

"No, this is far in advance of what the Russians tried. If you remember, that left a blotchy image where you could tell something had been changed. This is designed to strip and fill the image with the surrounding detail. Thing is, now we know what we are looking at, you can see the faint distortion."

"How long do you think this has been going on?" the supervisor asked.

"I don't know the answer to that, yet. And I may never find out." Rashid hated stupid questions, although he kept his tone benign.

"I have faith in you, mate." Mate! *Why does he always call me mate*? Rashid briefly looked at the other people in the partitioned area of the command hub. He couldn't tell what any of them were thinking. Was he impressing them?

"What I do know is that now, I should be able to crunch this down and find the errant software causing it much faster. Also, now that we have some of the biometrics of her face, I should be able to have the system actively search for it. If she shows up again on any of our cameras, we should be able to track her in real time."

"Really?"

"Hello, genius at work here," Rashid said. "If her face appears, a nice big red square will appear around it with an alert that would wake the dead." There was no denying he was one of the best GCHQ had. That was undoubtedly why his sometimes grating personality was tolerated.

"Do you think you will be able to get a full image of her face?" the Home Secretary asked.

"We don't need to," Rashid said. The video taken by the tourists hadn't captured her face full on. Partly because of the angle, but also partly because the woman had been wearing glasses and a covering to her mouth. "The computers can extrapolate from what we have. If you want a full image, though, I can only get an approximation for you."

"Do that," the Home Secretary ordered. Rashid wondered if he alone noticed that their VIP guest kept scratching at his arm.

"It still won't be easy. Biometrics doesn't just cover the face. It's in the way we walk, the way we hold our shoulders. This amateur video doesn't give us this. If she doesn't show her face, we may still struggle to find her. That's why we will still need to hunt out the virus."

"Do you think there are more of these people out there?" the Home Secretary asked. "I have intelligence that suggests there might be."

"Most certainly," Rashid said. "You don't go to this level of incursion into one of the most secure systems on the planet for the benefit of one person." He could tell he owned the room. They would all feel better knowing he would find this assassin and the code that hid her. And then more praise would come. He would never be a national hero, for his work required secrecy. But people like Rashid still required validation and recognition. Perhaps a promotion, which he would gladly accept. To get out from his supervisor's hapless influence would be ample reward.

"I want this made a priority," the Home Secretary insisted.

"I'm sure we can see to that," Rashid's supervisor said reassuringly. We? Where will this *WE* be five hours from now when I'm still here crunching numbers?

42.

London, UK

The folder Vicky carried made for shocking reading.

Patient name: Responds to the names Damien Morningstar and Legion.

Age: 31 stated on questioning, although no birth records have been found

Address: No known address

Distinguishing features: Burn scar on right side of face. Pentagram tattoos on the backs of both hands. Missing left ring finger up to second knuckle. Hair blonde, eyes brown/blue.

Reason for admittance: Accused of 47 counts of murder. Held on remand pending trial.

Record of care: To undergo evaluation under the supervision of Professor Frank Schofield. Vicky Richards, the assigned psychologist.

Warning: Patient to be kept in handcuffs during interview. Also, to be placed on suicide watch as strong chance of self-harm. Prisoner to be held in segregation.

That was the first page in the folder. There were far more shocking revelations in the rest of it.

Despite the disturbed sleep of late, Vicky found herself strangely excited. It wasn't every day you got to examine one of the most prolific serial killers the country had ever seen. The man called Damien had been ordered by the court to undergo psychiatric assessment to determine his capability for trial whilst being held on remand. There was little doubt as to Damien's guilt, but the court needed a reassurance of where to put the man on sentencing. It would not be advisable for the truly insane to be put into the normal prison population.

"How is he?" she asked the prison warder escorting her. This prison, due to its proximity to London, held many of the worst offenders Britain had been able to produce. For Vicky, it was a collection of fascination, although the building itself was oppressive. It felt sick to her, as if the ailments afflicting the prisoners had escaped and infected the walls that attempted to keep Britain safe. If evil really was a malevolent force, this would be the kind of place you would find it roaming free.

The clutched folder was a display of why Damien was in this place.

"Quiet," the prison officer said, his body filled with nervous tension. "You need to be careful with him when you are in there. Even with his restraints, I wouldn't want you to go anywhere near him."

"You have him restrained?" That was unusual.

"You're damned right we have him restrained. He's attacked two of us since being brought here. He's too big and strong for even four of us to safely handle. It's one of the reasons we have him segregated." Attacks on the prison staff weren't unusual. The violent sometimes needed a constant way to express themselves. But it was rare that a prisoner couldn't be brought under control without resorting to desperate measures. If Damien continued on like this, he was looking at a lifetime of brutal, mind-destroying isolation.

"Has he hurt anyone?"

"Broke my mate's arm," the prison officer stated. "Jumped on him just as the bastard was being taken down a flight of stairs."

"Ouch." This didn't put Vicky off. Her professional curiosity wanted to see what this person was like. She was surprised, though, being still quite junior in her psychology career. Her mentor, Professor Schofield, had insisted she was ready to help with the examination and questioning of the patient. That meant there would be two people under assessment when she spoke to Damien. The killer and herself. No doubt Schofield would be watching every moment and every twitch she made.

Was she ready for this? Her own self-doubts said no.

More officers were there when she turned the bend in the corridor, outside the room Damien was in. Both men were big, obviously picked for their size. She knew the senior of the pair, had met him several times on her visits here. He had a reputation for having a temper, but if he ever unleashed it on any of the prisoners, nothing had ever been proven. His name was Bob, and his love of beer was evident from the belly that thrust against his uniform.

"Mrs Ralph, I need you to listen very closely to me now," Bob said as she approached. Vicky had chosen to keep her married name.

"I know the drill, Bob," she replied.

"I'm still going to say what needs to be said. This is a bad guy, worst I've ever seen."

"Are you sure you aren't exaggerating?" Some of the staff sometimes liked to play games with those who entered their little sphere.

"No, I'm not." She didn't think she had ever seen Bob so serious before. "The patient is restrained, but he is still dangerous. Do not hand him anything and do not get within reaching distance of him. Do not pass anything to his side of the table and if you at any time feel unsure about your safety, retreat from the room. I will be in there with…"

"No, you won't," Vicky insisted.

"He isn't safe, Mrs Ralph."

"I appreciate that, but I need to be alone with my patient."

"I would advise against that," one of the other officers added.

"Look, I need him to trust me. I can't do that with any of you in the room." Bob looked at her doubtfully. "What are you really worried about Bob?"

"This one scares me." That answer surprised her. She'd never known Bob to show that kind of fear before, not openly. The other guards seemed to agree with him.

"You securely restrained him?" she asked.

"Yes, but…"

"And you will be right outside the door?"

Bob nodded. "I don't want to be responsible for this," he informed her.

"Don't worry, you won't be."

"No, sorry Mrs Ralph, I can't let you alone in there." She could see he wasn't going to be persuaded.

"Okay, but only one of you." Bob hesitated, the fingers of the key he held almost white. Finally, he forced that key into the door's lock and turned it. She could tell he didn't want to go in with her, but he did so anyway.

When Vicky stepped through, Damien was looking right at her. He was huge, a bulk of muscle that was being kept in one place by metal loops that seemed far too thin. This maniac's neck was wider than Vicky's thigh. The prison-issued jumpsuit he wore bulged with the muscles he had been genetically blessed with. Normally those on remand could wear their own clothes, but those found at the scene on Damien's arrest were logged as evidence.

It occurred to Vicky that maybe it was a good idea after all having a few protective men in with her. But their presence risked showing that she was afraid of Damien, which she suspected would be counterproductive.

"*He likes to talk, and he's self-assured. He thinks he has been right in everything he's done.*" That was the initial warning Schofield had given her. "*He refused to talk to the first two psychiatrists I assigned, which we are surprised about. I'm hoping you can charm him.*"

The room wasn't designed for comfort. The metal table was bolted to the floor, as were the chairs. Damien was handcuffed, his arms restrained to a loop on the table. There was little give in those restraints, Damien's body forced into a slightly head down posture. He could sit with his shoulders back, but that would cause discomfort in his wrist and arms.

It was unusual for the prison warden to authorise such precautions. More evidence of Damien's madness?

Vicky could see why Bob felt the way he did. There was a malevolence to Damien, an evil that pulsed out of him. She tried not to let her own unease show on her face.

"Good morning, Damien," she said, placing the folder on the table in front of her. There were no staples or paperclips in that folder, so the sheets within were all loose. Vicky tried to keep her voice placid, devoid of any emotion that could be misinterpreted. "For the record, I am Vicky Ralph. I'm a psychologist assigned by the court to determine your mental status pending trial."

Vicky sat in the chair opposite the man and did her best to hide her own apprehension. This was a powerful and dangerous maniac, if everything she had been told could be believed.

Some of her peers would have been shocked to think that she would consider using such an archaic word as maniac, but she believed in saying it how she saw it. If you could paint a picture of what it was to be insane, this patient would tick every box in that regard.

Damien licked his lips. He took his time, caressing every fold.

"So, you are here to get inside my head?"

"I'm here to assess you, Damien. The more honest and open you are with me, the sooner this will be over with."

"Why would I want this over with? It's so rare to be trapped in a room with a beautiful woman." Bob, standing behind Damien, tensed.

"We'll have less of that, please," Vicky insisted. Her voice was stern.

"Forgive me. That was in bad taste." Damien tried to shrug, but the cuffs prevented it. Sitting down closer to him highlighted how massive he actually was. He could have squeezed the life out of her with a single hand. Christ, she felt intimidated, despite the restraints. Physically, he had the edge on her, but how would their intellects compare? If she could get through to him and get him speaking, it would do a lot for her credibility. Two psychiatrists had failed to get him talking so far, and yet here he was, chattering away as soon as she entered. Strangely to Vicky, her own mentor had yet to interview the prisoner.

If she was honest, she was hesitant to be here, even with the potential of this case for her career. The things Damien had allegedly done sickened her, and she found it difficult to step to the side and view the case impartially. There was no doubt as to his guilt on two of the murders, and probably not the others either. Damien definitely looked like the kind of person who could commit such atrocities. It was as if he had been shaped from her own imagination.

Children and adults, Damien hadn't cared who he'd turned his knife on. Just not females.

This was not a man you wanted to find yourself at the mercy of. It wasn't just his size, but his utter reported ruthlessness that made him so dangerous. Her brief research into his past revealed Damien to be one of the worst serial killers the country had ever spawned. He might not have the body count of some of his contemporaries, but what he did to his victims set him apart.

"I will be asking you a series of questions. You can really help yourself by answering them as honestly as possible." The guy seemed eager to flap his gums at her.

"Ask away," he said. "Maybe I can teach you a few things." To Vicky's amazement, he winked.

"Okay, let's start the ball rolling. I am going to ask you some baseline questions to start. It's important you answer openly and honestly."

"What if I lie?" Damien asked mischievously.

"Then I won't be able to help you."

"I'm not sure I need your help. A place like this, it can't really hold me." Such arrogance.

"It seems to be holding you pretty effectively right now," Vicky pointed out.

"Only because I wish it. But please, ask your questions." Vicky had a sense he was enjoying this.

"Well, first question is pretty standard, really. Tell me, what do you remember about your father?" Vicky thought she had seen the worst that humanity could create, but being in this room with this man, she knew that she hadn't come close. There were people in this world who were too dangerous to be left free.

Some would say there were people too dangerous to be left alive.

"Which father? That's quite a complicated question when you get into the meat of it."

"Who raised you?" Vicky wondered if he was being deliberately awkward, although she had been advised of the events during his police interview.

"Ah yes, such a weak man."

"Did you respect him?"

"Ha!" Damien exclaimed. "I could only pity such a broken soul."

"Did he beat you?" She knew the answer, but it was best never to assume you knew the facts.

"Oh, he did more than that. For a time, at least." Vicky used silence then, letting it fill the room, sitting back slightly as she watched her patient. "I guess you want me to keep on talking?"

"Only if you want to."

"I'm happy to tell you everything, because nothing I tell you will matter in the long run."

"And why do you think that?" Vicky asked.

"Because I won't be here for very long."

"I'm afraid you are mistaken there. You are going to be imprisoned for a considerable time." She was astonished by the smug grin that developed on his face.

"It is you that is mistaken. Because I know something you don't." He sang the last part, his hands swaying slightly. My God, he *was* enjoying this.

"Why do you say that?"

"Because of what's coming," Damien answered. "I don't expect you to understand, but it's better for you if you do."

"What's coming, Damien?" That was when he leaned forward, his muscles tensing. Despite herself, Vicky reared back.

"The end of all things." The words were said without emotion.

"As in, the end of the world?"

"And all the delights that entails. You see, my father, my true father, he craves the world." Vicky could see the delusion taking shape around her.

"Is that why you took the name Damien Morningstar?"

"A little joke at his expense," Damien stated.

"I don't understand."

"No," Damien said, "your kind never do."

"Tell me more about the man who raised you."

"Must I? He was such a pathetic creature."

"But he did beat you?" It was rare for the victims of such abuse to show pity for their tormentors.

"Numerous times. Legion helped with that."

"Legion? Tell me more about Legion." This was the other thing that excited her about this patient. A definite case of split personality with recordable physical changes. Damien cocked his head into the air, a distant tune ensnaring him.

"No, not right now. You aren't asking me the right questions."

"What do you want me to ask?" She was happy to let him lead the conversation, for now at least.

“Why don’t you ask me why I killed so many people.”

“Okay.” Damien looked at her expectantly. Obviously, she would need to say the words. “Why did you kill so many people?”

“I’m glad you asked me that, Vicky. The answer is quite simple. They were a blight upon the world, as am I. But I am the only one who is worthy of what is to come.”

“Why do you use the word blight?” She flashed a glance at Bob, who was looking decidedly uncomfortable. Bob was no doubt confused at how cooperative Damien was being.

“They were a sickness, a force for evil. Like me, they had all been sired by dark seed. But more than anything, I killed them out of selfishness and greed.”

“What do you mean by that?”

“This is not something to discuss now,” Damien insisted. “I’m still not fully sure you are worthy to get the whole picture just yet.”

“That’s your choice, of course. What do you think needs to happen for me to become worthy?”

“Time,” Damien answered. “There are forces at work here that you couldn’t hope to understand.”

“You said in your police interview you all shared the same father. I’m assuming this is not the father that raised you.” Damien craned his neck around to look at Bob.

“She’s a smart one, isn’t she?” Damien said to the guard.

“Don’t talk to me,” Bob insisted. Damien turned back to look at Vicky.

“Why doesn’t he like me?” Damien said, his face a mockery of concern.

“Because you have been violent during your brief stay here. You shouldn’t act like that.”

"But I get so bored," Damien insisted. "To answer your question, the father I refer to is not of this realm. He is a resident of Hell. You might have heard of him. Lucifer? Got into a bit of a spat with God and got cast out with the other rebels. A terrible business."

"Your father's the Devil?"

"Ah, no. That's a common error. Satan is the devil. Lucifer is just another archangel who got too far up himself." Why was it people always seemed to get that wrong, his gaze seemed to ask? "If only you knew what they had planned for the world."

"That's somewhat unbelievable." Vicky wasn't going to significantly challenge the patient's deep held beliefs, not this early on. That would come later.

"And yet it is true. All those I killed were like me, spawned by his corruption. I couldn't let any of them usurp my rightful place." Damien flexed his biceps, the muscle rippling. "That is why I have the strength I have, both physically and mentally. That is why I was able to kill my mother and the man she shared her bed with. And that is why I allowed myself to be here."

"Allowed yourself? You were captured by the police."

"Yes, I've been thinking about that. I've been wondering about how they could have found me."

"I believe it was a tip-off. It seems you finally got sloppy." Vicky instantly regretted the words. Goading someone like Damien wasn't going to be an effective strategy.

"No, that isn't it. There's only one person who could have turned me in."

"Oh?" Vicky was curious where this delusion was going.

"My father."

"The dead one or the one from Hell?" Bob asked.

“Oh, it speaks,” Damien responded. The gaze he gave Bob caused the officer to step back a step.

“Can you appreciate how incredible this all sounds, Damien?” Damien turned his head back towards Vicky.

“Most certainly. I’d be surprised if you believed a word I said.”

“So why would Lucifer turn you into the police? That seems a bit weak for someone as powerful as Lucifer.”

“Don’t be too impressed by my father’s reputation,” Damien said. “He isn’t anything special. He needs a vessel to walk this ground,” Damien said, stamping one foot. “The time isn’t quite right for that, though.”

“Sound pretty special to me.” Vicky was amazed by how deep this delusion went. That was her purpose here, to explore the beliefs that drove Damien to murder. There was no point trying to refute those beliefs, because they would undoubtedly adapt to the evidence thrown at them. “Was your biological father not a vessel for him, though?”

“Briefly. Lucifer can corrupt at times of violence and lust. That’s my understanding of it.”

“I’m still curious how you think you have any chance of escaping from here. This is one of the most secure prisons in the country.”

“Would you like a demonstration?”

“What did you have in mind?” Vicky wasn’t expecting what came next.

“I think it’s time you met a friend of mine.” Damien once again went through his metamorphosis, the eye colour changing, shoulders swelling. There was no way Vicky could deny what she had witnessed. But it didn’t end there.

With strained effort, Legion began to pull on the handcuffs binding each wrist. Bob shifted in position, eyes bulging at what he was seeing. Grabbing Vicky, Bob pulled her from her seat and pushed her towards the door.

The handcuffs broke, blood seeping from the wounds inflicted on both wrists.

"There is a darkness around you, Vicky Ralph. I can see it. They are coming for you. I can already taste their stench on your flesh." This wasn't the voice of Damien.

Bob banged on the door, the lock opening, the door flinging wide. Bob and Vicky were out of the room before Legion was able to rise from the table, despite Vicky's resistance. The words he had said, the darkness. What did he mean by that? Bob expected Legion to come charging at them, but instead the killer remained standing, unnervingly passive after his display of strength.

How the hell had the police managed to catch this man?

"Next time we talk, make sure you bring me a Cherry Coke," Legion said from behind the door. Vicky found herself wondering if maybe Damien had been right.

Could this place hold him?

***

Lilith's motorbike had been chosen for performance and reliability, not style. Unlike her face, the registration wasn't blanked from the system. There were too many police cars that could randomly check her licence plate. If nothing came up on a live check, that in itself would be suspicious. Instead, the registration she presently used was linked to an address over a hundred miles away, and she never parked the vehicle anywhere near the murders she committed. Every two months, a fresh set of plates was delivered to her address by an unknown courier.

There were easier countries in which to be anonymous.

Worming her way through traffic, she couldn't fail to notice the two mopeds behind her. To a normal motorist, such a presence wouldn't have been of any concern. Lilith knew the danger they represented as soon as she saw them.

It was simple to test her theory, random turns that they jointly followed telling her trouble had arrived. She kept moving where she could, confident that they would only try to take her when she stopped. In the past, their kind wouldn't have wanted much in the way of eye witnesses, but lately they didn't seem to care.

Whoever these people were, it was evident that they weren't here for her, but for her motorbike. The more formidable foes she fought would have come for her in vehicles that could have been used to force her off the road, and they wouldn't have lagged behind, either. Demons would have attacked as soon as possible. The police, should they have cause to arrest her, would have been there with blues and twos roaring, backed up by helicopter overwatch. The more secretive human organisations wouldn't have been so inept in their pursuit.

This was just bad luck.

There had been a spate of bike and moped jackings in London recently, errant youths emboldened by the poor police response. Whilst Lilith preferred to try to avoid such trouble where possible, sometimes that trouble forced itself upon you, insisting that she address it. The other thing that gave the game away was that each moped had two people on them.

She nearly managed to avoid them. If the lights had been favourable, she could have sped up onto a nearby dual carriageway and that would have been the end of that. But the lights turned red, cars pouring across the intersection. Lilith considered going up on the pavement, but a collection of fluorescent vest-wearing children prevented that.

"So be it," she mumbled under her breath, one of her knives already free. The first mopeds pulled up to the side of her.

"Nice bike," the man to her right said with his helmet's visor now raised. His attempts to distract her whilst the other moped sidled up didn't work on Lilith. To call him a man was perhaps an exaggeration. If he was over eighteen, he was obviously blessed with youthful looks. Lilith didn't speak. Instead, she used her mirrors to watch her would-be attackers, the crash helmet having the undesirable effect of blocking her peripheral vision. The knife she held remained hidden.

The passengers each moped carried leapt off, and they came at her, one grabbing hold of the bike's rear, the other coming around to grab the handle bars. The man in front of her, whose age she couldn't ascertain, reeled back when Lilith's hot steel sliced through the flesh of his neck. He hadn't been expecting it, and he fell backwards as blood spurted from the slashed blood vessels. In the same movement, Lilith brought the knife to her right, letting go. Barely dripping blood due to the speed of the cut, it hit the talkative youth in the chest, burying itself deep in his flesh, six inches fully embedded. Leather was no protection against this brand of laser-sharpened steel. The rider fell back, the moped going with him, trapping a leg under the hunk of metal.

Instant justice.

The knife she was happy to abandon. It held none of her DNA and wasn't special in any way. Behind her, the man holding her bike let go, the reflection in her mirrors showing him running away, which was a sensible thing to do given the circumstances. The driver of the other moped let his vehicle rest on its kickstand whilst he came to the aid of his friend, the one whose neck was still spurting.

Killing human scum didn't hold the same satisfaction as ending the presence of demons on this planet. The second moped driver ripped his helmet off, tears streaming down his face. This was a child, but children could be some of the most dangerous foes a warrior could face. Lilith raised her visor, curious as to the relationship between the bleeding and the grieving. Brothers most likely.

"Learn from this," Lilith said loudly. "Change your ways."

"Bitch," was the only response she got. Lilith flipped the visor back down, the lights finally changing. All around her, the spectators were present, no doubt some of them recording on their accursed mobile phones.

She needed to get out of here, and she needed to ditch this bike.

43.

Moscow, Russia

The Lear jet came to a stop at a secluded area of Vnukovo International Airport. Cardinal Esposito made no move to depart the plane. There would be no official record of his visit, the flight a relatively comfortable one for someone who had no time for such luxury. It was perhaps better that Esposito made this journey, for he could do it in silence and without gaining the attention of the world's media. To the world, Esposito was nobody, whereas the Pope was a force of nature. Wherever the Pope went, the world followed.

The person he was here to meet was one of the few people he could trust when it came to such matters. Alek Popoff was one of the most powerful men in Russia, perhaps more powerful than the President himself. Although he didn't hold the reins of power, Alek had something more important under his thumb. He was the Director of the FSB, the Russian federal security forces. Alek Popoff was thus one of the few people who could order the execution of Russian citizens with impunity, and his organisation was essential to those who ran the country. He was a kingmaker, happy to let others take all the public glory.

Popoff was also one of the few individuals outside the Order of Tyron who knew of the existence of the demonic horde that threatened the world.

Looking out of the window, Esposito was not surprised to see the black limo already waiting by the side of the plane. At the front of the Lear jet, the pilots opened the passenger door, the steps descending to the cold ground. There were no other crew on this flight, as Esposito didn't need servants pouring his wine for him. His stay here was also to be brief. Words said that needed to be relayed face to face.

Both pilots departed the plane. For the briefest of moments, Esposito was alone with the world, but that wouldn't be for long.

Two men exited the limo. They scanned the area, more guards exiting the two black SUVs that flanked the luxury vehicle. A third door opened, nobody exiting. The guards stood with their hands ready, weapons mere seconds away from being drawn. Although he couldn't see them, Esposito knew that both pilots would be searched.

Three intimidating men entered the plane, their eyes serious and threatening. Popoff hadn't reached such heights of power without being cautious. It had been like this the last time Esposito had made such a visit, although the previous occasion hadn't been so spur-of-the-moment. Esposito nodded to the men as they approached, groaning as he stood. There was no objection from him as they searched his body, their roaming hands thorough and sometimes intimate. The intent was security, not an invasion of his personal space.

"If you will follow me, your Eminence," one of the guards said after they were satisfied.

"Gladly," Esposito said. He was not unfamiliar with such precautions, but his relative anonymity had always been his greatest protection. Who would have any interest in a mere Cardinal? Especially one dressed in such casual attire. Before he exited the plane, Esposito wrapped a scarf around his face to hold back the biting wind, but also to protect against the distant use of photographic equipment. Nobody other than the FSB director was expecting him here, but there was always a chance Popoff himself was being surveyed. If that was the case, then Esposito would be a mystery for them to chunter over.

Whilst there were numerous individuals and cults who had, over the years, made the mistake of messing with satanic forces, most of the countries of the world denied the existence of the demonic threat. It existed in the realm of fiction and nothing more. The Americans had briefly danced with the knowledge in the 1970s, but anything they had discovered was filed away in a deep hole along with the remnants of their paranormal research program. Whatever they had discovered, they had managed to keep secret from the curious eyes of the Inquisition.

Russia was different, because in 1972, Russia had, totally by accident, opened up a portal to Hell. There were no official accounts of the experiment that caused it, and most of those involved in the episode were no longer alive. Esposito was one of the few people on the planet to be aware of the events of that fateful day.

Experiment 4563 had been simple in nature. It was supposed to test the effects of a new sleep deprivation drug that the scientists had great hopes for. One of the biggest problems for soldiers in the field was sleep fatigue. If they were to win a conventional war against the bourgeois capitalists, then they would need an army that could fight longer and harder to make up for the technological edge that the Americans and their allies were developing.

The drug had been a catastrophic failure. Whilst it did indeed cancel out the need for sleep, the scientists had got carried away with themselves, pushing the experiment beyond what humans were supposed to be able to endure. By the twelfth day, half the experimental subjects were either dead or in comas. The other half found they could no longer sleep. And that was when the problems really started. Sleep, it seemed, was the body's natural defence against unwanted possession. Remove that ability and all manner of creatures could come through.

Esposito leaned into the back of the limousine. He didn't take a seat inside.

"This is a rare pleasure," Popoff said.

"Thank you for seeing me on such short notice." Both men spoke English, the only language they shared. This wasn't the sort of conversation you wanted translators involved in.

"I assume I should be worried."

"That will all depend on what you have recently experienced."

"Things have been quiet," Popoff said. "I think our demonic friends know not to come here. I suspect you can't say the same."

"No," Esposito said gravely. "Things are worsening. We have evidence that demons are working together. If that continues, our inquisitors are likely to be overwhelmed."

"Which means eventually our defences will also come under threat."

"We suspect something else," Esposito added.

"I hope you aren't going to say what I fear you are going to say."

"Prophecy." Esposito only needed one word.

"Ah, you Catholics and your books." Despite his knowledge of the dark place, Popoff was a long way from being religious. He agreed with his own scientists that the demons, rather than representing a biblical threat, were invaders from another dimension.

"It doesn't matter if you believe. All I need to know is if you are prepared for what might come?"

"We are prepared," Popoff stated. "We have our own ways of dealing with these creatures." Russia had learnt the hard way that this menace couldn't be ignored. That was why there were no inquisitors in Russia or many of the Eastern European states. They simply weren't needed. Russia had their own soldiers for that.

44.

Cheltenham, UK

Rashid replayed the attempted bike jacking and his intuition told him that this was the break he needed. At the same time, he watched the live feed being relayed from the Hendon operational command unit. Street CCTV, along with any cameras on Transport for London property as well as a multitude of government properties were all being linked through Hendon to GCHQ. Rashid wasn't involved in the hunt for this woman. The Met police were coordinating the response. He was an interested observer along for the ride.

Of the two monitors he had in his little part of GCHQ, the left one had the recorded feed. The other cycled through the various relayed images, allowing him to follow the search for the murderous woman.

Because it had been a busy intersection, a real live human being had been watching the altercation as it happened. Police had been dispatched to the scene, but then the CCTV operator had watched in disbelief as the lone motorcyclist turned the tables on her attackers. All that had been recorded, because the virus had no way of knowing who it was on the bike.

That was when Hendon had taken over, organising a response to try to apprehend the person who, at that moment, had been marked down as a random vigilante. By the time the police arrived at what was a huge traffic jam, the motorcyclist was already gone. Her progress was followed through the streets of London, although not as enthusiastically as Rashid would have liked. Some of those searching for this lone force for justice had initially been somewhat subdued in their reaction, the karma of the situation appealing to many of them. This, and Lilith's general skills in evasion, allowed her the time she needed to disappear from the surveillance grid.

Thirty minutes into the hunt, the bike had been found abandoned.

The woman they were chasing didn't so much disappear as enter one of the growing number of dead zones in the nation's capital. Just as with the ever-present moped gangs, there had been an increasing trend for the CCTV surveillance on some of the less affluent estates to be destroyed by those who didn't like their illegal activities monitored. Though those cameras were eventually repaired, funding limitations and the perseverance of the vandals meant whole areas weren't presently covered. It was on one such estate that the motorbike had been discarded.

It didn't take long before someone at Hendon suspected that their knife-wielding woman might be somehow connected to the case MI5 and the Home Secretary were going ballistic about. That meant phone calls were made, which brought in extra resources, the great beast of the UK surveillance state going into overdrive. As the evidence of what had occurred at the traffic intersection was reported in from the boots on the ground, more assets were brought into the hunt.

There weren't that many women who could so expertly kill with knives. The deaths had been taken ruthlessly and efficiently.

And yet, their prey still eluded them.

"It's as if she knew where to go," Rashid said to his supervisor, who once again stood behind Rashid.

"But if she's invisible, how do we find her?"

"She's only invisible to being recorded, and only then if her face is recognised by the virus. We are watching this live. Sooner or later a lone woman is going to come out of this area. She'll have discarded her helmet. The system has aspects of her face locked in. If she shows up anywhere, we'll likely have her." The computers would search for every biometric marker they had. Whilst they still hadn't found the virus that was plaguing their system, that didn't matter now. The live feeds could also be recorded via cell phones, so that they would have a record of what went down if needed. "The Met will follow and track down anyone who gets close to being our suspect."

"That's assuming she doesn't live on that estate," the supervisor pointed out.

"We just have to let the police do their job."

The surveillance grid had been compromised, but there were ways to counter the best hackers. Right now, that was by human eyes, watching dozens of screens and boots on the ground.

"You really think this is who we are after?"

"Do you know many commuters who are so proficient with an edged weapon?" Rashid asked. "She took those two down like they were nothing." Rashid zoomed in on the high-definition replay. "Look at that throw. Christ, I can't toss my trash in the bin next to my desk without missing half the time."

Rashid had no doubt now that this was the woman everyone was after. Even the clothes were similar to those in the tourist recording. *Make it easy on us, just show your face.*

45.

Slough, UK

The nightmare from the night before had caused Vicky a sense of foreboding when it finally came time to lay her head down. The words uttered by Legion hadn't helped, either. Emily was asleep, the terrors of school fortunately not extending into her daughter's nocturnal slumber.

Vicky had hoped for uninterrupted sleep, but at three in the morning, her eyes opened. She didn't know what had roused her, so she listened to the house, hopeful she wouldn't detect anything out of the ordinary.

Faint shadows played across the ceiling, just enough light from the streetlights to break through the gaps in her curtain. The noise of distant traffic could be heard, the hum of a city that was always alive. The world around her seemed calm, the warmth of her bed reflecting how safe she should have felt.

But Vicky didn't feel safe. Far from it, and she tried to turn her head to see what time it was. Only her head wouldn't move. That sparked something in her, a terror she had hoped never to experience again. Her body felt numb, unresponsive, and a scream began to grow deep in her lungs.

The scream would not be given voice.

"Here she is," a malevolent voice said from the corner of the room. Outside, a car passed, its headlights briefly scanning across the ceiling. Whatever made the voice wasn't captured by that light.

"Here is my little prize, a tasty morsel for me to chew on." The words were thick with an accent that she couldn't recognise, as if their owner hadn't spoken English for a thousand years. "And what delights we have in store for you, my precious little thing." She heard movement then, something coming closer, the chair in the corner of the room groaning as someone abandoned it.

Vicky wanted to say something, anything, but her voice was denied her.

From the corner of her eye she saw a shape, a blackness that seemed to soak up the available light, a presence that she couldn't fathom. It came closer, pulling at the duvet, the bed sinking as a great weight was pressed on it. Whatever this was, it was here for Vicky. Worse than that, it was here for Emily, too.

Would she have been so vulnerable if she hadn't been alone? She had chosen not to move forward with any romantic aspect of her life, feeling that nobody could fill the void left by her dead husband. She knew that was, in a way, selfish of her. Not selfish to others, but to her own chance at happiness. It was as if she somehow deserved this fate that had befallen her, a penance to be paid for some crime she wasn't aware of. Vicky regretted that, would have given anything for someone else to be in her bed at this moment.

She felt something wet caress her foot. Her mind told her it was a tongue, but it felt too coarse for that, almost abrasive. The moisture rose up to her ankle and along her calf, some hideous form slithering under the duvet with her. Vicky could make out the mound rising. Then it was gone, the duvet flat once more.

"Hmmm, she tastes good," the voice said. It wasn't a compliment, and Vicky's eyes began to sting with the tears that were welling in them. Just breathing felt like it took all her energy.

Leave me alone, her mind reeled, but her lips remained stubbornly closed. Better to keep quiet, a part of her said. Better not to wake Emily.

"You must let me in," the voice insisted, the space above Vicky turning black as a cloud of chaos formed above her. It hovered there, enrapturing Vicky's full attention, a coldness seeming to pulse onto her face.

No, get out, get away.

"So mean. I *will* have you, and then I will have my fun." The darkness seemed to spread, falling down upon her, stifling Vicky, trying to force itself into her mouth. "Just let me in. It's such a little thing."

No, I won't, Vicky roared inside. She knew it would be so easy to accept whatever this was, to open herself to the possibility. But she knew that what would follow would be beyond her ability to imagine.

"So ungrateful," the voice said. In the darkness, two eyes manifested, a corroded orange that glowed. There was insanity in those eyes, the promise of pain and unforgettable torment. This was not a force of this world.

You can't have me.

"So you say. But I will have my way." The eyes dropped closer, as if the face they were attached to was coming in for a kiss. They threatened violation. Vicky felt as if her mind would break, and she cursed the thing silently. "Just think of the fun we can have together."

"Fuck you." At first, Vicky didn't think she had said the words, but the blackness retreated, the eyes flinching from unknown pains. Closing her eyes, Vicky fought the numbness with all her might. The malevolence retreated further, weakening.

"So, not today then," the voice said. It sounded distant, cast out.

"Never. You will never have me."

"We shall see about that," the voice warned, warmth returning to the room as normality returned. Vicky lay there, the panic still present, her heart beating frantically. The sheets below her felt suddenly damp, sweat having exploded across her skin. She wanted to fling herself from the bed, to run to her daughter and check that Emily was safe. But sleep took Vicky again, wrapping her up in its confusing embrace.

When Vicky awoke to daylight, her logical mind was able to take charge. The only explanation that made sense was a night terror. None of it had been real, the whole experience a manifestation of her own mind. The kind of thing she had so obviously dreamt about did not happen in the real world.

Such lies weren't even worth telling children.

46.

Inquisitor training camp. 14 years earlier

"You must learn to make the cold your friend and your ally," Father said. They were once again outside, thick snow coating the hard earth. In the distance, the high mountains loomed ominously over them, a natural barrier Lilith knew she would one day be forced to cross. Before she could attempt such a mammoth trek, however, she first had to learn to control her own body.

So cold was it that the children thrust their hands under their armpits, the clothes they were wearing in no way adequate to combat the snow that was threatening to obliterate the visible world. Lilith's vision kept being blurred by the flakes that seemed drawn to her eyelashes.

"You were born naked into the world, and you must learn to survive as nature intended. The clothes you wear, the tools you wield, these are all sent to make you weak in the face of the enemy. In the Pit, the demons know how to live in the scorching fire. You will learn to live in the purity of ice."

Before them, one of the three priests began to remove his robes. The cold air swirled around him, his breath steaming as if to prove the foolishness of his present actions. It occurred to Lilith that, for the last two months, she hadn't remembered a moment when she had been warm. The meagre blankets they had been provided had been stripped from them, meaning they slept naked. There was no shame or embarrassment in that, for they had not been indoctrinated into a world that saw nakedness as a vulnerability to be avoided.

"Through the power of breath and the concentration of the mind, your body can resist the coldest of natural temperatures. This is a skill you will all learn, or you will die trying. For some of you, this will be your undoing. For the rest, this will see a transformation within you."

Lilith listened intently, resisting the chattering that her body was trying to force on her. She was just shy of her thirteenth birthday.

In front of them, the priest removed his trousers, white briefs all he retained. His feet were bare, and he sat cross-legged in the snow, fresh flakes falling all around him. As with his exhalation, steam seemed to rise from his body as his body fought the freezing moisture that landed upon it.

Another of the priests approached, a dripping blanket held in his hands. Carefully, the second priest draped the sodden fabric over the first priest's shoulders. Kneeling there, the first priest's chest went through rhythmic expansions as he practiced the breathing technique mastered centuries before.

"We show you this so you can believe. If you believe, you will be able to perform feats of endurance that would be fatal to the sheep who we protect." Father walked over to the first priest, who was deep in a self-induced trance. Already the snow gathered around the priest's legs was beginning to melt, such was the heat this man was able to radiate. Now Lilith knew why they had been subjected so much to the cold. It was a means to acclimatise them so that they could better learn what might one day save their lives.

"Gather round this blessed vessel," Father said, indicating the priest. They all huddled further, awe etched on some of their faces. As so often happened, Lilith found herself next to Lucien, and they shared the briefest of glances. As the two best students, they didn't have a rivalry. Instead, they had developed a respect for themselves and each other. Whenever one bested the other, they saw it as a sign that there was scope to improve.

Although they would ultimately be working out in the world alone, they would still be part of a team. And a team didn't need heroes. It needed people that could help improve those around them, to forge and mould the group into a single unit that worked for the greater good, not individual glory.

"Sit," Father ordered, the children doing so. Instantly, the wetness soaked through Lilith's thin cotton trousers, the chill painful as it bit into her. Nobody complained, Father walking between them, his dark eyes searching for signs of weakness and objection.

"In the cold, the extremities of your body begin to shut down." Father's words floated over Lilith as she paid attention to the way the priest was breathing. The inhalations were forced, to their maximum extent. On exhalation, the priest seemed to let the breath go, no pause in between it and the next in breath. She could see the rhythm there that was, in itself, almost hypnotic. "Your body does this to protect your organs, retaining the heat at your core at the expense of your fingers and toes. In this temperature, frostbite will set in within roughly thirty to forty minutes." Lilith suddenly felt a hand descend on her head. "Lilith, do you think you would be much use to our Lord with no thumbs?"

"No, Father." Lilith shoved her hands into their protection just that bit more.

"But can you fight your enemies with your hands hidden in such a warm place?"

"No, Father." Lilith reluctantly drew her hands out of their concealment and let them fall into her lap. The other children did the same. If one was told something, it was for the benefit of all. Satisfied, Father continued on his patrol of the young bodies he was here to instruct.

"Be assured, none of you will be harmed today. The cold you feel is here to teach you. By the end of this week, you will be able to do what this priest can do. Do you believe my words?"

"Yes, Father," they all shouted.

"Your lies will be your undoing." Lilith couldn't be sure, but she could have sworn Father smiled at that point. Lilith thought she believed, but the ice that was eating into her skin told her that what the priest was doing wasn't possible. And yet, the evidence of his accomplishment was there in front of her, trails of water running off his bare legs as the snow melted before it had any real chance to settle. The blanket over his broad shoulders showed no snow, either. Lilith had seen some things during her time here, but she found this incredible. She was about to say as much, but Lucien put his hand up before she could speak.

"Yes, Lucien?" Father asked.

"I don't see how this can be done. I see the evidence with my own eyes, but can I trust what I see?"

"Do you believe the Lord is all around us?"

"Of course, Father." There could be no doubt about that.

"And did our Lord bring us naked into the world without the means to survive?"

"It would seem unlikely."

Father did smile at that response.

"Then you have your answer. When you achieve this yourself, then you will understand. But to allay any further doubts…" Father stepped over to the priest and stripped the blanket from his back. With his good arm, he threw it at Lucien, who caught it in the air.

The blanket was merely damp, a vast difference to the sodden cloth it had been before.

"We teach you this, so you are ready. We teach you this so you will be stronger than your enemy. The demons come from the heat of the Pit, they do not like the cold. This will give you an advantage against the weaker of them."

Lilith had been here so long, and yet the days of her training seemed to fly by. The beatings were less now, the priests slowly relenting as their young minds and bodies transformed into adulthood. And the true training hadn't started yet. This was still the preparation phase, the moulding of their flesh and minds to accept what they must become. Lilith was not impatient to start the next phase. She knew that would begin only when she and her fellow students were ready.

You couldn't rush the training of an inquisitor.

47.

Silicon Valley, USA. Present Day

Normally, Stone's visions came to him in his dreams. Not today. Sitting at his desk, he felt the world around him shift. It began subtly, a darkness caressing the periphery of his sight. He was so enraptured by the book he was reading that, at first, he didn't notice the change. Then, when it finally dawned on his perception, Stone ignored it.

He couldn't ignore the words on the paper moving though, his whole vision gradually disrupting as reality seemed to dance and cascade down into chaos. In another time, he would have been concerned, afraid that something was wrong with his brain. But he was past that. Stone knew he wouldn't have been pulled this far off course only to have his own body fail him. Although he didn't understand why he had been chosen to scribe during the fall of mankind, he had accepted it, accepted his place in this new world.

Pushing his chair back, Stone let the change in perception take him. The surrounding walls melted away, opening up into the huge expanse he was now familiar with. The air he breathed became part of his hallucination, the stench of thick black smoke corroding his nostrils. Once more, he found himself on the cliff edge, a charred and shattered city extending below him to the horizon.

"*Do you see?*" the voice asked.

"Yes," Stone answered. "I see it all."

"*Do you accept what I give you? Do you accept your part in what is to come*?"

"Yes."

"*Are you prepared to pay the price?*"

"What price?" What more could be asked of him? The world probably thought he was dead. He had nothing except the books his new owner granted him. Oh, and his life, but what was that worth?

"*Everything*," the voice said. Such a simple word. "*You will be there to see it all, to record it all. You will suffer as your species suffers and you will fall as your people fall.*" The heat around Stone began to rise, the skin on his hands turning red.

"Will I hear the truth of it all?" He had learnt so much over the past few days. Stone's mind was still reeling from the change in his understanding of the world. Most of his adult life, he had written about something he thought to be false. Now he was learning it was all true, and that he was destined to be at the centre of it.

"*You will see it all. You will know it all. At the end it might break you, but before then you will have such knowledge and understanding as to make you almost one with those on high.*"

The skin on his hands began to blister, the smoke mingling with the sudden stench of burning hair. He was on fire, and he didn't care.

"Then I accept the price."

"*It's not like you had any choice.*" The voice was no doubt mocking him.

Stone turned. The throne was there once again, bigger, glowing with an impossible light. He felt a dullness come over him, the pain from his sizzling flesh detached and a thing he barely cared about. Deep in his thoughts, a brief flash reminded him that none of this was real. He wasn't on fire, and he wasn't on a cliff face overlooking a vast and ruined city. He accepted it all anyway.

"What will I become?"

"*Everything you ever dreamt of. And everything you ever despised.*" There was no reassurance in the riddle.

"Why me?" Stone cried out, his arms spreading wide through some powerful external force.

"*Why not you? Someone had to be chosen. And you monkeys all look the same. Don't for one minute think you are in any way special. In fact, you will rapidly learn what a curse it is that has been laid upon you.*" Stone felt his body beginning to rise into the air, a searing pain breaking through the dullness as something penetrated both wrists. He turned his head and tried to look, but an invisible hand seized his chin. "*Look at the throne, damn you.*"

Stone did, tears threatening to obscure his vision.

Before him, the scroll manifested, the seven seals still intact. It pulsed with an ethereal light, the power within anxious to escape and begin it all. Stone suddenly found himself thankful that he couldn't move his arms. He felt compelled to reach out and grab the scroll as he had before, only this time he knew that to touch it would be the end of him. It would consume whatever was left of his soul and leave his body a dried out and lifeless husk.

"*It is time.*"

"Why are you doing this to us? We don't deserve any of this."

"*Don't presume to tell me what humanity deserves. You have reached this time, the moment of your ultimate potential, and you have squandered it with your petty squabbles and your addled minds. All this is because you have been found unworthy to live on this planet anymore. You are, however, worthy of the suffering that can be unleashed upon you.*"

"Who are you?" Stone realised he had never thought to ask that question before.

"*I am the I am,*" came the response, followed by laughter that rocked the heavens. After the thunderous noise calmed down, the voice spoke again. "*You will have to forgive me. I'm enjoying this immensely*." The scroll drew closer, its brightness painful to Stone's eyes. Despite that, he had no power to close his eyelids or look away.

"God shouldn't be this evil." That was the only explanation that made sense.

"*You think I'm God? Are you so consumed by your own importance that you think God would talk to you? You bloody fool. God doesn't concern himself with my affairs, never mind yours. God doesn't care for any of us because he already knows what the future holds. Everything we do has already been written.*"

"But the images, the things I'm seeing?"

"*That all comes from inside you. What you see is your own mind trying to understand what it should never be able to see. You are seeing what you want to see. I'm just riding on that, amazed at how warped your primitive mind is. It amuses me to think that I've just been mistaken for that malodorous prick*."

"If not God…"

"*Try looking down for a change instead of shoving your nose up God's holy arse*." The force holding him tipped Stone's head forward so that he was able to witness the ground open up before him. There was no mistaking what he was looking at, the burning rocks around the edge of the pit that were forming glowing with a vile redness.

"But I thought…"

"*So now you know. You have agreed to pay the price, which will be your immortal soul*." What had he done?

"You tricked me."

"*No*," the voice cautioned. "*You tricked yourself. I am, after all, just in your imagination*."

"I never agreed to any of this." Things with indistinguishable shapes began to crawl out of the pit. Dark things, creatures of pure evil. Their long thin arms reached up for him, not to attack Stone, but to honour him.

"*See? See how Hell's pets value you. You will bring the word of the Fallen to the world. You are the one who has been chosen by fate and the flaws in your own character.*"

"I no longer want this." Stone struggled against the forces holding him, but he would have had more chance pushing over a mountain.

"*Then why is the first seal breaking?*" came the response. Stone looked, the first of the seven seals clearly fracturing as the wax failed. With an unnerving silence, the seal finally gave way, the whole world trembling beneath him. "*You say you don't want this, but we both know that's a lie. You want to know what God knows, to see what God sees. You want to be there to witness the majesty the Fallen archangels will create when they are freed.*" Below him, the dark ones retreated back into the pit, the hole sealing itself up. The smoke that had been billowing and consuming him suddenly cleared, the sky above brightening as the light broke through. "*You might try to deny it, but I see the truth in you.*"

The throne and the scroll vanished. It was as if they had never existed.

The force holding Stone relented, his arms freed, dropping him to the ground. The skin that had all but charred off was whole again, no wounds where his wrists had felt as if they had been penetrated.

"*It's not so bad to follow the satanic cause, son,*" the voice said.

"I'm not your son," Stone spat, his throat still filled with the soot and dust that made him retch.

From the heavens a mighty voice roared the word *COME*, the very clouds seeming to vibrate with the importance of it.

"*No, but he is*." Stone was about to ask who the voice was referring to, but over the hill a figure appeared. Stone knew who this was instantly, the white horse carrying the hooded figure. The horse seemed to drift rather than walk, the ground beneath its hooves undisturbed.

"It can't be?" Stone insisted. The first horseman. The one brought forth by the breaking of the first seal.

"*But it is. Meet the new boss, worse than the old boss*." As the horse came closer, the figure pulled its hood back to reveal a man Stone had already met. Stone closed his eyes. He didn't want to see any more. He didn't want anything to do with this. Around him, the temperature diminished, the world shrinking back to the prison he had become trapped in. When he eventually opened his eyes again, Stone wasn't surprised to see Horn standing there.

"I guess you're ready then," Horn said with a smile. "Now you know who I really am. Let me tell you what I want you to write."

The Inquisitions ranking of the hierarchy of Hell

Satanael

The Fallen - Lucifer, Belial, Azazel, Leviathan, Mammon, Belphegor, Asmodeus

Kings - Baal, Paimonia, Beleth, Purson, Asmodai, Vine, Balam, Zagan, Belhor

Dukes - Amdusias, Agreas, Valefar, Barbatos, Gusion, Eligos, Zepar, Bathin, Saleos, Aim, Buné, Berith, Astaroth, Focalor, Vepar, Vual, Crocell, Allocer

End of Book 1

Ready for book 2?

If you enjoyed this book and want to read the second in the series, just follow the links below

Amazon.com - https://www.amazon.com/dp/B08BNVMK5N

Amazon.co.uk - https://www.amazon.co.uk/dp/B08BNVMK5N

ABOUT THE AUTHOR

Facebook - https://www.facebook.com/seandevillesnovels/

Website - https://seandeville.com/

Get free chapters to try before you buy, as well as a free book.

Building a relationship with my readers is the best thing about writing. I occasionally write blogs and send newsletters with details on new releases, special offers, and occasional free gifts relating to my books. And if you sign up to my mailing list, I'll send you all this free stuff:

- **The zombie apocalyptic short story "London lost"**
- **The vampire apocalyptic story "Legacy of Ashes"**

You can get these for free by signing up at

https://seandeville.com/

Did you enjoy this story? If so, you can make a big difference.

Reviewers are the most powerful tool in my arsenal when it comes to getting attention for my books. Much as I'd like to, I don't have the financial muscle of a big New York publisher. I can't take out full-page ads in the newspaper or put posters on the subway.

(Not yet, anyway).

But I do have something much more powerful and effective than that, and it's something that those publishers would kill to get their hands on. A committed and loyal bunch of readers.

Honest reviews of my books help bring them to the attention of other readers. If you enjoyed this book, I would be grateful if you could spend just five minutes leaving a review (it can be as short as you like) on the Amazon page.

Thank you very much.

ALSO BY SEAN DEVILLE

THE HIDDEN HAND CASE FILES

Hellgates (Book 1)

Some secrets are worth killing for.

Hellgates.

Interdimensional portals that lead to a parallel world some call The Pit. Others call it Hell, a place of brutality, torture, and unbelievable suffering. There is only one force that can protect the Earth from the vile creatures that crawl out of these Hellgates.

The Hidden Hand.

It is a ruthless and secret organisation that guards the world of humanity. For centuries, its agents have hunted down the invaders from that other world. Be you human or monster, the Hidden Hand will show you no mercy.

A second chance?

Special Forces officer Craig Armstrong made a mistake and innocent people died. With his career in ruins, he faces disgrace and ten brutal years in military prison. Instead, he is offered a chance at redemption, and joins the elite ranks of the Hidden Hand.

There's just one problem.

His first month on the job and the Hidden Hand is faced with its greatest threat yet. Worldwide, the Hellgates are waking up, threatening to unleash the apocalypse upon the Earth. Craig is about to discover that keeping secrets comes with a terrible price.

Hellgates is book 1 in the Hidden Hand Case Files, a pre-apocalyptic horror series.

UK: https://www.amazon.co.uk/gp/product/B0BS8GY1DW

US: https://www.amazon.com/gp/product/B0BS8GY1DW

THE NECROPOLIS TRILOGY

Cobra Z (Book 1)

What if one day you find your world suddenly torn apart? Entranced by your daily routine, you hear the terrifying news that makes your blood run cold. A devastating man-made virus has been unleashed on the world, a virus so lethal that it rapidly turns everyone it infects into rabid, blood-crazed killers. Maniacs so devoid of humanity that their only goal in life is to rip the flesh from your very body, and kill or infect the people you love the most.

Would you panic? Would you rush from your desk in a frantic attempt to save your children? Would you hunker down, and hope the infection somehow passed you by, praying to whatever God you think will help? And what if the very people you care for so deeply are the ones clawing at your door, their blood-smeared faces screaming for the destruction of your soul?

How would you survive in such a world? And would you even want to?

THE LAZARUS CHRONICLES (a 5 book series)

The Spread: Book 1

Scientists told us the dead would never walk the earth. They were wrong.

- What if the members of a secretive and powerful death cult created a man-made virus with a 99.9% mortality rate?
- What if that virus escaped into the wider world, spreading to nearly every country on the planet?
- What if that virus re-animates those it killed, creating millions of blood crazed creatures of carnage?

That virus exists.

They call it Lazarus.

It spreads... it infects... it kills... it resurrects.

Clandestine government operative, Nick Carter, finds himself at the heart of the UK's first outbreak. In the depths of the ensuing slaughter, Nick and his team rescue a single survivor, a woman called Jessica.

Immune to the virus, Jessica's blood could be our only chance of salvation?

With cities across the world already falling to the undead hordes, Nick and his team are given a new mission... keep Jessica alive long enough so that the secrets of her blood can be unlocked.

The thing is, it isn't just the zombies Nick needs to worry about.

Or is it already too late?

U.S.: https://amzn.to/2MEGFlK

UK: https://amzn.to/2F3leIP

Printed in Great Britain
by Amazon

42843328R00179